Death Makes
a Prophet

Death Makes a Prophet

John Bude

With an Introduction
by Martin Edwards

Poisoned Pen Press

Originally published in 1947 by Macdonald & Co.
Copyright © 2017 Estate of John Bude
Introduction copyright © 2017 Martin Edwards
Published by Poisoned Pen Press in association with the
British Library

First Edition 2017
First US Trade Paperback Edition

10 9 8 7 6 5 4 3 2 1

Library of Congress Catalog Number: 2017946810

ISBN: 9781464209024   Trade Paperback
        9781464209031   Ebook

Poisoned Pen Press
4014 N. Goldwater Boulevard, #201
Scottsdale, Arizona 85251
www.poisonedpenpress.com
info@poisonedpenpress.com

Printed in the United States of America

Contents

Introduction   1

Part I   *Welworth Garden City*   5

    I   The Children of Osiris   7

    II   Mrs. Hagge-Smith Has a Vision   16

    III   Eustace Writes a Letter   31

    IV   The Missing Crux Ansata   47

    V   Penpeti Turns the Screw   61

    VI   Mayblossom Cut   75

    VII   The Man in the Teddy-Bear Coat   88

    VIII   Near Miss   102

Part II   *Old Cowdene*   107

    IX   Sid Arkwright Listens In   109

    X   The Letters in the Case   121

    XI   The High Prophet Plans a Theft   133

    XII   Overture to Murder   145

    XIII   Inspector Meredith Gets Cracking   149

    XIV   Unknown Visitor   162

    XV   Fatal Effect   172

    XVI   Terence Through the Hoop   187

    XVII   Pow-Wow with Penpeti   201

    XVIII   The Poison Puzzle   216

XIX	A Young Lady Gives Evidence	225
XX	Mr. Dudley Talks	235
XXI	Death Down the Lane	244
XXII	Final Facts	254
XXIII	Meredith on Form	262

Introduction

Death Makes a Prophet, first published in 1947, illustrates John Bude's versatility as a crime writer. In common with many of Bude's books, it features Inspector Meredith, but the series detective does not appear until the second half of the story. The punning title is matched by the light tone of the first part of the story, in which humour is much more to the fore than in most of Bude's earlier work; perhaps, in the austere aftermath of a world war, he felt that his readers needed cheering up.

Cults of various kinds have long fascinated crime writers, perhaps because seemingly eccentric beliefs and practices offer fertile ground for murderous antics. As a result, cults have featured in a surprisingly large number of detective stories, especially in the classic crime fiction written during the first half of the last century. G.K. Chesterton characteristically indulged his love of paradox in a notable example of this kind of story, "The Eye of Apollo"; at the end, Father Brown says: "These pagan stoics always fail by their strength." In "The Flock of Geryon," a story included in the collection *The Labours of Hercules*, Agatha Christie allowed Hercule Poirot to mock the disciples of a Devonian cult known as The Flock of the Shepherd. Another Queen of Crime, Ngaio Marsh, had Roderick Alleyn investigate the mysterious death of a new initiate at the House of the Sacred Flame in *Death in Ecstasy*. Across the Atlantic, cults of one kind or another appeared in a wide variety of crime novels produced by authors as distinguished as Dashiell Hammett (*The Dain Curse*), Ellery Queen (*And on the Eighth Day*) and Anthony Boucher (*Nine Times Nine*, a notable "locked room mystery").

Writers of classic crime stories tended to be rational thinkers who regarded cult leaders as at best naive, and at worst charlatans, determined to exploit the gullibility of their followers for personal advantage. Bude seems to have been as interested in the comic potential of Cooism as in its suitability as the context for a whodunit plot, but in the later stages of the book, the storyline begins to resemble those so often found in the work of Freeman Wills Crofts (another author whose work has been reprinted in the British Library's series of Crime Classics). Crofts was the creator of Inspector French, a detective even more relentless than Meredith when faced with the challenge of breaking down a seemingly impregnable alibi, and his meticulous approach to writing crime fiction plainly influenced Bude's methods.

John Bude was the pen-name adopted by Ernest Carpenter Elmore (1901–57) when he turned to writing crime fiction. For his early books, starting with *The Cornish Coast Murder* in 1935, he chose settings and titles featuring a variety of attractive locations. This, like his choice of pseudonym, was a simple enough marketing ploy, but it proved increasingly effective as he developed into a very capable craftsman. Meredith was introduced in Bude's second mystery, *The Lake District Murder*, and is an example of the appealing, if lightly characterised, British police officer (such as Inspector French) who emerged during the Golden Age of detective fiction between the wars.

When war did return, Bude—who lived in a rather idyllic house called Crooked Cottage in Sussex—joined the Home Guard, and arranged for his daughter Jennifer to be sent to the safety of Devon, where she stayed with her grandmother. Bude was kept busy dealing with the aftermath of "doodle-bugs" which landed in the neighbourhood of Crooked Cottage, but perhaps to compensate for the absence of his daughter, he started work on a children's book. Chapter by chapter; he mailed it to a delighted Jennifer. The book was eventually published in 1946, under his real name.

Jennifer recalls that since

> 'Crooked Cottage' was 500 years old, it had no drinking water so each day my father had to walk to a deep well in the woods and fill two buckets. The round trip was about a quarter of a mile. His writing room was a low building attached to the house but accessed from outside. It had a long low window so that when he was writing he could sit and look out at the garden and hills beyond. Nobody was allowed in without permission!
>
> After the war, life carried on much the same as before except, to his delight, in 1946 he had a son Richard. Our parents then became very busy, building on to the cottage. The other memorable excitement was getting the Rover out of the garage and onto the road, so that we could all get around other than by bicycle. As a result, once again, we were able to go to plays, ballets, concerts, and so on in London.

The sense of humour so evident in *Death Makes a Prophet* was typical of a man whose wit, and love of practical jokes, are still fondly remembered by his daughter. Rather like Inspector Meredith, Bude was evidently a likeable fellow, and this novel, like the other titles of his reprinted in the Crime Classics series, displays his talent for writing likeable mysteries.

Martin Edwards
www.martinedwardsbooks.com

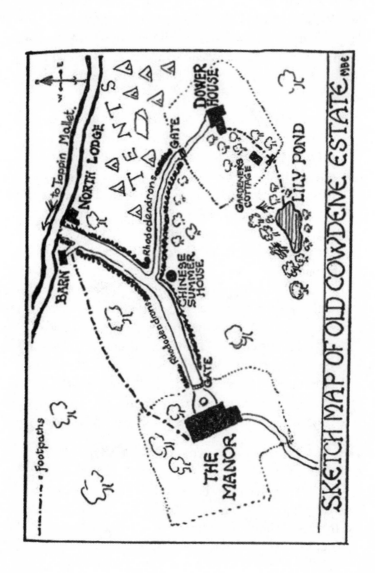

SKETCH MAP OF OLD COWDENE ESTATE MBE

Part I

Welworth Garden City

Chapter I

The Children of Osiris

I

"An Englishman, as a free man," said Voltaire, "goes to heaven by the road which pleases him." If there are many roads that lead to perdition, then there are as many that lead to salvation; and England probably houses more diverse, odd and little known religions than any other country in the world. And of all places in this island most conducive to the flourishing of these many beliefs, none can equal the little town of Welworth. Welworth is not an ordinary town. It is that rarefied, mushroom-like, highly individualistic conglomeration of bricks and mortar known as a Garden City. There is no house in Welworth over thirty years old. There are no slums, monuments, garden-fences, bill-hoardings or public-houses. There is a plethora of flowering shrubs, litter-baskets, broad avenues, Arty-Crafty Shoppes, mock-Tudor, mock-Georgian, mock-Italianate villas. There is, of course, a Health Food Store selling Brazil Nut Butter, cold spaghetti fritters, maté tea and a most comprehensive and staggering range of herbal pills and purgatives. Per head of the population, Welworth probably consumes more lettuce and raw carrot than any other community in the country. A very high percentage of the Welworth élite are not only vegetarians, but non-smokers, non-drinkers and non-pretty-well-everything-that-makes-life-worth-living for less high-minded citizens.

They weave their own cloth, knit their own jumpers and go their own ways with that recherché look common to all who have espoused the Higher Life. Many favour shorts and open-work sandals. A large number do barbola-work or dabble in batik. Some are genuine, some are not; but all bear with them the undeniable stamp of individuality and burn with the unquenchable fire of their particular faith. It may be Theosophy or Babaism; it may be Seventh Day Adventism, Christian Science, Pantheism or what you will—but in a naughty world full of atheists and agnostics, Welworth is a refreshing centre of spiritual élan and a complete refutation of the theory that sectarianism in this country is on the wane.

It is claimed (with all due deference to Mr. Heinz) that there are fifty-seven varieties of religion in Welworth. It speaks highly of the town's tolerance. Some are orthodox. Some are unorthodox but well known. Others are unorthodox and unknown. And among the latter, probably the least orthodox and the most exclusive, is that queer, somewhat exotic sect, founded by Eustace K. Mildmann in the early nineteen hundreds, called the Children of Osiris.

For the sake of brevity in a busy world, the Children of Osiris, adopting the initials of their full title, referred to their doctrine as the Cult of Coo, or more simply, Cooism. (Not to be confused, of course, with Coué-ism.) The gods of Cooism were those of Ancient Egypt—Osiris, Isis, Horus, Thoth, Set, and so forth—but this rich mythology had been modernised and modified by the inclusion of many dogmas

borrowed from less remote religions. The result was a catholic
hot-pot compounded of a belief in magic numbers, astrology, auras, astral bodies, humility, meditation, vegetarianism, immortality, hand-woven tweeds and brotherly love. It
was, in short, an obliging religion because one could find in
it pretty well anything one looked for. Eustace Mildmann
found everything in it. It was his child, his passion, his whole
life. He had created Cooism and because, before seeing the
light, Eustace had been a nonentity, it might be said that
Cooism had created Eustace Mildmann. It had lifted him
out of a small provincial bookshop and set him down in
Welworth with five elderly female acolytes, an enormous
and contagious enthusiasm for his faith and a small overdraft
at his bank. His sincerity was not to be doubted. Cooism
to Eustace was the key to all life's mysteries. It was the only
straight road that led to salvation. He believed it could solve
everything—even the overdraft at his bank. And like many
men of unswerving belief he found his optimism justified.
He found in Welworth an intellectual coterie ready and willing to listen to him. His five female acolytes soon became
ten, fifteen, fifty zealots of both sexes. He found a small tin
hall left by some improvident sect that had gone theologi-
cally and financially bankrupt. It became the first Temple of
Cooism. And finally, like a Parsifal who at length discovers
his Holy Grail, he found the Hon. Mrs. Hagge-Smith. After
that Cooism, so to speak, was on the map.

II

Before he left his bookshop and moved to Welworth, Eustace
had become a widower. It was shortly after the death of his
wife, in fact, that he set out to evolve the first principles of
Cooism. His best ideas had always come to him when sunk
in a self-imposed trance, or, as he more pithily expressed it,

"during a phase of Yogi-like non-being". ("Non-being" figured as a very important factor in the Cult of Coo, though
nobody seemed able to define its exact significance.) Whether
the original idea of Terence, his only child, had also occurred
to him when in a state of "non-being" seems doubtful, for
at such periods Eustace was a receptacle for *good* ideas and
Terence was probably the worst idea he'd ever had. For Terence was the antithesis of his father. Where Eustace was mild,
dreamy and soft-spoken, Terence was athletic and practical,
with a booming bass voice. When Eustace had first moved
to Welworth, Terence was still a very junior schoolboy. At
the time when this narrative opens he was a gradely young
man of twenty-one, with a healthy appetite, wholesome
ideas and the physique of a boxer. In the interim, his father
had done everything to undermine his normality. He had
sent him to a co-ed school with an ultra-modern, one might
almost say, post-impressionistic curriculum; clamped down
on his tremendous appetite with a strict vegetarianism; made
him a Symbol-Bearer in the Temple of Osiris; and with the
inhumanity of a fanatic with a one-track mind, kept him
very short of pocket-money. To say that Terence disliked
his father is not an exaggeration. He simmered with resentment under the restrictions placed upon him. He thought
Cooism the most incomprehensible twaddle. He thought
the Children of Osiris the most embarrassing collection of
cranks in a town where ordinary men seemed odd. He rated
vegetarianism as an unnatural vice. He thought co-education
sloppy. He considered the Hon. Mrs. Hagge-Smith a blot
on the face of creation. And yet, being naturally inarticulate
and obedient, Terence dared not come out in open rebellion.
He just suffered in silence like a goaded ox. Sometimes there
was a look in his eye that was strangely reminiscent of an
ox—a look of patient resignation that gave way every now
and then to a gleam of ominous hostility.

The Mildmanns, father and son, lived in the mockest of mock-Tudor mansions on Almond Avenue. It was a big, secluded house standing in an acre of well-kept garden as befitted the High Prophet of Cooism. It was run by an efficient lady-housekeeper, a widow by the name of Laura Summers, a handsome, even striking, blonde, with perfect manners and a cultured voice. In the emancipated atmosphere of a Garden City this arrangement raised no breath of scandal. Merely a rip-snorting tornado of vilification that would have pulverised any man less innocent and unworldly as Mr. Mildmann. As it was he never even thought of Mrs. Summers as a blonde. She was his housekeeper and a convert (though not a particularly reliable one) to Cooism. Between Terence and Mrs. Summers there was considerable sympathy and understanding. Her late husband had been a man with a big appetite and few ideas. She felt sorry for Terence in his over-tight shorts, his sandals and open-neck shirts. He looked so like a little boy that has grown out of his clothes that the mere sight of him roused all her maternal instincts. They formed a sort of nebulous alliance against the soft-fingered influences of Eustace Mildmann. They shared little private jokes over many things that the Children of Osiris held sacred. Misplaced, perhaps, but very human. In particular over Mrs. Hagge-Smith—the very sight of whom always reduced Terence to a state of unutterable boredom.

Ostensibly the Archbishop—or in the nomenclature of the order, the "High Prophet"—of Cooism was, of course, its founder, Eustace Mildmann. But the force behind the movement, the financial prop, the true director of policy, was Alicia Hagge-Smith. She paid the piper and so, naturally, she called the tune. She was quite accustomed to calling the tune. She had been calling it all her life, for the simple reason that her late husband had made a million out of mineral waters.

Right from her earliest years Alicia had taken to religion as other women take to golf, bridge or pink gin. She had, so to speak, a nose for odd religions—the odder the better. She had feasted at the tables of many a faith, but always in the long run she had suffered spiritual indigestion and retired in search of a more assimilatory diet. At one time she had actually turned her back on the problems of salvation and taken up Eurhythmics. Unfortunately, a generous build coupled with an artistic fervour out of keeping with her mature years, had led her to rick her back during one of the more advanced exercises, leaving a vacuum in her life which was quickly filled with Cooism. And in Cooism, Mrs. Hagge-Smith seemed to have found a spiritual pabulum that suited her to a T. She gobbled up the movement lock, stock and barrel and, thereafter, allowed Eustace five thousand a year to act as figurehead whilst she steered the ship. Luckily, Eustace (probably during a phase of "non-being") recognised on which side his bread was buttered, and sensibly accepted Mrs. Hagge-Smith's patronage with open arms. In less than no time Cooism thrust out tentacles, though its central body still remained in Welworth, and, within four years of Alicia's enrolment as a Child of Osiris, its membership numbered over ten thousand and Temples sprang up in London and the provinces. Within five years its subscriptions and donations covered all disbursements. In six, Cooism was making a handsome profit and Eustace found himself saddled with a far more elaborate hierarchy for the running of his movement. He needed his Bishop of York, so to speak—a worthy successor who, in the event of his sudden demise, could step into his sandals. It was thus that the office of Prophet-in-Waiting was created and paved the way for the sudden, flamboyant entry of that enigmatic personage, Peta Penpeti.

III

From its inauguration Cooism had attracted a very distinct type of initiate. It was a cult for the few rather than the many; and the few for the most part were well able to afford the exclusive entrance fee that was deliberately imposed by Mrs. Hagge-Smith in order to sort the sheep from the goats. Alicia, when backing her enthusiasms, preferred quality rather than quantity. She liked her religion to have a certain *ton,* a certain *je ne sais quoi* of good-breeding about it. She often felt that Eustace, as High Prophet, was a trifle too democratic in outlook. To him all converts were grist to the mills of his particular creed, irrespective of their accents and incomes. Even as High Prophet, Eustace himself was not quite…and here Mrs. Hagge-Smith would twiddle her fingers and shake her grey locks.

Then, enhaloed in mystery, there had arrived in Welworth Garden City a man after Alicia's own heart. A man with poise and personality; a man with a black beard and dark, hypnotic eyes; a man with an exotic accent and the manners of a French count.

"Penpeti," declared Mrs. Hagge-Smith, "is not only a man—he's an experience!"

Be that as it may, Peta Penpeti soon rose in the ranks of the order. He brought a new and exciting mysticism into the meetings, an oriental spice that had previously been missing from the hot-pot. His name alone stirred the imagination, for wasn't Penpeti a genuine ancient Egyptian surname? It meant "divine father", and that, in fact, is what Penpeti soon became to many of the more impressionable and younger daughters of Cooism. Although there was nothing divine in his appearance, his attitude to these young ladies, however, was strictly paternal and his devotion to the Movement seemed irreproachable. He claimed to be a reincarnation of a certain Pen Penpeti, a priest in the temple of Amen-Ra at Thebes, but his more immediate origins remained shrouded in mystery. It was rumoured that he had actually been born within sight of the Nile, that he had later led a life of dissipation in Cairo, run through a considerable fortune, repented of his ways and arrived in England in search of salvation. He had been tutored, so it was said, by a Scotch dominie, which doubtless accounted for his faultless use of the English language.

Mrs. Hagge-Smith found him delightful. His polish and urbanity were refreshing after Eustace's rather dreary humility. She liked the jaunty angle at which he wore his fez and the long black caftan he wore beneath his black cloak. She liked his oriental exaggerations, his long, mystical silences, his air of culture and assurance.

In Welworth, Penpeti was probably the finest single advertisement that the Children of Osiris had ever received. Comment on him invariably led to some mention of Cooism, and Cooism to some mention of Eustace Mildmann. So, in a way, Eustace was bathed in reflected glory. After the advent of Penpeti, Mrs. Hagge-Smith was able to double the annual subscription and, out of the resultant profits, Penpeti was voted a salary of five hundred a year. He seemed to have no money of his own, which was not surprising since he was supposed to have squandered a fortune. He lived modestly in a Garden City Council House in Wistaria Road—that is to say, an ordinary Council House with blue-painted frames and doors, two bay-trees in scarlet tubs and a flagstone path. He took most of his meals at the Rational Feeding Restaurant, a vegetarian dive on Broadway, Welworth's main thoroughfare. A daily woman came in and "did" for him. Penpeti, in short, for all his extravagant appearance, lived in an atmosphere of monastic isolation. But whether by choice or necessity nobody was prepared to say.

But there they were, this exclusive, intelligent coterie of seekers-after-truth—eccentric, temperamental, "different", perhaps, but at bed-rock moved by those passions, great and small, which are the arbiters of human action. On the surface the Children of Osiris seemed to reflect indeed all the uncomplicated and lovable traits of the very young. They seemed to be banded together by their common faith, imbued with an almost excessive consideration for each other's feelings. But appearances, even in a Garden City, are deceptive. Beneath this concealing crust of Cooism a ferment was at work; small hostilities were growing; vague jealousies were gaining strength; little intrigues swelling into obsessions. And far off, no more than a dark speck beyond a distant horizon, wasn't there a nebulous hint of approaching tragedy in the air? Big oaks from little acorns grow, and viewing events in retrospect there seems little doubt that the jumping-off point of this tragedy was Alicia Hagge-Smith's "vision". Without her "vision" circumstances favourable to a murder would never have materialised. And without a murder, Inspector Meredith would never have heard of the Children of Osiris. As it was, he always considered it to be one of the most interesting, bizarre, and exacting of all his cases.

Chapter II

Mrs. Hagge-Smith Has a Vision

I

"My dear," said Mrs. Hagge-Smith, as she swept into the breakfast-room of Old Cowdene, "don't speak to me for a moment. I want to sit perfectly silent and let the Influences flow into me. I've had a vision! A wonderful, inspiring vision!" She sniffed appreciatively. "Ah, am I right in suspecting walnut steak? Yes, my dear, you can serve me with a small helping and pour my coffee. It's wrong to neglect our earthly bodies. We must never forget that they're the temporary dwelling-places of our Better Selves."

She was addressing her secretary, a young and extremely pretty brunette with a stylishly slender figure and a nice deferential manner that went well with her position in the household. That this manner was the only false thing about her, Mrs. Hagge-Smith had never realised. That behind her charming presence Denise Blake concealed an unswerving dislike of her employer was something so fantastic that Mrs. Hagge-Smith would have refused to credit it. She was used

to deference, smiling faces, quick obedience and good service—the result, she felt sure, of an irresistible personality
rather than a bloated bank balance. She liked to have Denise
about because she was quiet and efficient and deft. She had,
moreover, a pale blue aura which Alicia had always found
particularly soothing.

Having crossed to the sideboard and served Mrs. Hagge-
Smith, Denise poured her coffee and returned to her own
place at the breakfast-table. She began to nibble her toast,
slyly watching Alicia from under her long lashes. There was
no doubt from the smile of beatitude on her face that the
Influences were flowing in. Denise wondered what form her
latest enthusiasm would take and just where it was destined
to land them. From a certain congested look about those
raddled and monumental features there was no doubt that
the vision was a thumping big one.

At the end of ten minutes, Mrs. Hagge-Smith came out
of her state of "non-being" like a cork from a bottle. She
reached for the toast and marmalade, demanded a second
cup of coffee and rapped out:

"We shall be leaving for Welworth on the ten-ten. You
will come with me. See that Millie has me packed by nine-
thirty sharp and order the car round for nine-forty-five."

"Yes, Mrs. Hagge-Smith."

"And ring the Endive Hotel and reserve our rooms for
a week."

"Yes, Mrs. Hagge-Smith."

Denise, despite the gloomy November day beyond the
window, brightened considerably. Anything to get away from
the deadly dull routine which reigned at Old Cowdene. Even
Welworth Garden City would seem like Paris and Buenos
Aires rolled into one after this waterlogged, isolated corner
of Sussex. Although she had been with Mrs. Hagge-Smith
for nearly six months, she had never before accompanied

her on any of her many visits to this Canterbury of Cooism. She had often tried to imagine what Mr. Mildmann and Mr. Penpeti and many other of the Coo celebrities looked like, for at one time or another Mrs. Hagge-Smith had dictated letters to all of them. Now she would have the chance to see for herself. She imagined the experience would be rather amusing.

Out in the hall, she got through to the Endive Hotel and was informed with regrets that every room in the place was booked up for at least a fortnight. There was a Hand Weavers Conference due to start that very day. Denise went up to Mrs. Hagge-Smith's dressing-room and gave her the information.

"How tiresome, my dear. But we mustn't lose control. You must telephone Mr. Mildmann at once and see if *he* can have us. Tell him it's urgent. Tell him I've had a vision in connection with our great work. I must discuss it with him without delay."

"Yes, Mrs. Hagge-Smith."

Ten minutes later it was all arranged. Mr. Mildmann, who really had no option, said he'd be only too delighted to accommodate Mrs. Hagge-Smith and her secretary under his humble roof. He would expect them for lunch. Little did Denise realise as she turned away from the phone that the Hand Weavers Conference was destined to alter the whole future aspect of her existence. Little did she realise, as she packed her well-worn, imitation leather suitcase, that she was moving towards an experience before which all previous experiences would pale into insignificance.

II

Lunch—spaghetti and lentil pie with prunes and custard to follow—was over. Mrs. Hagge-Smith, aflame with impatience, drew Eustace aside into the latter's study. Eustace eyed his patron through his pince-nez with a nervous, rather apprehensive look. He conducted her to a chair and threw an extra log or two on the fire.

"Well, Alicia?"

"Eustace, my dear," announced Mrs. Hagge-Smith dramatically. "We simply must have it! We must bend all our energies to its creation. We must organise it without delay. It all came to me last night in a vision."

"It?"

Eustace looked utterly fogged. Mrs. Hagge-Smith threw wide her arms as if embracing her large and invisible idea.

"Our Summer School!" she cried. "Our very own al fresco Convention! A gathering of all our children, *all* of them… at Old Cowdene."

"Old Cowdene?" echoed Eustace bleakly.

"All our children!" repeated Mrs. Hagge-Smith with a moist expression. "All of them."

"All?" echoed Eustace, still more bleakly. "But my dear Alicia—"

"Eustace!" exclaimed Mrs. Hagge-Smith. "Don't tell me that you haven't the wildest enthusiasm for my idea. It would break my heart if I thought I couldn't rely on your support. We shall have to put it, of course, to the members of the Inmost Temple. But as you know, we never have the slightest difficulty in overriding *their* objections. Well, what do you say?"

"It's all so sudden, so extensive in scope, I've barely had time to grasp it all. You mean you are prepared to throw open your estate at Old Cowdene for a general convention of the Movement?" Mrs. Hagge-Smith nodded. "But how would you house them? We have, as you know"—Eustace coughed deprecatingly—"a present membership of over ten thousand. Even if only half of them were able to attend—"

"Tents!" broke in Mrs. Hagge-Smith with a snap.

"Tents?" echoed Eustace. "You mean we could accommodate them in tents?"

"I was granted an astral manifestation of it, my dear Eustace. Rows and rows of delightful tents with all our happy and devoted children wandering among them. With the Chinese summer-house converted into a Temple and a huge marquee for meals. It was all there—perfect in every detail. Even the cook-houses. It was all so beautiful, so idyllic, so *right,* that it brought tears to my eyes. I confess it, Eustace. When my vision faded I just lay in bed and wept with joy."

"What if it rains?" asked Eustace in a tentative sort of way.

"It won't," said Mrs. Hagge-Smith decisively. "I have a feeling about these things. And I *feel* it won't rain. I'm always lucky with my weather. It runs in the family."

"And Peta?" asked Eustace. "How do you think he'll react?"

"Yes, there is Mr. Penpeti," said Mrs. Hagge-Smith, her previous self-assurance suddenly modified. "You rang him as I suggested and told him to come round at once?"

Eustace nodded.

"He should be here at any minute. I know you value his opinion on matters of grand policy."

"I do. I think he's an exceptionally gifted man. So hypnotic. A Gemini, of course. Like Shakespeare."

"Umph," commented Eustace with a hint of sourness. "I'm not sure if we can trust these astrological labels. Shakespeare himself said 'It is not in our stars...', didn't he? And Gemini," he mused. "The Heavenly Twins. I often think it is the sign of the two-faced. I have nothing against Peta, of course. But I sometimes think you overrate his sincerity."

"Eustace!" gasped Mrs. Hagge-Smith. "Don't tell me you're jealous of Mr. Penpeti. You, the High Prophet of our order, allowing the grosser human emotions to..."

Mrs. Hagge-Smith got no further since at that moment the maid announced the arrival of Mr. Penpeti himself. He came into the room, still wearing his fez, with a smile of welcome on his pallid features. Ignoring Eustace entirely, he crossed the room with a pantherine tread, seized one of Mrs. Hagge-Smith's large and capable hands and raised it to his lips.

"An unanticipated pleasure," he murmured. "All day I have been filled with a strange sense of expectancy. And now…" He stood back with a soft, ingratiating smile. "And now *this*!"

He made to seize her hand a second time, but unfortunately Mrs. Hagge-Smith in the interim had unearthed her handkerchief to attend to a slight catarrhal trouble to which she was subject. Penpeti's manœuvre, therefore, much to Eustace's delight, was merely an embarrassment for both of them. He crossed to a chair and, somewhat stiffly, sat down.

"I called you round," said Eustace haughtily, "because Alicia…er, that is, Mrs. Hagge-Smith, has a matter of considerable importance to discuss with us."

"Indeed?"

"Mr. Penpeti!" exclaimed Mrs. Hagge-Smith. "I am sure I can look to you for the enthusiasm which dear Eustace has lamentably failed to exhibit." Penpeti gave a little bow. "I have been blessed with a most wonderful inspiration. Last night in bed I—"

And for the second time Mrs. Hagge-Smith set out the details of her vision. Penpeti's reaction was startling. He sprang from his chair, seized both Alicia's hands, kissed them each in turn, and whipped round on Eustace.

"But this is a superb, incomparable idea! Of course we must have a Summer Camp. Why haven't we thought of it before! We must ensure that we have representatives from every branch. My dear Mrs. Hagge-Smith, the Movement already owes more to you than it can ever repay. Now, alas, we're more than ever in debt to you. And when do you suggest that we—?"

"Next June," broke in Mrs. Hagge-Smith, whose organised mind had already worked out the general details of her scheme. "That will give us six months to prepare. We must, of course, have running water laid on, with proper drainage, shower-baths, electricity, telephone extensions, laundry facilities, washing-up machines—"

The list seemed to prolong itself interminably and as the magnitude of Mrs. Hagge-Smith's conception dawned more fully on Mr. Mildmann's mind, his nervousness seemed to increase. As a small provincial bookseller he was not used to thinking in a big way. The whole project not only staggered but frightened him. Carrying out the ceremonies of his faith in the snug and familiar atmosphere of the Welworth Temple, he was happy and confident. But this super-epic à la Cecil de Mille left him apprehensive and miserable. He dropped into a sulky silence whilst Alicia and Penpeti continued to discuss the scheme with ever-increasing liveliness. Only once did he look up and murmur a timid objection.

"But the expense…the expense of it all! Have you thought of that, Alicia?"

Mrs. Hagge-Smith dismissed his objection with an airy wave of her hand and returned with redoubled fervour to Peta Penpeti. She was thinking it was a thousand pities that Cooism had been created by such a spineless creature as Eustace Mildmann. Otherwise Mr. Penpeti might have been its High Prophet—a splendid, forceful, inspiring leader, a man after her own heart. Together they could have lifted the Movement to new and exalted heights, expanding its influence, furthering its publicity until it was known from one end of the country to the other. This Summer Convention was but a trial spin. Mrs. Hagge-Smith could see the tentacles of Cooism reaching out over the Continent and beyond, to India, Africa and Asia, even to America. Cooism—a World Religion! And why not? With Penpeti by her side she was ready to dare anything. If only Eustace were not such a wet blanket, such a cautious old maid, so provincial in outlook! Alicia sighed. Life, even if you had a million, was very exasperating.

III

In the large, severely-furnished drawing-room across the hall another conversation was in progress. It was by no means a fluent conversation. In fact, silence and speech were mixed in about equal proportions. The room itself was not exactly conducive to light and witty badinage. There was a vast amount of hard polished wood underfoot, with here and there an unreliable rush-mat which, at the slightest provocation, would skid from under one with all the consequent social embarrassment. Hard wooden chairs were set about, defying the intruder to make himself comfortable. Strange appliquéd figures, representing scenes from the Book of the Dead, marched in stiff procession round the wooden-panelled walls. Two stone Thoths, one Anubis, three Hathors, a Beb, a Mut and a Set were the principal ornaments, save for one enormous imaginative oil-painting over the wooden fireplace depicting Am-Mit, the Eater of the Dead, enjoying with immense gusto the unvarying *plat du jour*. A few scraggy sprays of "everlastings" stuck up from the necks of several wooden vases and to either side of the door, like the immobile sentinels of a past epoch, stood two anthropoid coffins of carved and painted wood.

Yet by far the most wooden object in the room at that particular moment was Terence Mildmann. He was sitting on the very edge of a small upright chair, his brawny knees gleaming in the firelight, his two ham-like hands clasped over his thighs. Despite the raw November day he was dressed, save for walking-stick and rucksack, like a hiker. His expression was difficult to analyse but among the more fleeting emotions it was possible to isolate delight, incredulity and acute bashfulness. Seated opposite to him on a small, hard, wooden coffin-stool, was Denise.

Neither was prepared to say just what had happened to them over the luncheon-table. Once, twice, perhaps three times, their eyes had met for a brief instant, yet within that flash of time something incredible had transpired. Terence, at any rate, knew that he had never seen anything quite so breathlessly lovely as Denise, and Denise knew that she had never met anything quite so pathetically helpless as Terence. Once they were in the drawing-room he had offered her a cigarette. She said she didn't smoke. Terence said he didn't, either. He wasn't allowed to. His father didn't like it. After that they both looked into the fire and said nothing for a time. Then Terence tried again:

"You work for the Blot, don't you?"

"I beg your pardon?"

"I say!—I shouldn't have said that. I meant Mrs. Hagge-Smith."

"Yes, I'm her secretary."

"Phew!"

After which expressive ejaculation there was again a long silence. This time it was Denise who stepped in.

"Don't you find it cold wearing shorts in the winter?"

"I have to. My father believes in rational clothing."

"But he doesn't wear shorts."

"I mean, he believes in it for other people."

"I see."

"Mind you, I'm pretty tough." Terence crooked an arm to show off his biceps and threw out his barrel-like chest. "I do dumb-bells and clubs before my open window every morning. I can do the mile in four minutes, twenty seconds. Not bad, is it?"

"It's jolly good," said Denise warmly. "I'm not very hot at that sort of thing. I was in the second eleven hockey at school. But even that was rather a fluke."

After a further pause, Terence enquired:

"Do you believe in all this Children of Osiris stuff? I know I oughtn't to talk like this. After all it was the Guv'nor's idea. I suppose it's all right if you like that sort of thing. But I don't. I'm keen on sports. Er...do you belong?"

"Well," admitted Denise, "I'm a member of the Order, if that's what you mean. You see in my job it would be a bit awkward if I wasn't. Mrs. Hagge-Smith more or less made me join when she engaged me. And as I have to earn my own living..."

"I say, what rotten luck. Of course, my father being the High Prophet, I can't very well get out of it. I'm a Symbol-Bearer in the Temple. But I'm not much cop at it." He boomed happily: "I'm awfully glad you're going to be staying here for a bit. It will cheer things up for me no end."

Denise flushed with pleasure at the compliment, but not knowing quite what to say, she wisely said nothing. Terence scratched his knees, which were burning in the heat from the fire, shot a quick glance at the miracle in his midst and asked abruptly:

"I say, don't think this rude of me, but do you have manifestations?"

"Manifestations?"

It sounded as if he were referring to insects or pimples.

"Yes, you know—astral visions and all that sort of thing. Spirit shapes."

"No—I can't say that I do. I dream rather a lot after a late supper. But I'm not at all psychic, if that's what you mean."

"I am," announced Terence, to Denise's surprise. "I'm always having astral manifestations. I get quite a kick out of it." His eyes assumed a dreamy expression and then suddenly narrowed, as if he were trying, there and then, to penetrate the Veil. "It's marvellous sometimes how clearly I see things. They're so terribly realistic."

"Things?" enquired Denise. "What things?"

"Steaks mostly. But sometimes it's mutton-chops or steak and kidney pudding. I just have to close my eyes, relax my mind and body, and there they are." He passed a healthy red tongue round his lips and swallowed rapidly. "You think it's blasphemous of me to see things like that, don't you? I know it's not very high-minded, but—"

"I don't think anything of the sort. I think it's very clever of you to see anything at all."

Terence shot a quick glance at the door, shied away from the painted glaring eyes of the mummy-cases, and lowering his voice, went on:

"I just can't help it. I suppose it's a kind of wish fulfilment, as the psychologists call it. The point is, I've got a pretty healthy appetite and all these vegetarian fripperies leave me cold. I've no interest in the food I'm supposed to eat, only in that which I'm not allowed to. Sickening, isn't it? I mean I just can't work up any real enthusiasm for peanut cutlets and raw cabbage. Pretty low-minded of me, isn't it?"

"Oh I don't know. I'm only a vegetarian myself because in Rome one has to do as the Romans do. But then, I never worry much about food."

"You never worry?" said Terence with a shocked and incredulous look. "Never worry about food!" For the second time he lowered his voice and cast a guilty glance at the door. "Look here, can you keep a secret?"

"Of course."

"You promise not to give me away?"

"Of course."

"Then I'll let you in on something. Last week I went on the binge. And it's not the first time, either." There was a proud and defiant ring in his rumbling bass voice. "Yes, I sneaked out last Tuesday night and went on the binge."

"Where?"

"Wilson's Restaurant in Chives Avenue." He sighed profoundly and his eye was lit with a retrospective gleam. "Gravy soup, sole à la bonne femme and a double portion of silver-side! Oh boy!" He chuckled happily. "What a binge! What a glorious, all-in, slap-up binge! I'd been saving up for that. Ten weeks' pocket-money gone in a flash. You can't keep that sort of thing up on sixpence a week. There are long blank periods in between, worse luck!"

"Oh you poor boy!" breathed Denise, genuinely moved by his predicament. "Fancy you getting only sixpence a week at your age."

"Father's pretty stingy, you know. He doesn't believe in money. At least, not for other people."

"Like rational clothing."

"Yes—that's it. Like rational clothing."

They laughed happily together, each conscious of the undercurrent of sympathy which was flowing between them. Already they were fast overcoming their shyness.

"I say—what's the Blot doing here? Any idea?"

"None at all at present. I daresay we shall soon find out."

"Well, whatever she's got up her sleeve," observed Terence sagaciously, "I'll wager it's going to land us in all sorts of trouble. Whenever she turns up in Welworth things start to happen. And the trouble is you can never tell where they're going to end!"

Which was about the wisest and most penetrating remark Terence Mildmann had ever made.

IV

Mr. Penpeti stayed to tea. He also stayed to dinner. Even Eustace could not entirely detach himself from the wild enthusiasms swirling about him. A complete scheme for the Summer Convention had been drawn up. Numerical and astrological influences had been worked out so that the most suitable period of June could be chosen. Denise, under Mrs. Hagge-Smith's direction, had already drawn up a summons to the members of the Inmost Temple to attend a committee meeting on the following day. Eustace and Penpeti had even sketched out a rough schedule of lectures, discussions, rituals, and so forth. Aware that Denise would almost certainly have to attend the convention, Terence was prepared to admit that Mrs. Hagge-Smith's latest and most grandiose idea wasn't such a bad bet after all. As for Penpeti, he was at his most forceful, charming and persuasive—every now and then veiling his hypnotic eyes behind their heavy lids, slipping away into a state of "non-being" and coming out of his trance with ever new and more splendid suggestions.

But behind all this activity it grew more and more evident that Eustace was simmering with irritation. He resented the free-handed way in which Penpeti gradually took command of the proceedings. Once or twice Peta actually overrode Mrs. Hagge-Smith's opinions and substituted ideas of his own. And what was even more disturbing, Mrs. Hagge-Smith appeared quite ready to submit to his dictatorship. Everybody seemed ready to bow down before him.

When he left "Tranquilla" (which was the name of Mr. Mildmann's mock-Tudor mansion) Penpeti was delighted with the way in which everything was progressing. His position inside the Movement was growing more and more secure and his influence over Mrs. Hagge-Smith more comprehensive. He sighed with the deepest satisfaction.

His rise had been swift. In less than eighteen months he had been promoted from a mere nonentity to the second most important person in the Order. Of course, he had been forced to walk warily, *very* warily; but now his patience and caution were beginning to pay big dividends. It was not only that he enjoyed the kudos and the five hundred a year that went with the office of Prophet-in-Waiting—it was more than that. Much more. The whole point was that, after a period of almost unbearable suspense, he was *safe*! Safe at last from the—

But at this juncture Peta Penpeti's thoughts sheered away from all recollections of the past. It was better that way. Why summon up those dark unwanted spectres when he could exorcise them by a simple refusal to think about them? It would be only too easy to allow those smoky shadows of the past to haunt him and hound him into a pit of the deepest depression. But that way lay madness! After all, for eighteen months now he had been safe. And if safe for eighteen months, why not for ever? The fear that had once sniffed at his heels now seemed to have turned tail and given up the hunt. He was free once more to look ahead and relax. He must still walk warily, of course, but...

Suddenly, not five yards from his own front-gate, Penpeti stopped dead. In a flash all his reassuring arguments fled. A chill trickle of fear ran up his spine and left him trembling. From the gloom ahead a figure in a seedy mackintosh and black felt hat sidled up to him and placed a detaining hand on his arm. Penpeti recoiled as if from the clammy touch of a snake.

"Well?" he demanded in a low voice. "What is it? What do you want?"

"I think you can guess."

"But look here, Yacob, you know I damned well can't—"

"Think again, my dear fellow. Er...for *your* sake."

For an instant Penpeti hesitated, then with a quick glance up and down the road, he muttered angrily:

"All right—come inside. I don't want to be seen hanging about here with you."

"That's perfectly understandable," said Yacob.

Penpeti opened the gate and Yacob followed him up the flagstone path and into the tiny unlighted hall. Not until he had groped his way into the little sitting-room and carefully drawn the curtains, did Penpeti switch on the light. Yacob blinked owlishly in the sudden glare, threw his black hat on to the settee and sat down beside it. Penpeti stood over him and scrutinised with unconcealed hatred those swarthy, dark-jowled features, the tawny, malignant eyes that looked up so mockingly into his own. Just now, of course, he had been wrong. Too optimistic. There was always Yacob—the predatory, unpredictable Yacob, wandering back at odd intervals into his life and forcing him to remember all he wanted to forget.

Perhaps, after all, he wasn't quite so safe as he imagined. No, despite all his reassuring arguments, there was always Yacob!

Chapter III

Eustace Writes a Letter

I

It would be impossible to describe the various forms of ritual practised by the Children of Osiris without writing an exhaustive treatise on Cooism. There is such a book available to the general public—*The Development, Practice, and General Principles of the Cult of Coo* by Eustace K. Mildmann—Utopia Press—21/-. The work is in two volumes. The reading is not, alas, very much snappier than the title. But a word about the constitutional side of Cooism is, perhaps, essential.

Apart from the High Prophet and the Prophet-in-Waiting, the fortunes of the Movement were presided over by the members of the Inmost Temple. These numbered six—three High Priests and three High Priestesses. Among the latter, of course, was Mrs. Hagge-Smith. For all her airy assumption that she had this governing body in her pocket, Mrs. Hagge-Smith was more optimistic than accurate. There were at least two other members of the Inmost Temple who carried nearly as much weight in the order as she did—Penelope Parker and Hansford Boot. Both had money, which made them quite independent of Mrs. Hagge-Smith's whims and prejudices. And both had brains which in Mrs. Hagge-Smith's case were at a premium. Alicia admittedly had energy and enthusiasm but when it came to academic matters she was a broken reed. Hansford was Eustace Mildmann's stoutest champion. Penelope backed Penpeti. The other three members of the Inmost Temple, although less influential, had, despite Alicia's insidious propaganda remained loyal to the founder of the Movement. But the rift dividing these two factions had been steadily widening and at the meeting convened to discuss the idea of a Summer Convention matters reached a new high level of tension.

"Wrong approach. Stupid!" exclaimed Hansford Boot, who spoke a kind of shorthand English peculiarly his own. "Tents. Trees. Arcadian idyll angle. Ridiculous. Laughable. Too frivolous. Don't like it."

"I must say…" began Eustace with a nod of approval, "that as the founder of the order I—"

"Balderdash!" shot out Mrs. Hagge-Smith. "We must carry Cooism out into the world. This parochial attitude shows a deplorable lack of spirit. We must grow and grow and grow!" She made a gesture of expansion which caused the committee-men on either side of her to lean back quickly in their chairs. "We must no longer hide our light under a bushel. We want to gather more and more children to our bosom." She made a gesture of gathering children to her bosom, which enabled the committee-men to tilt forward again, though they kept a wary eye open for any further hint of expansion. "I know that I have the full support of our splendid Prophet-in-Waiting and I suggest we call upon dear Mr. Penpeti to express his views."

Penpeti did so with voluble charm, his rich voice resounding under the tin-roof of the temple and causing a frisson of voluptuous pleasure to course down Penelope's spine. The weaker section of the opposition began to waver. Hansford came back with a further series of staccato objections. Eustace again attempted to back him up, only to be interrupted a second time by his redoubtable patron. Penelope said nothing. Penpeti painted a noble and imaginative picture of thousands of sunburned, smiling devotees in rational clothing, strolling happily under the immemorial elms of Old Cowdene Park. Hansford sketched in an impressionistic picture of those same thousands clad in mackintoshes and goloshes squelching about in the mud beneath immemorial elms that dripped and whipped in a cold June wind. Mrs. Hagge-Smith said: "Balderdash!" Eustace put in timidly: "As High Prophet I do beg of you to allow me—" But this time it was Penelope, speaking for the first time, who interrupted him.

She spoke languidly, mystically, in her soft attractive drawl for ten minutes without a break. Her slender hands wove esoteric patterns on the air. The gauzy veil over her corn-coloured hair was like an aura about her and the pale oval of her face was lit with the beauty of pure devotion. The male section of the committee, with the exception of Penpeti was held spellbound. Yes—even Eustace's weak eyes were expressive of tenderness and admiration. He gazed at Penelope as if she were the reincarnation of some ancient goddess, of Isis herself, perhaps, the hallowed wife of Osiris. In fact he had always believed that she was Isis reborn. In the same way, with the most abject humility of course, he wondered if he might not be a resurrected Osiris. Beyond that he dare not think without exercising the more profane side of his imagination. He only knew that Penelope's presence was a kind of sweet torment, a perilous distraction.

Unfortunately Eustace was one of those prize idiots who fondle the belief that no man over fifty can fall in love. He was unable therefore to diagnose his state-of-mind with any accuracy. Actually Eustace was climbing the first rungs of a ladder that was to lead him to dizzy heights of foolishness and mental anguish. Fate, in short, had earmarked Penelope as his Achilles heel.

When, therefore, Penelope declared herself in favour of Mrs. Hagge-Smith's idea, Eustace's opposition collapsed. The matter was put to the vote, and the motion, with the single exception of Hansford Boot, received the full support of the committee. Mrs. Hagge-Smith's vision was already well on the way to becoming a reality.

II

When the other members of the Inmost Temple had departed, Hansford Boot drew Eustace aside into the vestry. He looked glum and grim.

"Well, Hansford?" enquired Eustace gently, "what is it you are so anxious to see me about? You look depressed."

"I am. Don't like it. Hate hostility. But felt I must speak up."

"And the trouble?"

"Penpeti!" snapped Mr. Boot. "In collaboration with Mrs. H-S."

And then it all came out—an impassioned, yet well-reasoned belief that there was treason in their midst. Hansford Boot was emphatic. Unless Eustace took a strong line there was a danger that the Temple of Cooism would be split asunder. Wasn't Eustace aware of the growing conspiracy among certain elements of the Movement to deny the original ethics of Cooism, in favour of new and disturbing principles? This Summer Convention was a perfect example of his theory. There was no doubt that Mrs. H-S and Penpeti were filled with ambition. They were hungry for power. Mrs. H-S would like to see Penpeti elevated to the position of High Prophet. She was working to that end and, if Eustace were unprepared to retire with good grace, then, declared Mr. Boot, the Penpeti-Hagge-Smith element would break away and start a kind of bastard Cooism of their own. Such a tragedy, at all costs, must be avoided. Hansford Boot was even more emphatic.

"Shall do all I can to cook their goose. Must rally round you with unflinching determination. Vital! Something strange about Penpeti. Intuition tells me. Undesirable influence. Hypocritical. Mrs. H-S too simple to see it. Led by the nose. Penpeti using her for his own ends."

His telegraphic speech gathered force and speed. His evident sincerity was impressive and Eustace warmed to his old friend. Such devotion was touching and he felt unworthy of it. But deep down he knew that Hansford's suggestions matched up perfectly with his own unspoken suspicions. If only he were less timid. If only he had the courage to go to Mrs. Hagge-Smith and point out to her that as the Father of Cooism his word was law. If only he had the fire and eloquence of an Old Testament prophet to sway the dissenters and bring them back into the fold. But those gifts were unfortunately with the opposition, with Penpeti himself. A sudden surge of anger swept through him at the thought of Penpeti's overweening conceit and presumption. And this anger increased when he thought of Penelope Parker's obvious admiration for his Prophet-in-Waiting. He resettled his pince-nez at a more aggressive angle and drew himself up to his full height. At that moment he would have revealed to anybody with psychic powers an aura of flaming, unequivocal red.

"My dear Hansford, you're right. By Geb, you are!" It was the one oath he allowed himself. "Something must be done about it. We must act. And we must act quickly. We must nip this unhappy conspiracy in the bud. But how? How?"

"Leave it to me!" exclaimed Mr. Boot stoutly. "You must do nothing. Lower your dignity. Undermine your prestige. Fatal! I'll handle this. Think of a way. We're not alone remember. Thousands of orthodox believers behind us. Encouraging!"

"But I beg of you, Hansford—nothing violent. I would prefer an appeal to Peta's sense of loyalty rather than any direct recriminations. The Movement can't suffer an open breach in its ranks without the very loss of dignity and prestige you're so anxious to preserve. We must have no brawling—nothing of that kind, please."

"Leave it to me!" rapped out Mr. Boot for the second time. "Never fear. Always diplomatic. But time ripe for action. Strong action. Rely on me!"

III

Hansford Boot in the days that followed made no effort to tackle Peta Penpeti directly about the matter. He followed the far more diplomatic course of waylaying Mrs. Hagge-Smith at every conceivable opportunity. He argued, with considerable common-sense, that Penpeti by himself constituted no real danger. It was only in alliance with Mrs. Hagge-Smith that he might try to undermine poor Eustace's authority and wreck the Movement by dividing it. The great thing was to drive a wedge between Penpeti and his admirer.

Luckily for Hansford, it was about that time when Penpeti made a fateful mistake and played into his hands. It was a mistake that anybody in similar circumstances might have committed. Penpeti, quite unaware that he was about to touch off a keg of gunpowder, merely asked Mrs. Hagge-Smith for a loan. Now, if there was one thing that Mrs.

Hagge-Smith hated beyond all other things, it was being touched for money. She was prepared to pay good salaries, subscribe generously to charities, lay a small fortune at the altar of her particular faith, but to be *asked* for money roused her to a fury. And in the case of Penpeti she felt it was even more irritating and inexcusable. Hadn't she already granted him an annual emolument of five hundred pounds? And since he had no family to support, wasn't that more than ample for his means? Wasn't a simple life compatible with his status inside the Movement? Why did he want this extra money? Penpeti refused to say. It was in connection with a private matter.

"Pooh!" exclaimed Mrs. Hagge-Smith. "What right have you and I to private lives? We should have no life outside the Cause! None! I'm deeply shocked to hear you talk like this. And my dear Mr. Penpeti, never, never, never come to me again and ask for money!"

Penpeti departed from the presence a wiser and sadder man, and Hansford Boot realised that his criticism of the Prophet-in-Waiting was not falling on deaf ears. From that day there was a marked cooling off of Alicia's interest in Penpeti and a new and welcome tendency to listen to Eustace without interrupting him. After all Eustace had never *asked* for a penny. Apart from the upkeep of a household worthy of his exalted position in the order, Eustace never spent a penny on his personal pleasures. He was annoyingly humble and unassertive but, bless the man, a sincere and devout servant of his faith. Alicia wondered if she hadn't been a little hasty and misjudged Eustace.

In the meantime Penpeti, suddenly realising the new precariousness of his position, became increasingly worried. He had got to have that money. But how, in the name of Thoth, Set, and Mut, was he to raise the wind? Eustace? There was absolutely no hope in that direction and in any case he hated the idea of being under any obligation to Eustace. He had never liked his superior's pious manner and undoubted integrity. It made him feel rather cheap and uncomfortable. Moreover it was Eustace who stood between him and the incredibly handsome salary of five thousand a year. Mrs. Hagge-Smith had made that quite plain. The High Prophet designate once he stepped into Eustace's shoes, would automatically receive a High Prophet's salary. The whole matter had been legalised through her solicitors. Even in the unlikely event of Mrs. Hagge-Smith's premature departure into the arms of Osiris, that five thousand a year was assured. But what real hope was there of immediate promotion? None. Eustace with his rational feeding and simple tastes would probably last for years. It was a tantalising situation and one that made Penpeti's present position even more unbearable.

And then, with a flash of sheer inspiration, Penpeti thought of Penelope Parker. She was not his type and her anaemic mysticism annoyed him profoundly. He disliked her floating veils, her tendency to go off into trances at the slightest provocation, but as a possible pigeon to pluck she had one great advantage. She admired him without reservation. She had made this clear to him, more than once, with a frankness that was embarrassing. But as his taste in women was nearer to Rubens than Burne-Jones, Penpeti had remained austere and correct. His attitude to her had been monastic. But now, on the principle that beggars could not be choosers, Penpeti squared himself up for conquest. He decided to see Penelope alone on every possible occasion, to steal aside, as it were, her gauzy veils one by one, until he came (as he felt quite sure he would) to the eternal Eve lurking beneath them.

IV

Terence was living in a dream. Previous to Denise's arrival he had always found it extremely difficult to put himself in a state of "non-being". Now he found it damned hard to get out of. The girl had got him in a flat-spin. Perhaps nothing was more indicative of this than the fact that he suddenly felt utterly disinterested in eating. He no longer had astral visions of cutlets and filleted soles. Instead there was Denise, gently smiling, welcoming him to her bosom with open arms; Denise with her shapely head thrown back inviting his kisses; Denise, in an exquisite evening-frock, waiting to waltz with him; and once, turning his brick-red face even redder, Denise sitting on the edge of her bed in heliotrope pyjamas.

Unfortunately the Blot, in a frantic whirl of activity, more or less monopolised her secretary's time. Terence, himself, since leaving school, had been forced to help his father in a similar secretarial capacity, with the result that he and Denise practically never saw each other alone.

One evening, however, about a week after Mrs. Hagge-Smith's descent on Welworth, she and Eustace went into a huddle in the latter's study over a little matter of ritual. Mrs. Summers, who had already divined which way the wind was blowing, tactfully kept clear of the drawing-room, leaving the young couple to take their coffee alone. The graven images about the room seemed to stare at them expectantly. Even the Eater Up of Souls seemed to pause a moment in his eternal task to cast a priapic eye at them. Terence blew his nose. Denise, without putting sugar in her coffee, stirred it vigorously.

"My sun sign," said Terence suddenly, "is Taurus the Bull. What's yours?"

Denise knew this was astrology and not having lived with Mrs. Hagge-Smith for nothing, she answered brightly:

"I'm Capricorn the Goat."

"I say, that's marvellous. Taurus and Capricorn are supposed to go awfully well together. In fact they're almost twin souls. It's jolly encouraging, isn't it?"

"Why?"

"Well, you see…I rather want to get on well with you. I feel we're both a bit lonely, you know. All this occult stuff's jolly nice if you're keen on it, but when you're just a normal sort of person it's terribly boring. Do you skate?"

"Yes, a bit. Why?"

"I was wondering if you could come skating with me to-morrow. The ice on the Long Pond is supposed to be perfect. Will you come?"

Denise shook her head.

"Impossible, I'm afraid. Mrs. H-S won't let me off. I've just oodles to do at present. I'd love to come, of course."

There was silence for a space. Terence rose, poked the already blazing fire and, greatly daring, reseated himself next to Denise on the hard wooden-backed sofa. His bare knees gleamed healthily in the firelight. Denise was acutely aware of his nearness. He muttered:

"I say, are you game for a bit of deception? There's a temple gathering to-morrow night and they'll all be there, of course. Couldn't you work up a sort of a headache at the last minute? I'll manage a sort of a cold, see? It would give us a chance to see more of each other, wouldn't it?"

"It might," admitted Denise cautiously.

"I'd ask you to come to the pictures, but as a matter of fact"—his embarrassment was enormous—"I haven't a bean. Not a bean! Otherwise…"

"Would you be terribly insulted if I offered to…" Denise abandoned the sentence in mid-air.

"You mean, would I let you…?"

"Yes, if you would. I'd love to."

"I say, that's awfully decent of you. It is really."

"I'm glad you've got no silly pride."

"Pride!" snorted Terence. "You can't afford much pride on a tanner a week." He jumped up and knocked a small hand-carved Ptah-Seker-Asar off a nearby table, stooped to recover it and, tilting the table as he groped, sent two Gebs, a Taurt, and a Nefer-Temu skidding off the polished surface. Denise went down on her hands and knees to help him recover this galaxy of fallen gods. And it was at that moment when a huge ham-like hand closed over one of hers and squeezed it violently. Denise winced, blushed and then protested. "You're marvellous," croaked Terence in a throaty bass. "A real sport. You're the most wonderful—"

Very gently Denise withdrew her hand.

"Now Terence, if you take me to the pictures to-morrow you must promise to behave. No nonsense, please. Promise."

"Of course," declared Terence. "Of *course!*"

V

But of course Terence didn't behave; and of course Denise didn't really want him to. They were young, fast falling in love, and Nature as usual had the last word. They walked home from the Welworth Odeon with their arms round each other's waists, speaking only by means of small physical pressures and long searching glances. They had worked it to reach "Tranquilla" before the meeting at the temple broke up, little realising that Eustace that very evening had, in theatrical parlance, staged the first night of a brand new ritual which he had been working on for some months past; a very much foreshortened version of the usual mid-weekly service. This was unfortunate. Doubly unfortunate was

Mrs. Hagge-Smith's decision to walk home with Eustace in the interests of her figure rather than use the car. Opposite the house, overcome by an extra-passionate interest in each other, Denise and Terence suddenly halted, twined themselves into a somewhat inexpert embrace and kissed each other furiously. And at that precise moment, emerging from the gloom beyond the lamp-post came Eustace and Alicia in a deep discussion concerning the significance of the Pestchet Neteru, a subject over which they had not always, alas! seen eye to eye.

Over this other subject they displayed *no* divergencies. Mrs. Hagge-Smith let out a wail of agonised astonishment. Eustace tut-tutted. Denise uttered a small embarrassed cry. Terence made no sound whatsoever. Still tut-tutting Eustace ushered the little party into the hall, where Denise with a murmured "Good night" pattered quickly up the stairs to her bedroom. He turned to Mrs. Hagge-Smith with an apologetic air.

"A regrettable contretemps," he murmured. "I'm sure you'll excuse me if—"

He waved a dismal hand at his son and nodded towards the door of his study. Taking the hint, Alicia bumped away up the stairs, leaving Terence to follow his father into the room.

"I've no need to tell you what a shock this has been to me," piped Eustace without preliminary. "Miss Blake is a guest under our roof and, therefore, under my protection. When I witnessed that disgraceful exhibition under the lamp-post just now I felt ashamed of you, Terence—profoundly ashamed." Terence wilted. He could have kicked himself for a fool. Lashings of darkness all around and he just had to embrace Denise under that confounded lamp-post!

"And it's not only that," went on Eustace sorrowfully. "It's the deception. You told me that you had a cold in the head, when in fact there was nothing the matter with you. I understood Mrs. Hagge-Smith to say that Miss Blake wouldn't be attending the meeting because—"

"I put her up to that," grunted Terence. "The whole blooming mess-up is my fault. You mustn't blame Denise. I've got a terrific influence over her. It's a sort of hypnotic power, I think. I make her do all manner of things that she doesn't really want to by just *willing* her to do them."

"I can hold no brief for anybody with mesmeric powers who abuses them. If you've been granted this wonderful gift, Terence, you should exercise it only for good and noble ends—not in the interests of your selfish desires. This must go no further. It's not only embarrassing for Miss Blake but a deliberate insult to dear Mrs. Hagge-Smith who naturally feels responsible for the girl's welfare. I can't ask Miss Blake to leave this house since she's employed by Mrs. Hagge-Smith. So you'll pack your things to-night and leave for your Uncle Edward's by the first train. Understand, Terence?"

"But, father—"

"When Mrs. Hagge-Smith returns to Old Cowdene I shall allow you to come home. In the meantime you'll make no attempt to see Miss Blake or correspond with her."

"But, father—"

"To think that a boy of your upbringing and education…"

"But, father—"

"Well, well—what is it?"

"I'm in love with Denise."

"In love? At your age? Don't be absurd, Terence. This is no time for levity."

"But I *know* I'm in love with her! I've just realised it!"

"Nonsense! Good night."

"Good night, father."

VI

But later, in the silent seclusion of his bedroom, Eustace experienced a sudden pang of remorse. Was he being quite fair to Terence? Wasn't he adopting a high-minded attitude which, in the circumstances, he had no right to adopt? Hypocrisy was an evil thing and he was perilously near to becoming a hypocrite himself. Or was he?

He paced about the room, restless and unhappy, trying to analyse the new mood which had descended upon him. That very evening, during the performance of his new ritual, he had found his mind wandering. The old powers of concentration seemed to have deserted him. Twice he had lost his place in the service. Twice he had turned to the left instead of the right, a lapse that had caused considerable confusion among his acolytes and symbol-bearers. His customary faultless touch had been lacking. Moreover, it was not only his mind that had wandered, but his eye. Time and again, ashamed of such laxity, he found himself casting swift and surreptitious glances at Penelope Parker. He seemed to draw inspiration from her as she stood by his side bearing the gilded Wings of Osiris on a red velvet cushion. But a personal rather than an ecclesiastic inspiration.

The previous evening, under the stress of an imperative emotion, he had written her a long delicately-worded letter expressive of admiration and gratitude. He had done his utmost to avoid any suggestion that he was writing to her as a man. It was the letter of a High Prophet to a beloved and loyal member of his priesthood. And yet, somehow, the warmer, more human phrases had crept in and Eustace had not found the courage to erase them. He even felt a kind of perverse thrill in his daring; and so anxious was he to post the letter before he grew faint-hearted that he had slipped out of "Tranquilla" and caught the midnight collection.

And that evening, after the service, Penelope had come up to him with the sweetest, humblest of smiles and murmured:

"I want to thank you for all the kind and lovely things you said to me in your beautiful letter. You make me feel so unworthy."

Returning home with Mrs. Hagge-Smith he had walked on air, until the sight of Terence with that girl in his arms had brought him to earth with a bump.

But wasn't Terence, perhaps, moved by emotions not unlike his own? Eustace frowned. No! No! The idea was ridiculous! What he felt for Miss Parker was a pure and *spirituelle* devotion devoid of all gross desires. Terence's behaviour was inexcusable. His deception unforgivable. Whatever happened it was his duty to guard his son against the lures and temptations of the flesh. He must, with constant vigilance, keep his son's purity unspotted. Such low desires must be sublimated. Terence must live on the Higher Plane as befitted the son of a man with a great mission.

Eustace ceased his prowling and gazed, fascinated, at his open escritoire. Several sheets of notepaper lay invitingly on the blotting-pad. His uncapped fountain-pen was ready to hand. But no! He must control his impulses. It would be quite wrong and very tactless to send Miss Parker a second letter so soon after the first. No! No! He must resist the lure to express the pleasure she had afforded him by her charming words. He must be strong, undress and get into bed. He ripped off his coat and waistcoat. He undid his tie and whipped off his tall starched collar. He unbuttoned his braces. And then, almost before he realised it, he was seated at his escritoire, pen in hand. He tried to struggle up. Something stronger than his own will pinned him to his chair. His pen was already travelling over the glossy notepaper.

My very dear Miss Parker, he wrote.

Then, with the temerity of an innocent man who finds he has sold himself to the devil, Mr. Mildmann cast all further restraint to the winds. He might as well be damned for a Casanova as a Dante, eh? He went the whole hog. He screwed up the sheet of notepaper and flung it into the waste-paper basket. Again he took up his pen.

> *My very dear Penelope,* he wrote,
>
> *I cannot tell you how moved I was by your reception of my very inadequate expressions of admiration and gratitude...*

It took twelve closely-written sheets to convey all he had to say. And when he had sneaked out and posted his letter, Mr. Mildmann was far from realising that he was formulating a habit that in the long run was to bring him infinite distress.

Chapter IV

The Missing Crux Ansata

I

If Penpeti was a well-known character in Welworth, Miss Minnybell was famous. For one thing she had lived in the place since its inauguration and for another, where Penpeti was silent and aloof, Miss Minnybell was talkative and utterly unselfconscious. She waylaid any and every citizen at the slightest provocation. She revealed to them with unblushing gusto all the intimate problems and actions of her circumscribed existence. But nobody minded and nobody was unkind to Miss Minnybell—for Miss Minnybell, poor soul, was "not quite all there".

For twenty-five years she had tested the patience and tempers of the Welworthians, but she had never harmed a soul. She had her obsessions, of course, but she was not, and never had been, dangerous. Her story was a tragic one. At the age of twenty-one she had taken up missionary work in Turkey and for five happy years had devoted herself to this service. And then late one night poor Miss Minnybell had found herself struggling in the arms of her Turkish male servant, who was endeavouring, with considerable intimacy, to embrace her. Luckily she had been rescued by a member of the mission before she had suffered any real damage, but the incident so preyed on her mind that she eventually had a nervous breakdown and was forced to return to England. Although she recovered her bodily strength, her mind, alas, lagged behind. From that day to this Miss Minnybell had a horror of and a hatred for anything Turkish. Even Turkish Delight. She was known in the Garden City as "Mad Minny", but it was kindly meant and everybody felt genuinely sorry for her. She was just a harmless old lady who was not quite right in the head.

And then one December dusk Miss Minnybell first set eyes on Penpeti. He was just coming out of a bookshop and the light from the window illuminated every detail of his odd attire. But it was not his cloak, his caftan or his purple umbrella that arrested Miss Minnybell's attention. Her whole interest, with a sudden uprush of fear and loathing, was centred on his fez! It was the first time she had seen a man wearing a fez since she had left Turkey nearly forty years before. The shock to her nervous system was profound. Her old obsession flamed higher. With the cunning and patience of a plain-clothes man she "tailed" Penpeti home through the December twilight. Then, with equal cunning, she began to find out all about him. She was convinced that he had turned up in Welworth with designs, not this time, alas, on her virginity, but on her life. She was absolutely certain that Peta Penpeti and Ali Hamed, her one-time servant, were one and the same man. The beard was merely part of a disguise. Beneath his caftan she was sure he concealed a long jewelled dagger, whose destined target was her own heart. It was revenge he desired—for through the swirling mists of her memory Miss Minnybell seemed to recall that

Ali Hamed had been sentenced to two years solitary confinement for assault.

Thereafter, at night, she barricaded the doors with tables and chairs. She contracted with a local builder to fashion her a set of stout wooden shutters for every window—shutters that she barred and bolted the moment it was dark. From among the effects of a recently deceased brother she unearthed a large and cumbersome revolver and a box of ammunition. Then she went to the Public Library and, with the aid of the *Encyclopædia Britannica,* learnt how to load and cock this instrument of defence. Every night she slept with it under her pillow. It was for Miss Minnybell a period of intense activity and suspense.

And although, with the passing of months, nothing happened, Miss Minnybell's conviction remained unshaken. The would-be assassin was biding his time. She was being too clever for him. She wasn't giving him the opportunity to lure her into a dark corner, where he could commit his crime unseen and in silence. Meeting Penpeti in the street, Miss Minnybell would take not the slightest notice of him until he had passed by—then she would skip into a doorway and watch him, or dodge after him from tree to tree like an enthusiastic Boy Scout out for a good day's "tracking". She soon learnt all about his connection with the Children of Osiris. Often she hid in the laurel bushes that surrounded the corrugated-iron temple and spied on his movements. As long as she knew where he was and what he was up to, Miss Minnybell felt comparatively safe. But when she went home after dark she always kept to the most frequented and best-lighted streets. Luckily she lived only a stone's throw from the town centre.

And of this flapping, fluttering female in his wake Penpeti remained unaware. He was probably one of the few people in Welworth who were ignorant of "Mad Minny's" existence. After all, the oddity of her dress and behaviour were probably less noticeable in Welworth than they would have been in any other town in England. It was her conversation that marked her down. And to Penpeti Miss Minnybell never spoke.

II

Although Hansford Boot had noticed with satisfaction that Mrs. Hagge-Smith had suddenly cooled towards Penpeti, he refused to let the grass grow under his feet. In another week Mrs. Hagge-Smith would be returning to Old Cowdene, which gave him exactly seven days in which to widen the rift between them. Seven days that he devoted to a constant and subtle broadcasting of anti-Penpeti propaganda. Perhaps Hansford's desire to wreck Penpeti's position in the hierarchy of Coo was not entirely disinterested. True he was wildly anxious to avoid any split in the Movement, but deep down he was also jealous and envious of the Prophet-in-Waiting. As one of the cult's oldest members, he felt that the office should have been his. With Penpeti discredited in the eyes of Eustace and Alicia, he had no doubt that the office *would* be offered to him. This was his great opportunity, and he must seize it.

He began by underlining Penpeti's reticence about his past. Who was the man? What was his background? Why was he so elusive about it? Didn't it suggest to Mrs. Hagge-Smith that Penpeti had something to conceal? And the very name Peta Penpeti—didn't Alicia feel that it had a false ring about it? It was too beautifully ancient Egyptian to be true—surely? Wasn't it possible that Penpeti had deliberately adopted the name to further his own position in the Order? Perhaps he was using them all as pawns in some clever game of his own. Perhaps his devotion to the cause was, so to speak, all my eye and Betty Martin. Wasn't it possible that Penpeti was no more than an unprincipled opportunist who hoped to make something out of his connection with the Children of Osiris? And was that something…money?

It was the word "money" that first convinced Alicia that there might be something in Hansford Boot's suspicions. Penpeti had come to her and tried to borrow money. He refused to say for what he wanted the money. It was certainly odd. And aware that the seeds of doubt were beginning to germinate in Alicia's mind, Hansford sought around for further evidence of Penpeti's shiftiness.

And then, like manna from heaven, came the alarming disappearance of the Crux Ansata from above the temple altar. It was a beautiful piece of work, fashioned of solid gold and set with semi-precious stones, centring on a single faultless ruby. Needless to say Mrs. Hagge-Smith was the donor of this magnificent symbol. Night and day it stood in a small niche directly above the altar-piece. The temple itself was always kept locked and the windows, set high in the walls, were fitted with metal grilles. Three people owned keys to the building—Eustace, Penpeti and Mrs. Williams, the caretaker. The latter, a decent elderly widow with an unimpeachable record, lived in a bungalow adjacent to the temple itself; an arrangement which enabled members, anxious to meditate in the quiet and privacy it afforded, to call on Mrs. Williams at any time of the day and get her to unlock the door and lock it again after their departure.

It was Mrs. Williams herself who first gave news of the Crux Ansata's disappearance. She sent her daughter, Annie, post-haste to Mr. Mildmann with a brief yet dramatic note.

Sir,

When I went to cleen up same as ushal this mornin the Crooks and Sarter was gorn from its place abuv the alter. I carnt say how its gorn but am wurred and remain.

yours truly
Sissie Williams.

Eustace at once informed Mrs. Hagge-Smith who was in the drawing-room dictating letters.

"Send for Hansford immediately," she said. "We must go round to Carroway Road at once." She turned to Denise who was seated demurely at her portable typewriter. "Tell Arkwright to bring round the car in ten minutes."

Hansford, who lived only a short distance from "Tranquilla", was there five minutes after receiving the news over the telephone. Five minutes later, Arkwright, in his plum-coloured uniform, drove the sleek, forty-horse Daimler round to the door. This luxurious monster was another of Alicia's "little gifts" to Eustace, who prior to her munificence had bounced about Welworth in a decrepit Austin Seven. This Alicia considered out of keeping with the dignity of his office. And with the Daimler had come Sidney Arkwright—a young and handsome under-chauffeur from Old Cowdene, a staunch disciple of Cooism and one of Alicia's many "finds".

Having piled into this glittering barouche, Alicia, Hansford, and Eustace were swiftly transported to Carroway Road. The agitated caretaker was waiting for them at the gate of her bungalow and the whole party at once entered the adjacent temple. There Alicia began to cross-question Mrs. Williams with typical efficiency.

"You first noticed the Crux Ansata was missing when you came in to clean up this morning, Mrs. Williams?"

"That's right, mum."

"When did you last see the Crux Ansata in its proper place?"

"Yesterday morning, mum."

"So it must have been stolen sometime during the last twenty-four hours."

Eustace broke in:

"But I was here early yesterday afternoon. Arkwright drove me round about two o'clock. I left the building about half-an-hour later. The Crux Ansata was certainly in its niche when I left."

"A most useful piece of evidence," boomed Mrs. Hagge-Smith with a nod of approval. "Now, Mrs. Williams, did you let anybody into the temple after two-thirty yesterday afternoon? Think carefully. This is a very unsavoury business, remember."

Mrs. Williams adopted an expression which she considered appropriate to careful thinking and announced:

"Why to be sure now, Miss Parker came round about six and stayed until nearly seven. That's her usual time, of course."

"Usual time for what?"

"Meddlytating, mum."

"You're sure you locked up securely after Miss Parker left?"

"Yes, mum."

Mrs. Hagge-Smith turned to the others.

"We shall have to ring up dear Penelope and see what *she* has to say." She pivoted again towards the caretaker. "And you didn't open up the building again until this morning?"

"No, mum. But I saw Mr. Penpeti a-coming out of the place a little after nine. He's got his own key, of course."

"Mr. Penpeti! Why on earth didn't you tell us this before? But how did you know it was Mr. Penpeti? Surely it was dark, Mrs. Williams?"

Mrs. Hagge-Smith sounded like a persuasive yet malicious K.C.

"I was just coming back from my sister Aggie's, mum, and saw his figger against the open door before 'e turned out the light. There's no mistaking Mr. Penpeti, is there, mum? I mean with that there little tasselled 'at of 'is."

"Did you speak to him?"

"No, mum. I'd reached my own gate before 'e'd finished locking up—and 'e never was a talkative gentleman at the best of times."

"Think now!" broke in Hansford sharply. "Mr. Penpeti— was he carrying anything? Any sort of parcel? Bundle? Eh?"

"No, sir—but I did notice 'e had a little bag in his hand. A sorta doctor's bag, if you take me."

"Umph!" Hansford exchanged a meaning glance with Alicia.

Mrs. Hagge-Smith concluded her cross-examination.

"You, yourself, know nothing about the disappearance of the Crux Ansata, Mrs. Williams? You're quite sure there's nothing on your conscience? I promise you that anything you say to us here will be treated in the strictest confidence."

"I 'ope you're not suggesting," bridled Mrs. Williams, drawing herself up with outraged dignity, "that I pinched that there Crooks and Sarter? Because if so, mum, you can kindly look elsewhere for a caretaker. I'm as put about by this nasty business as any of you. And if I thought you was—!"

"Come now, Mrs. Williams," broke in Eustace soothingly. "Mrs. Hagge-Smith was only posing a very natural question. But now that you've answered it so clearly, I'm sure we're all more than satisfied."

"I should 'ope so, sir!" snorted Mrs. Williams, still fuming. "And if there's nothing further I'll be getting back to my 'ousework. Anything on my conscience indeed! I never did!"

The moment Mrs. Williams had stumped out of the temple, slamming the door behind her, Hansford turned to Alicia.

"Must ring Penelope. If the Ansata was there at seven o'clock—looks fishy. Penpeti, I mean. Carrying a bag. Note that. Know he's pushed for money. Ansata worth a packet, eh?"

"Oh I'm sure such a dreadful thing's out of the question," bleated Eustace forlornly. "It's unthinkable."

It was Alicia Hagge-Smith's turn to ejaculate that queer indeterminate word which is usually written down as "Umph!"

III

Penelope, her lovely drawl trickling along the wires like spilt syrup, was emphatic. When she had left the temple shortly before seven o'clock the Crux Ansata was gleaming in its niche above the altarpiece. Hansford Boot hung up the receiver with a sigh of profound satisfaction. His intuitive reading of Penpeti's character was even more accurate than he had imagined. Not only was he an opportunist and a scrounger but now, so it appeared, a common or garden thief. It was too good to be true!

He hastened to Eustace and Alicia in the study and handed on Penelope's information. Eustace's face crumpled with dismay.

"But how terrible," he breathed. "If our suspicions prove to be correct…how truly terrible! We must see Peta without delay and give him the chance to show us how wrong we are in suspecting him."

"No," said Hansford shortly. "Wrong approach. Even if true, he'd deny it. What then? We couldn't *do* anything. We couldn't *prove* anything. Agreed?"

"Then what do you suggest," enquired Alicia with an impatient glance.

"Police. Get them to investigate. Know how to cross-question. Find clues. Drive home guilt. Their job."

"Oh no, no!" wailed Eustace unhappily. "What ever happens we must avoid any undesirable publicity. We can't afford a scandal. We simply mustn't call in the police!"

"That's all very well," put in Mrs. Hagge-Smith practically. "I spent a great deal of money on that Crux Ansata. It was an expensive one. Even if you're content to let the matter slide, Eustace, I'm the one who should really be asked to make any decision. Personally I entirely agree with Hansford. We've got to recover that Crux Ansata. And we've got to discover the thief. We'll go to the police-station without delay."

Eustace's watery eyes gleamed defiantly through their pince-nez.

"I refuse to come with you."

"Very well," said Alicia with a sniff of disapproval. "Hansford and I will go alone. At once! Come along, Hansford."

Arkwright drove them to the police-station. It was a sedate mock-Anne building in Lavender Lane with a beautifully espaliered wistaria trailing over its red-brick façade. They were ushered at once into Inspector Duffy's office, where with admirable clarity Hansford laid the facts of the case before the alert bullet-headed little man behind the desk. The inspector made voluminous notes.

"And this Crux Ansata?" he asked, puzzled.

"It's the Ancient Egyptian symbol of eternal life," explained Mrs. Hagge-Smith. "A cross with its upper arm bent into a loop. The loop being a circle, and a circle, as you know, is the nearest geometric expression to something that has no beginning and no end. Which is, of course, eternity!"

Inspector Duffy scratched his head and pushed a slip of paper towards Mr. Boot.

"Perhaps you'd better draw it for me, sir." Hansford did so. "And what would be the approximate value of the missing article?" continued Duffy. Mrs. Hagge-Smith suggested about four hundred pounds. Duffy whistled. "I see—quite a nice little sum. And this Mr. Penpeti…what makes you suspect that…?"

Hansford etched in the details, stressing Penpeti's apparent lack of funds and his attempts to "touch" the determinedly "untouchable" Alicia.

Duffy nodded.

"Well, sir, until I've something more definite to go on, I can't do more than put this Mr. Penpeti through an ordinary cross-examination. And even then he's under no obligation to answer my questions. Of course, he may be anxious to put forward an explanation. He may have his alibi. You've got no real evidence to suggest that he stole the missing article."

"Quite," admitted Hansford, "but felt it easier for you to put the questions. Difficult for us. Embarrassing. Agreed? Can only hope he's cleared. Unpleasant if not. Create a scandal. Member of our faith. High up in the order, too."

It was Inspector Duffy's turn to say "Umph."

IV

Penpeti looked glum. He *was* glum. Even the very excellent rissole à la Bernard Shaw, which was the *plat du jour* of the Rational Feeding Restaurant, failed to relieve his depression. Sitting over his lunch he tried to take a more optimistic view of the future, but no matter in which direction he gazed the outlook was black. It was just one damned thing after another. First Yacob's untimely visit; then the sudden loss of Mrs. Hagge-Smith's patronage, and, finally, his utter inability to make any headway with Penelope Parker. Financial headway, that is. His headway in other directions had been both startling and swift. At his second visit, Penelope, with the brazen shamelessness of a woman who knows exactly what she wants, declared that she was in love with him. At the third visit, for decency's sake, he was forced to take her into his arms and kiss her. Beyond that dangerous moment he dared not think. He only knew that his original surmise was correct. Beneath the mystic veils lurked a really virulent specimen of the Eternal Eve. In less than a week he had landed himself in a very ticklish situation.

But Penelope's purse-strings were as obstinately knotted as Mrs. Hagge-Smith's. His hints had been broad enough, but not a penny-piece was forthcoming to make this amorous adventure worth-while. Penpeti felt desperate. In another week Yacob would come sneaking back into Welworth demanding the money that Penpeti had been unable to pay out on his previous visit. Yacob had given him just fourteen days in which to find, what he always referred to as, "the necessary". Either "the necessary" was forthcoming, or else… and Penelope was his last hope!

Then there was another upsetting complication. Penelope had warned him that Hansford Boot was out to sabotage his position in the Movement. Penelope swore that Boot wanted the office of Prophet-in-Waiting for himself. He was working day and night to set Mrs. Hagge-Smith against him. Well, there was some truth in that! Alicia certainly seemed cold and unapproachable these days. She was constantly in Hansford Boot's company. Yes—it was all very depressing.

Penpeti had always detested Boot. No definite reason— just an instinctive antagonism. His dislike was coupled with the firm belief that he'd met Boot before. He couldn't for the life of him say where and when, except that it was during the period of his life in which Yacob had so expansively figured. Perhaps Yacob would remember. But no matter in what circumstances he had previously met Boot, the idea lingered that the fellow had been connected with something shady, something secret, even criminal. Penpeti decided that when Yacob next turned up in Welworth, he would show him the group photo of the Coo hierarchy taken outside the temple, and see if Yacob could identify Boot. After all it would be very, very useful to know something about Boot, that Boot himself might be anxious to conceal. Such knowledge could be used as a lever. Or would "chisel" have been the better word?

And then, startled by the coincidence, Penpeti was suddenly aware that Hansford Boot had entered the restaurant and was escorting Mrs. Hagge-Smith to an adjacent table.

Penpeti hastily clapped his napkin to his mouth, hiding his beard, and bent lower behind the tall vase of cape gooseberry. Once the couple were seated he knew he would be safe from discovery, for the tables at the Rational were separated from each other, like loose-boxes in a stable, by a series of low partitions. The wood of these partitions, however, was so thin that it was possible by listening carefully to overhear at least the gist of any conversation that took place behind them.

From the moment they had settled down and given their order, Penpeti's interest was aroused. In the very first sentence he heard mention of his name, and fast on the heels of that, his own name in connection with the police. He listened intently, almost holding his breath, whilst Hansford quickly slashed his reputation to shreds in his peculiar telegraphic English. From mention of the missing Crux Ansata, he passed on to a detailed exposition of his belief that he, Penpeti, was the only possible person who could have stolen it. It all sounded devilish clever and convincing and there was no doubt that Hansford's reasoning was cutting a great deal of ice with Alicia.

Penpeti's hackles rose. So Penelope was right, by heaven! Hansford *was* out to besmirch his good name in the eyes of the one woman he was most anxious to impress. Damn the man! It was intolerable, despicable! Somehow, by hook or by crook, he must put an end to this devilish slander. But how? Was Yacob the answer? Was it possible that Yacob's memory would prove to be more alert than his own? Was it possible that Yacob would recall just *where* he had met Hansford Boot before? Yacob was smart. He forgot nothing. If there was anything shady in Hansford's past record then, by God, Yacob was the man to know all about it!

"But the police," he thought. "No—that's more serious."

It was obvious that they had got the police on to the job of recovering the missing Crux Ansata and that he, himself, was destined to be put through some sort of cross-examination. And, at that moment, an interview with the police was something that struck Penpeti as peculiarly distasteful. But how to avoid it without rousing suspicion? Damn this fellow Boot!

Well, he'd have to wait until Yacob turned up to collect the money he didn't seem likely to get. Unless, of course, at the last minute, Penelope…?

But Penpeti, for all his prowess as a high-powered Casanova, had little hope in this direction. He shook his head dolefully and dug a vicious spoon into his sickly-looking fig mould. His world seemed to be falling apart.

Beyond the partition, the hateful voice of Hansford Boot was saying: "So secretive about his past. Sticks in my gullet. Never been happy about his reserve. Suggestive. But mustn't influence you, my dear Alicia. Unfair. Fellow not here to defend himself. But queer, eh? Air of mystery. Personally I don't like it!"

Chapter V

Penpeti Turns the Screw

I

Inspector Duffy didn't keep Mr. Penpeti waiting long in suspense. Barely had the latter arrived home from lunch, when the gate clicked and the dapper little figure of the inspector came briskly up the path. Penpeti, steeling himself for an ordeal he was most anxious to have done with, showed Duffy into the somewhat cramped yet comfortable sitting-room. Then with a carefully assumed expression of bewilderment he asked:

"What exactly do you wish to see me about? I trust there's nothing wrong? It's not bad news is it, Inspector?"

Penpeti's foreign accent had never been more pronounced. He seemed to have heightened it deliberately for this unpleasant interview. But Duffy, who had never spoken to him before, was naturally unaware of the deception.

"Bad news?" smiled the inspector. "Maybe you've already heard about the theft from the Osiris Temple in Carroway Road?"

"Theft?" exclaimed Penpeti with enormous innocence. "I've heard nothing."

Duffy consulted his notebook.

"It appears that a valuable piece of altar-plate was stolen, presumably between the hours of seven yesterday evening and nine o'clock this morning. I understand that you visited the building *after* seven o'clock. So we're hoping you may be able to give us some information, Mr. Penpeti."

Penpeti looked genuinely astonished.

"I visited the temple? Never! I haven't been near Carroway Road, Inspector, for the last two days. What exactly is missing?"

"I understand you call it a Crux Ansata."

"The Crux Ansata!" breathed Penpeti. "But, good heavens, that's worth—"

"A great deal of money, eh, Mr. Penpeti? You can see why we're anxious to gather in all available evidence."

"But as I didn't enter the building yesterday, I'm afraid I can't help you."

"But, look here, sir—you were seen by the caretaker coming out of the place just after nine o'clock. How about that?"

"I can only suggest that Mrs. Williams was the victim of an optical illusion. Unless she had some form of psychic materialisation. She may have seen *somebody*, but most certainly it wasn't me!"

"But she claims that the figure she saw was wearing a fez. Not exactly a commonplace form of headgear in this country."

"Quite."

"And you still uphold that you didn't enter the building last night?"

"Most certainly."

"Then may I ask what you were doing, say, between the hours of eight-thirty and nine-thirty?"

"I was here in this room, writing letters."

"Can you produce a witness to corroborate this evidence?"

"No—I'm afraid not. You'll just have to take my word for it. Apart from a daily help, who leaves at midday, I live here alone."

"I see. Not very satisfactory, of course. However…" Duffy shrugged his shoulders and jumped up from his chair. "Well, there's no need for me to trouble you any further, Mr. Penpeti. I'm only sorry you haven't been able to help us."

"So am I," retorted Penpeti wryly. "Profoundly sorry. Because naturally, until you discover who it was that Mrs. Williams saw coming out of the temple, everybody's going to assume that it was me. And it wasn't. Rather unpleasant for me, as you'll admit."

II

And it was unpleasant—decidedly so! But as is so often the case, no sooner has Fate landed an upper-cut, when it will as swiftly put out a helping hand. With a single powerful yank, some two hours later, Fate hauled Mr. Penpeti out of the dark pit of depression into which he had fallen. This slice of good fortune was even more agreeable because totally unexpected. When Penpeti had gone round to Penelope's house later that day, he had not expected to come away with a cheque for fifty pounds in his pocket. But that is precisely what happened. After a particularly passionate interlude, in which all reason and restraint were thrown to the winds, Penelope suddenly abandoned her previous miserly attitude. In the afterglow of Peta's tempestuous love-making, her infatuation reached new heights of abandonment and when for the umpteenth time Peta mentioned his "temporary financial embarrassment", she abruptly reached for her chequebook and fountain-pen.

Penpeti was elated. If his little goose had laid one golden egg then, according to all natural laws, she would probably lay another. And another and another. The possibilities were inexhaustible. And Penelope, with the veils of her mysticism torn aside, was a far more attractive woman to make love to than Penpeti had dared hope. She wasn't his type, admittedly, but in this most imperfect of worlds it was no use baying for the moon.

Now, at any rate, he could await Yacob's return with equanimity. In fact, with the money in his pocket, Penpeti did something he had never done before. He wired Yacob to travel down to Welworth without delay. He had sound reasons for his apparent impatience. Ever since overhearing Hansford Boot's virulent tête-à-tête with Mrs. Hagge-Smith, the conviction had grown that he and Yacob had met the fellow before. And Yacob had the memory of an elephant.

Two days after the disappearance of the Crux Ansata, therefore, Yacob came slinking up the flagstone-path between the scarlet bay-tubs and slid like an animated shadow into the house. Once in the little sitting-room, Penpeti drew the curtains against the wet November dusk, poked the fire into a more cheerful blaze and got down to business. First, with a casual air, he slapped a wad of notes onto Yacob's knee and watched him count them. Yacob was satisfied…at least, for the time being. He nodded amiably.

"Well, that's all fine and dandy. I won't ask how you raised the necessary. Tactless, eh my dear fellow? But I'm damned if I can see why you were so impatient to settle your little debt. I gave you fourteen days. Still four days to run. What the devil's come over you? You're usually pretty reluctant to—"

Penpeti pushed a large unframed photograph under Yacob's nose.

"Take a good look at that, will you?"

"Good God! What is it? Amateur dramatics?"

"That," explained Penpeti with a certain hauteur, "is a photo of the high officials of our order, taken in their ceremonial robes. Do you recognise anybody?"

Yacob indicated a figure with a yellow-stained fingertip.

"You," he chuckled. "The spit and image of Svengali, eh? Good God! If they only knew."

Penpeti silenced him with a look.

"Take another look," he suggested.

Yacob did so. Suddenly he jerked out:

"By heaven! This chap standing in the back row with the bald head and horn-rims. If that's not Sam Grew I'll swallow my watch and chain! But what the devil's he doing in this crowd? You remember Sam Grew, surely? Only in the old days he had more hair and swagger little moustachios."

"Sam Grew!" repeated Penpeti softly; adding with a malicious smile: "Oh yes, I remember Sam Grew all right. So *that's* who it is! I knew I'd seen the fellow before. It's all coming back to me now." He gave a little whistle. "Yacob, I'm not sure, but I *think* we're in clover. I think we're going to make things pretty uncomfortable for Mr. Sam Grew. I think we're going to twist Mr. Sam Grew's tail until he squeals for mercy."

"You mean," shot out Yacob, suddenly interested, "that there's money in him?"

Penpeti nodded.

"I couldn't recall just where I'd met the man before. What's more I couldn't recall the exact nature of his business. But now you've given me his real name, it's jerked my memory into action. Moldoni's Dive in Soho, wasn't it?"

"You've said it! Dope peddling. Snow was his stock-in-trade."

"Cocaine! The drug racket! Of course."

Yacob nodded appreciatively.

"Sam did pretty well for himself until the dicks got him on the run. Made a pretty tidy fortune, I reckon. Then he folded up. Just vanished from the scene and was never heard of again." He grinned and added with a meaning wink: "Until now. Until *now,* my dear fellow."

"Exactly. And since I knew Sam Grew far better than he knew me, I think I've got him just where I want him." Penpeti slowly closed his fist. "In the palm of my hand."

"You mean, *we've* got him just where we want him!" shot out Yacob with sudden suspicion. "I'm in on this, my dear fellow. Get that clear from the start."

"I see no reason why you should be," contested Penpeti with a scowl. "If I take the risks then I take the profits. I'm not asking you to turn the screw, am I?"

"Maybe not. But I think you're going to give me a twenty per cent rake-off."

Penpeti was aghast.

"Twenty per cent!"

"If you start squealing I'll make it fifty-fifty. So you'd better watch your step."

"But my dear Yacob—" began Penpeti pleadingly.

"Aw! Cut that out," snapped Yacob with a gesture of impatience. "Either I get that rake-off or…" He stuck a cigarette in his mouth and lit it in leisurely fashion. "For God's sake, have a little common-sense. You're in a jam and a man in a jam isn't in any position to bargain. I suppose you take me for a sap. Aw shucks!" He spat viciously into the fireplace. "I don't want to squeeze you dry, but fair's fair. I'll take twenty per cent—understand? Neither more nor less. Twenty ruddy per cent. Get me?"

Penpeti nodded.

"All right, Yacob—if you insist. But don't forget it's just possible that he won't—"

Yacob cut in scornfully:

"Oh he'll play ball, if that's what's biting you. His kind always do. Looks as if he's been sitting pretty here for ten years. Worked up a nice steady little alibi, too. It's on the cards that he's actually done a repentance act and decided to go straight. So much the better, eh?" Yacob clapped his hat jauntily on his head and sprang up. "Good God! It'll be like taking milk from a blind kitten."

"There's always a risk," pointed out Penpeti.

"Not in his case, there isn't. He can't afford to ask for police protection from a nasty-wasty little blackmailer, can he? The nasty-wasty little blackmailer holds all the pretty-witty cards. My dear fellow, it's money for jam! Money for jam! And twenty-wenty-per-centy of it for poor hardworking little Yacob." His swarthy face was wreathed in smiles, as he added: "By the way, what's his moniker these days?"

"Boot," said Penpeti. "Mr. Hansford Boot."

III

With his customary energy Peta Penpeti wasted no time in cogitation. It was action he wanted—quick, neat, decisive action. The next day, therefore, shortly after breakfast, he walked round to Hansford Boot's mock-Victorian villa in Hayseed Crescent and rang the bell with considerable assurance. To say that Hansford was surprised when Penpeti was ushered into his study is to put it mildly. He was flabbergasted. Never before, due to the antagonism which divided them, had Penpeti put foot inside his house. Then what on earth had driven him to make this unexpected call? Was it something to do with the missing Crux Ansata? Had Penpeti lied to Inspector Duffy and, after a bad night of it, come along to confess to the theft?

Penpeti's first words disillusioned him.

"I suppose I have you and Eustace to thank for putting the police on to me, eh, Mr. Boot? Very stupid of you, of course. It would have been better to have checked up on Mrs. William's evidence before jumping to foregone conclusions. You were convinced that *I'd* taken the Crux Ansata, weren't you?"

"You? Not a bit of it! Hoped you might have useful information—that's all. Didn't suspect you. Of course not. Ridiculous!"

Hansford hummed and hawed uncomfortably, aware that Penpeti's dark eyes were fixed on him with a look of acid amusement.

"Really, Mr. Boot—be honest. You can't wriggle out of this, you know. I was on the other side of the partition when you lunched our dear Mrs. Hagge-Smith at the Rational. I overheard *everything*!"

"What? You what?" exclaimed Hansford, obviously disconcerted.

"And do you know what struck me as the most curious part of your unwarrantable behaviour, Mr. Boot?"

"No idea."

"That you should, in any way, want to make any sort of contact with the police."

"What the deuce do you mean?"

"I think you've a very shrewd idea."

"None whatsoever. Talking Greek. Don't follow. Obliged if you'd clarify."

"I will, Mr. Boot. And not without a certain justifiable pleasure. After all, you've given me little cause to like you. The opposite in fact. So you'll have to forgive me if I show evidence of enjoying this little tête-à-tête. Because I *am* enjoying it." Adding with a poisonous little smirk: "Immensely!"

"In heaven's name—!"

"All in good time, Mr. Boot. Now where shall I begin? Might I suggest Moldoni's Dive in Soho? It should prove a familiar starting-point."

"Moldoni's?" Hansford's face underwent a transformation that was startling. His rather bland amiable expression gave way to a look of wild apprehension. His eyes, behind their horn-rims, stared at Penpeti, fearfully, incredulously. "What do you know about Moldoni's?"

"Far more than is good for my peace-of-mind, Mr.Grew."

"Grew? What the—?"

"Yes—Sam Grew. For a long time I've been worried by your likeness to somebody I knew in earlier days. Now I'm no longer worried."

"But it's nonsense! Piffle!" blustered Hansford, his eye roving unhappily over his cosy familiar little study. "Ridiculous mistake. Often happens. We all have doubles."

Penpeti shook his head.

"I'm sorry you're going to be obstinate." His voice hardened and he flashed out viciously: "If you refuse to admit that I'm right, I'll go to the police. I'll tell them I've a strong suspicion that a certain Sam Grew, who disappeared some years ago, has turned up in Welworth. A one-time dope pedlar with a hide-out in Soho. I think Scotland Yard might be deeply grateful for the information."

"By God!" cried Hansford with a cornered look, "You wouldn't do that. What proof have you?"

"Oh, I should leave all that to the police. They have a neat way of getting at the truth. No, Mr. Grew, you wouldn't stand a chance under cross-examination, and you know it."

"You want to ruin me?" groaned Hansford, no longer trying to brazen it out but pale and trembling. "Is that the idea? But why? I've done you no harm."

"Really?" observed Penpeti coldly.

"For God's sake, give me a chance. Once I was a fool. I admit it. But that's over and done with. My heart's genuinely in my work here. I tell you, I'm a reformed man. A new man.

A different man. Sam Grew's dead. D'you understand? Dead and done for. Forgotten."

"Not by the police," Penpeti reminded him with a sarcastic smile. "Do you know, you're in a devilish awkward position, Mr. Grew?"

"What do you want?" asked Hansford on a sudden note of practicality. "What's your price, eh? What's your silence going to cost me. You didn't come here without a definite idea in mind. I'm not a fool, you know!"

"Shall we say a regular three-monthly donation to the upkeep of my official position as Prophet-in-Waiting? As a reward for my future discretion."

"Blackmail, eh? Just as I thought."

"Sound business, Mr. Grew."

"I always sensed that you were a twister. I've tried to warn the others. You're a fake, Penpeti. Using the Movement for your own ends."

"Oh and that reminds me," went on Penpeti smoothly, "from now on you will work to rehabilitate me in the eyes of Mildmann and our dear Mrs. H-S. You'll scotch the foul suspicions you've roused against me. Understand?"

"Is that part of our...bargain?"

"It is."

"I see. And how much...?"

"Oh I shan't be unreasonable. As the first of four quarterly instalments, shall we say fifty pounds?"

"Fifty pounds!"

"Preferably in one pound notes. Shall we say...by to-morrow, Mr. Grew? That will give you time to cash a cheque."

Hansford Boot at that moment had a murderous gleam in his eye, but he nodded dumbly as Penpeti took up his gloves and fez and crossed jauntily to the door. There he turned and said with a casual air:

"Oh, and by the way, it may interest you to know that I *didn't* steal that Crux Ansata. You were off the rails there, Mr. Grew. Your little chat with Alicia was dangerously near libel. But as you've enough trouble to cope with at present, I'm prepared to overlook the matter. I told you that I was never unreasonable. *Au revoir,* Mr. Boot. I shall expect you to return my visit to-morrow. And I advise you *not* to forget!"

IV

Mrs. Hagge-Smith, who had always looked upon Hansford as one of the most reliable and intelligent Children of Osiris, had good cause in the few days left before her return to Old Cowdene to modify her opinion. Hansford's volte-face concerning Penpeti bewildered her. Without the slightest warning he substituted praise for vilification, admiration for suspicion, and left poor Alicia in a flat spin. Hansford's explanation for this change of front, however, was both subtle and ingenious. He had, so he said, dreamed a dream in which the great god Osiris himself had appeared out of a cloud and spoken to him in a voice of thunder. His message was brief and to the point. Peta Penpeti was a good and noble man, worthy of the select position he held in the order. To believe anything else was to display a miserable lack of faith and perception. Hansford was to spread news of this important revelation. He was to make amends for his own wicked persecution.

It is easy to imagine what it had cost poor Hansford to concoct this beautiful story. But this *was* his story and he stuck to it. With the result that Mrs. Hagge-Smith, before she returned to Sussex, was once more prepared to accept Penpeti as her closest ally and confidant. Eustace's stock again slumped. Hansford breathed more freely.

But from that moment onward he was a man without any real peace-of-mind. He realised that as long as Penpeti held the threat of exposure over his head he was destined to walk the tight-rope. And Penpeti's silence was going to prove an expensive luxury, a sad strain on his finances. He could see no end to the situation—at least, no happy ending. After ten years of comparative ease and safety, his past, like a bolt from the blue, had struck him down. It was a bitter blow, for during those ten years he had worked energetically to wipe out the disgrace of his earlier activities. His devotion to Eustace and the Movement was genuine and wholehearted. He believed in Cooism. His one thought now was to serve the Cause.

And now *this*! Damn Penpeti! How had he discovered his guilty secret? Where had Penpeti seen him before? How was it he knew all about Moldoni's Dive in Soho?—for to know that cesspit was to be branded as a criminal. Hansford had only to close his eyes to see again the green-chequered table-clothes, the hardwood chairs, the reckless, ferrety, slick, sly clientele that patronised that basement inferno. But amidst that shifting and shifty crowd he had no recollection of Penpeti, not even of a man who might have been a younger, clean-shaven and less oddly-garbed Penpeti. If only he could place Penpeti in that nightmare of his past, then without doubt he, in turn, would discover something to hold against him. And with that knowledge he could bargain and free himself from his predicament. His silence for Penpeti's. And failing that? Sam Grew shuddered. To think along that line was madness! Silence was one thing, but everlasting silence… murder! No! By heaven, no! He must not and *could* not add any further burden to his conscience.

And yet?

A shadow of Hansford's tormented state of mind darkened the existence of the one man to whom he was blindly devoted. With the departure of Mrs. Hagge-Smith and Denise for Old Cowdene, Eustace found himself with far more time for uninterrupted reflection. True, Terence's return did something to mitigate the sudden silence that descended on "Tranquilla", but Terence was in a decidedly untalkative mood. Grunts and nods seemed to have usurped the place of speech. He eyed his father with a surly expression, determined to show him that his resentment was still on the boil. But it was not Terence's uncompromising attitude that tortured poor Eustace. It was his own over-deepening infatuation for Penelope Parker.

He had within ten days stepped far beyond the boundaries of pretence. Now he was writing her quite openly, without a blush, as *My very dearest and sweetest Penelope.* His moral deterioration had been so rapid that Eustace had barely noticed it. He only knew that when Penelope smiled on him and was kind, the sun blazed from a cloudless sky; that when she was cross or critical he was encompassed by a pea-soup fog of depression. He thought out a score of little ways to see her alone. He wrote her every day. He sent her expensive little gifts which he thought might amuse or charm her. And the more effective he became as a man, a male, the less efficient he was as a High Prophet of Coo. Disciples began to notice his air of distraction, his fumblings and absent-minded gaffes.

As for Penelope, launched on a full-blooded affair with her dark-eyed Penpeti, she felt she could afford to be generous. Eustace's outpourings at first piqued, then amused and, finally, touched her. He was so naïve, so pathetic in his frank adoration. Oh yes, she could afford to be generous. So Penelope replied to his impassioned letters and occasionally granted Eustace the luxury of seeing her alone. Once she squeezed his hand in the vestry. On another occasion she kissed him on the brow. But all the time she took the greatest care to conceal from Eustace the full significance of her relationship with Penpeti. She knew that they were hostile to each other and she didn't want to further any more enmity. In his present mood even the mild Eustace, bitten by jealousy, might prove a veritable demon of wrath!

Chapter VI

Mayblossom Cut

I

Sidney Arkwright was a young man with an excellent sense of humour. It would be more correct to say that he was *two* young men—the smart, well-mannered, plum-coloured chauffeur and the smart, slick-haired lady-killer who sallied forth when his day's work was done. His deferential manner was simply a bit of professional blah. He touched his peaked hat, opened doors, arranged the rugs and cushions because he was paid a decent salary to do so. When in Mrs. Hagge-Smith's employ, before being loaned to Eustace, he had professed a keen interest in the cult of Coo because he could see that such an interest would pay good dividends. And it did. He became more than Mrs. Hagge-Smith's under-chauffeur. He became her protégé, her latest "find", with privileges that were not extended to the less diplomatic members of her staff and a far bigger salary than was normally paid to under-chauffeurs. She, herself, instructed him in the elementary ethics of the Movement. When finally he was transferred to Welworth to drive for the High Prophet, he was selected as one of the two Temple Sistrum-Shakers. As, at one time, he had served as assistant behind Charlie's Cocktail Bar at Southend, he could shake a very pretty sistrum indeed. Older disciples of the Movement said he was the greatest virtuoso on the instrument that they had ever heard. Sidney Arkwright smiled modestly and said nothing.

But once clear of the atmosphere which surrounded his job, Sidney was a different cup of tea. His pin-stripe suits were the envy of the other lads about town. His ease and success with the local belles filled them with admiration or racked them with jealousy. In his private life he "shook a leg" at the local hops with as great a mastery as he shook his sistrum in the temple. On one occasion only had his particular cronies tried to bait him about his connection with the Children of Osiris. He selected the heftiest of the gang and, with consummate skill, knocked him down. After that he cooled off and explained just why he attended the meetings and services in Carroway Road.

"It's this way—see? It pays me pretty handsome to act a bit soft with that crazy gang. Lots of 'perks' attached to my job just because old Haggie thinks I'm a bit of a High Lifer." Sid winked. "But you fellahs get this straight unless you want one bloody nose apiece. I'm not listening to any wisecracks about the Guv'nor. That Penpeti guy makes me feel hot under the collar, but Mr. Mildmann's a proper sort of chap—a decent, straight-dealing, honest sort of chap. And don't you forget it!"

And Sidney made a prolonged and vibratory noise which in those enlightened circles was known technically as "a raspberry".

His whole-time girl at that period was Violet Brett—a flashing brunette with a perfect pair of legs and big ideas. Sid found her expensive to run, but with a classy kid like that he didn't mind throwing his money around a bit. On the dance-floor she was the tops and no mistake about it. She and Sid had been hitting the Garden City high-spots for about three months, when the Rollup Corset Factory advertised the fact that their annual fancy-dress dance was due to take place on the first Saturday in December.

Actually Sid had known for some time that this great event was on the way and he had prepared for it in advance. He had even managed to slip up to Town and visit a theatrical costumiers. Naturally he was taking Violet to the dance.

"Tell me, Sid, what are you going as?" she asked one evening as they were coming out of the pictures. "I'm fixing myself up as a pierrette."

"You wait and see," said Sid cryptically. "I reckon I'm going to raise a laugh."

II

Sid did raise a laugh! There was no question about his supposed identity. The moment he walked into the crowded canteen of the Corset Factory, where the dance was held, people nudged each other, pointed, sniggered, giggled and then started laughing. Sid had gone to considerable pains to get his sartorial details correct. His make-up was admirable. From the fez to the purple umbrella, from the black beard to the long black caftan, the illusion was without flaw. And having had ample opportunity to study his original at close quarters, even the walk and the accent were passably good imitations. At first glance one or two of the more gullible actually thought it *was* Peta Penpeti. Violet was enchanted. Sid was the hit of the evening and since he danced only with her, she was able to wallow in reflected notoriety. The sight of the well-known, dignified Prophet of Coo dancing the rhumba with the verve and abandon of a Carmen Miranda more or less brought the house down.

By popular acclaim Sid took the Gent's First Prize for the most original fancy-dress.

It was one of the grandest evenings he'd ever had in his life. Not only had he got his laugh, but he'd got it at the expense of the half-baked crowd that patronised him. He got a tremendous kick out of running with both the hare and the hounds, of having his cake and eating it too. After the last waltz, he gathered up Violet on the stretch of asphalt before the factory main-entrance and prepared to get down to the more serious business of the evening. With this in mind, he suggested escorting Violet home via Mayblossom Cut. And although Violet had no illusions about the perils which would result from agreement, she accepted his invitation with alacrity. They took a firm grip on each other's waists and, with his fez at a cocky angle, Sid piloted his inamorata towards the inadequately lighted Cut.

Mayblossom Cut, as its name suggests, was a narrow footpath roofed over by the interlocking branches of a double row of may-trees, running parallel with the railway embankment. Three widely-spaced lamp-posts were supposed to illuminate this arboreal tunnel. Naturally they didn't, and it was for this reason that Mayblossom Cut was highly popular with the younger and more enterprising couples of Welworth. To take a young lady for a stroll through the Cut was the last word in doggery. Needless to say it was not Sid's first visit there with Violet and, if Sid had his way, it wouldn't be the last. But as Destiny is quite indifferent to the hopes and desires of mere mortals, it *was* very nearly his last! Death lurks where he will—so why not in Mayblossom Cut?

Between the first and second lamp-posts, with a common-sense that Terence would have envied, Sid and Violet kissed. Then they murmured for a space and kissed again. Then Violet, with the age-old technique of her sex, suddenly went cold on Sid and refused him any further intimacy. They wrangled. Sid pleaded. Violet shook her head.

"Aw shucks!" said Sid. "What's come over you, Vi? Where's the harm in a kiss?"

"I don't want to—that's all. It's time I got back."

"Running out on me, eh?"

"You know it's not that, Sid. But we've been hanging about here long enough."

"Oh well, in that case…" muttered Sid, kicking sulkily at a stone, "there isn't time to show you something that I bought for you in London. Rotten shame, eh? Something rather slap-up, it was. I thought you'd rather like it."

"Coo! Let me see, Sid. There's a sport."

Sid shook his head.

"Naow! Can't hang about here, Vi. You gotta get back."

"Well, I might be able to stretch a point this once and—"

"Maybe I don't want to give it you now," said Sid in chilly tones. "When a chap gets something fancy for a girl, the least he expects is a bit of a come-back. Fair's fair, Vi."

"I didn't mean to go dumb on you, Sid. Come on—be a sport. Let's see it."

"Gimme a kiss, first."

"O.K.," said Violet, "only don't crumple my ruff—it's only hired."

They kissed—pierrette and her pseudo-Penpeti.

Then, by common consent, they moved on to the next lamp-post, where Sid halted and plunged his hand into his pocket. He drew out a small, flat, red-leather jewel-case, nicked open the clasp, and displayed to Violet's astounded and excited gaze a glittering bracelet.

"Aw, Sid!—it's luvly! Luvly! I never seen anything half so luvly before."

"S'gold," said Sid nonchalantly. "Studded with dimunds."

"Dimunds!" cried Violet. "Go on, Sid, you're kiddin'!"

"No, honest, Vi. Like it?"

Violet took the bracelet from its case and stared at it rapturously as it gleamed and twinkled in the lamplight.

"Do I like it? Aw, Sid, I'll never be able to—"

But Violet never completed her sentence. There was a sudden shattering explosion, a deafening stab of sound, followed almost at once by a second. Violet let out a piercing shriek. Sid gave a curious little grunt and collapsed, moaning, on the ground. He tried to say something, then, with a sigh, he seemed to pass out in a dead faint.

There was the sound of running feet receding up Mayblossom Cut. Then silence, save for Violet's tearful and agitated whispers, as she crouched over Sid's recumbent body.

III

Although it was getting late, Inspector Duffy was still at his desk dealing with arrears of routine work when the sergeant-on-duty came briskly into his office.

"Well, sergeant?"

"There's a young woman just showed up. Some story about a shooting affair up Mayblossom Cut. Thought you'd like to be informed, sir."

Duffy got instantly to his feet.

"A shooting affair, eh? All right. I'll see her at once."

Followed by the sergeant, he went through to the main office where an agitated and tearful Violet was seated in a chair by the fireplace. Her open coat revealed a sadly rumpled pierrette costume and in her left hand she still clutched the diamond bracelet that Sid had handed her just before he collapsed. Having run the whole way to the police-station she was still struggling to regain her breath.

"Well, young lady, what's all this I hear?" asked the inspector quietly. "Just take your time and tell me all about it."

"But I can't!" gasped Violet. "You gotta come at once. Sid's been hit. He may be dead for all I know."

"Sid?"

"Yes—my friend Sid Arkwright, what chauffeurs for that queer Mr. Mildmann. We was coming home from the Rollup Corset Dance."

"I see." Duffy turned to the sergeant. "You'd better get the ambulance and follow us up. Come along, young woman. You can give me the details on the way."

By the time Violet and the inspector reached Mayblossom Cut, Duffy was more or less cognisant with the complete layout of events. But like a sensible man he refused to advance any theories until he had learned the full import of the incident. A great deal would depend on whether Sid Arkwright were dead or alive.

On this point he was soon able to satisfy himself. As they approached the middle lamp-post in the Cut, a figure came limping towards them out of the gloom.

"Sid!" cried Violet, suddenly running forward. "Coo! You did give me a fright. I thought you was a gonner—honest I did!"

She slid an arm round his waist, whilst he leaned heavily on her shoulder to take the weight off his right leg.

"Sorry, kid," he muttered, obviously still in pain. "Winged in the back of the leg. Fainted, I guess." Then as Duffy drew level, he asked: "Hullo—who's this?"

"I'm a police inspector. Your young lady came along to the station. Here, put your other arm over my shoulder. We'll get you along to the end of the Cut. The ambulance should be there any minute."

In this estimate the inspector was right, for no sooner had they reached the road into which the narrow track debouched, when the police ambulance drew into the kerb. Once Sid had been helped into the interior of the vehicle,

Duffy drew up his trouser leg to examine the wound. A single glance told him that it was not serious. A bullet had passed through the fleshy part of the calf and, though the wound was bleeding fairly profusely, the inspector had soon checked the flow with a workmanlike bandage. Leaving Violet to sit with him and hold his hand, Duffy jumped up beside the driver and told the sergeant to follow on foot.

A cup of hot sweet tea laced with a spot of brandy soon put Sid in a more comfortable frame-of-mind, and Duffy felt justified in putting him through a brief cross-examination. As his story matched in every detail the one already told him by Violet Brett, the inspector realised that the facts of the case were unquestionably true.

"So you were coming home from a fancy-dress dance, eh?" He nodded towards the fez that Sid still gripped in his hand. "What were you supposed to represent? The Caliph of Baghdad? The Sultan of Turkey? Or what?"

Sid displayed a momentary embarrassment and fingered his false beard which, in the stress of events, had come partly adrift. Then, with a glance at Violet, he said sheepishly:

"As a matter of fact, Inspector, I was putting over a bit of a leg-pull. You know that chap that walks about in a fez and a long black coat affair—one of the big-shots up at the Osiris temple?"

"Mr. Penpeti, eh?"

"That's him. Well, I thought it 'ud be a bit of a joke to get myself up to look like him. Everybody in Welworth knows the chap. Got a good laugh, too, didn't it, Vi?"

"Sid ran away with the first prize," said Violet with an admiring look. "It was ever so funny, Inspector. A real scream."

"Umph—that's rather interesting," reflected Duffy, his mind suddenly reaching out to new possibilities. "You say you got no glimpse of your assailant?"

"No. Took us so sudden that we hadn't time to gather our wits. He was off up the Cut before we really knew what had happened."

"He?" snapped the inspector.

"Sorry—that was only a manner of speech. Might have been a woman for all I know."

"Do you think your assailant could have seen the bracelet you had just given this young lady?"

"I should think so. We were slap under the lamp-post."

"So the motive was evidently not robbery," commented Duffy.

"Strikes me," said Sid in injured tones, "there just *wasn't* any motive. Some loony, I daresay, out for a quiet evening's gunning."

"I suppose you've no rivals for the hand of this young lady?"

Violet blushed scarlet, but Sid merely chuckled.

"Oh there's one or two other chaps who'd like to cut me out, I daresay. Vi's a good-looker as you can see for yourself. But there's none of them *that* crazy about her. Damn it all, if I'd have been hit in a fatal spot, Inspector, it would have been murder. Can't get around that."

Violet shuddered and slipped her arm more tightly through Sid's, looking down on him fondly. The inspector nodded.

"Well, your explanation may be the right one—a homicidal maniac. On the other hand…"

"Well?"

"Suppose somebody really mistook you for Mr. Penpeti?" said Duffy. "It's a line of argument we shall have to follow up." The inspector rose. "And now if you're feeling better, I'll get the constable to run you home in the ambulance. Where do you live?"

"Over the garage at Mr. Mildmann's—'Tranquilla' in Almond Avenue. I have my meals over in the kitchen with the rest of the staff."

"I see. Well, we'd better let Mr. Mildmann know what's happened. You won't be fit to drive for a week or two. You'll have to get a doctor to look at that leg of yours. It's nothing serious, but wants watching. I'll come up and have chat with your employer to-morrow."

Sid enquired with a hang-dog look:

"I suppose you'll have to give him the low-down on my little leg-pull at the dance to-night?"

"Sorry—yes."

"The boss won't like it," said Sid slowly. "He won't like it at all. He's a damn decent old buffer but he's touchy when it comes to religious matters. It may mean the sack. Just bloomin' bad luck that we decided to come home through the Cut, I reckon. Otherwise I shouldn't have run into this spot of bother."

IV

But to Sid's lasting gratitude Mr. Mildmann made no mention of the matter. His anxiety for Sid's comfort was touching. It made Sid feel a little cheap and ashamed of himself. It struck him that in guying Mr. Penpeti he had been perilously near to guying Mr. Mildmann himself. From that moment onwards Sid was determined to make amends for his previous behaviour and was prepared to champion his employer against the slightest criticism.

Eustace himself, after a long talk with Inspector Duffy, felt curiously uneasy. He had a feeling that things, dark, unpleasant things were happening about him that he was powerless to diagnose or check. He was convinced that Duffy's theory was correct. The shots had been aimed, not at his chauffeur, but at a clearly recognisable simulacrum of Peta Penpeti, and, for one horrid instant, he recalled Hansford's words to him in the temple—"Time ripe for action! Strong action!" Then he dismissed such wild suspicions as absurd. Hadn't Hansford in these last few days suffered a complete change of heart towards his Prophet-in-Waiting? Hansford no longer suspected Penpeti of serving his own ends in the Movement. Hansford seemed to think that the threatened split had now receded. He was even apologising for his own previous suspicions.

Yes—it was all very queer and disturbing. And on top of all this stealthy unrest which seemed to surround him, Eustace had his own personal troubles to combat. Before leaving for Sussex, Alicia, as variable as a weather-vane, had suddenly turned nasty about a play she had written and was desirous of staging at the Summer Convention. This wretched play was an old bone of contention between them. Alicia had written it in a trance—or, in the parlance of Cooism, "the Divine Forces had used her as a medium through which to disseminate the Great Truths incorporate in the Ancient Wisdom of the Predynastic Gods". It was called *The Nine Gods of Heliopolis*. And it was a bad play. A *very* bad play. Even worse, it was a very bad play in blank verse. Ever since Alicia had swept like a whirlwind into the tranquil harbourage of Cooism, she had moved heaven and earth to get this play produced. Eustace had naturally submitted the MS. to the Cultural Committee of Coo—a panel of advisers with considerable artistic sense and ability. They had taken one look at the manuscript and turned pale. They told Eustace that if he wanted to inflict mortal injury on the fortunes of his order he had only to produce *The Nine Gods of Heliopolis*. Naturally Eustace bowed to their superior knowledge and told Alicia that there was, so to speak, nothing doing. Alicia was furious. Like all fond amateurs who think they can write a play without (*a*) any knowledge of writing and (*b*) any knowledge of the theatre, she was abnormally sensitive to criticism. Her pride was severely wounded; and it came naturally to her to blame the mild and apologetic Eustace.

For a time she had let the play, like the sleeping dog, lie—but now, with the Summer Convention looming ahead, the wretched thing had taken on a new lease of life. It was yapping and snarling and scrabbling at the door, demanding attention. Eustace sighed. It was going to take a lot of energy to keep that play off the suggested programme of events for the June rally at Old Cowdene. He knew that Alicia was working hard on Penpeti and Penelope to have the thing performed, baiting her hook by offering them the two fattest rôles in the cast. And he had an idea that Penelope rather fancied herself as an actress. It would cost him much to go against her evident wishes.

Eustace sighed again. It was not much fun being a High Prophet. In the old days, before Alicia Hagge-Smith had got her teeth into the Movement, it had not been so bad. Now his office bristled with difficulties.

But being a father was, he claimed, even more unpalatable. Terence grew daily more sulky and unapproachable. Eustace tried to jolly him out of his moodiness. The effort was a dismal failure. Terence looked at him with the repugnant expression of a vegetarian who finds a slug in his salad. Eustace tried to reason with him. The result was even more disheartening. Terence had suddenly jumped up from the dinner-table and shouted at the top of his basso-profundo voice:

"I'm sick of all these pi-jaws! I'm sick of Cooism, rational clothing, rabbit's food and all this High Life bunkum! I want to live as a normal low-minded, carnivorous, lounge-suited sort of chap. Damn it all, father, can't you realise that I'm old enough to decide things for myself? I tell you straight, if I have to knuckle under to this sort of goody-goody business much longer, I shall go crackers! Haywire! Stark, staring crazy!"

Eustace was shaken to the very core of his paternal soul.

V

But there was one bright spot amidst all this gloom. Quite unexpectedly the Crux Ansata turned up again in its niche above the altar-piece of the temple. It had apparently suffered no damage. So Eustace promptly informed the police and the queer incident of the missing Crux Ansata was quickly forgotten.

That is to say, by all save the man or woman who, for some mysterious reason, had stolen it.

Chapter VII

The Man in the Teddy-Bear Coat

I

Inspector Duffy's investigations of the shooting affair in Mayblossom Cut were slow and tedious. The evidence upon which to base any satisfactory theory was extremely slender. Two shots fired out of the night, the sound of running feet—beyond that, nothing! No description of Sid Arkwright's assailant. No apparent motive. Not even the certainty that the would-be murderer had *intended* to kill Arkwright; for always at the back of his mind Duffy entertained the belief that the shots were meant for Penpeti.

A careful examination of the locale surrendered some information. At a point not far from the middle lamp-post, where Arkwright and the girl had been standing, Duffy discovered that a patch of grass on the verge of the lane had been muddied and trampled flat, suggesting that the wanted person had been lurking in the gloom beyond the lamplight. Several Swan Vestas littered this little patch of ground. A fact which led Duffy to assume that Arkwright's assailant was of the male sex. For, since no cigarette-stubs were visible, it was reasonable to suppose that the matches had been used by a pipe-smoker. Doubtless in his keyed-up state of mind, he had allowed his pipe to go out more than once, though it was impossible to assess the time that the assailant had waited there from the number of expended matches.

The next point that puzzled Duffy was this. If the shots were directed specifically at Arkwright (or Arkwright in the guise of Penpeti) and were not fired at random by some homicidal maniac, how had the assailant known that Arkwright would be coming along Mayblossom Cut? This route had only been decided on as he and the young lady left the factory gates. It rather suggested that the man who had fired the shots had been present at the dance and had chanced to overhear Sid's conversation with Violet. The couple, at a further cross-examination in Sid's room over the garage, reckoned that they had taken about twenty-five minutes to cover the ground between the factory gates and the middle lamp-post. As Sid explained, with a wink, they had naturally lingered a little on the way—a point that Duffy was quick to appreciate. So if the assailant *had* overheard their conversation outside the factory, he would have had ample time to race ahead and take up his position in the Cut.

It was then that Duffy harvested a clue which he was inclined to rate as highly significant. Both Arkwright and the girl admitted that there were several people within a few yards of them when they had made their decision to go home via the Cut. Any of these persons might have overheard them making this arrangement. But it was Violet who recalled a somewhat curious fact that seemed to isolate one particular figure from the rest of the group. All the other dancers like themselves had been in fancy-dress and, although many had put on their overcoats, all the men in their immediate vicinity were wearing some kind of fancy head-gear. All, that is, save this one man. Both Violet and Sid had remembered noticing him for three very good reasons: (*a*) He was dressed in a well-fitting teddy-bear coat and tweed cap. (*b*) He was abnormally tall and broad-shouldered. (*c*) He was middle-aged and, as Violet graphically put it, "a wah-wah sort of chap". They further recalled that this unusual fellow had suddenly slipped away and jumped into a small car that Sid recognised as a Stanmobile Eight. They both felt sure that this man had not been attending the dance. He was of a different type and generation from the rest of the crowd. He appeared, in fact, to be a complete stranger.

Duffy was deeply interested. Suppose this man *were* the assailant. Wasn't it possible that he had driven his car all out to the far end of the Cut, making a small detour through the neighbouring streets, parked his Stanmobile at some inconspicuous spot, and gone on foot down the lane to the point where Duffy had discovered the trampled patch of grass? This would have given him plenty of time to intercept the couple. Plenty of time, in fact, to light and relight his pipe as he crouched there, waiting, with the revolver in his hand.

Revolver? Well, that, as the inspector was prepared to admit, was mere guesswork. Revolver, automatic, rifle—the exact nature of the weapon was uncertain. He had made a close search for the spent bullets, but the result was nil. In the circumstances he was inclined to suspect a revolver, but he was taking no bets on the matter.

But this tall figure in the teddy-bear coat had captured his imagination. Was he a citizen of Welworth or a mere visitor? Had anybody seen the man about the place either prior to or since the shooting incident in the Cut? Was he *really* connected with the crime?

That week Duffy had a small paragraph inserted at the foot of the column in the *Welworth Echo* which dealt with the incident. It ran:

The police are anxious to get in touch with a tall, broad-shouldered, middle-aged man, wearing a teddy-bear overcoat and tweed cap, speaking with an educated accent. It is thought that this person may be able to throw some light on the mystery surrounding the shooting. If any person has seen this man recently in Welworth or knows of his present whereabouts, they are asked to get in touch immediately with the local police.

It was two days after the insertion of this notice, that a rotund, bald, benign little man looked—or rather, peeped—into the main office. He claimed to have some information about the man the police were anxious to interview. The sergeant showed him through to Inspector Duffy.

Once seated, the little fellow placed his hat carefully on the inspector's desk, puffed out his cheeks, wriggled like a small child on his chair and chuckled:

"Dear, dear, to think of me in a police-station. My name's Pillick, by the way. Strange indeed are the quips and quirks of…Now, where was I? What did I…? But, of course. That paragraph in the *Welworth Echo*. It *was* the *Echo*, wasn't it? Not that nasty cheap mid-weekly *Gazette*, which my wife and I…My wife—yes! It amused her enormously when she knew I was coming here to…tut-tut! But my domestic life can't possibly…Now what *was* it I came here to give you?"

"Information," suggested Duffy, curbing his impatience with difficulty. "Concerning the—"

"Ah yes!—that's it. Information. But I can't for the life of me…But how ridiculous. It was in connection with your notice in the *Gazette*."

"The *Echo*."

"Naturally—the *Echo*. I can't imagine the police having any truck with a nasty, cheap…But don't let's waste time discussing the merits of our local newspapers. Both are utterly devoid of any literary…As a matter of fact, Mr. Manxton observed only the other day that…I mean, of course, Mr. *Fred* Manxton. Not Herbert. Herbert knows nothing. He has no critical faculties whatsoever. So different from his brother. Herbert, if you'll pardon my forceful termination, is a nitwit. He has absolutely no…Information! Yes. Yes. I mustn't wander. You mustn't let me. Bad habit. Information, of course. About the man in the teddy-bear hat."

"Overcoat."

"Dear me—of course. Overcoat. A teddy-bear hat would… Rather like that oriental gentleman in his fez, eh? I bumped into him—yes, last Saturday it would be—coming out of a gate not far from my little place in Bindweed Crescent. Tall, broad-shouldered—"

"You mean the oriental gentleman?"

"In what connection?"

"You mean you bumped into the oriental gentleman?"

"But, gracious me, you don't want information about *him,* surely?"

"No, sir, we don't. We want information about a tall, broad-shouldered, middle-aged man in—"

"Yes! Yes! I know. In a tweed cap and a teddy-bear coat. The gentleman I bumped into coming out of a gate near my house in…He emerged from the front door and walked so quickly down the path that I…Most unfortunate."

"You say this was last Saturday? That is, four days ago. Is that right, sir?"

"Oh yes, yes. There's no mistake about that. I always have a little game of contract every Saturday evening with…My wife doesn't play, of course. She finds the bidding overcomplicated. Her mind's adequate rather than…Yes, he came out of the gate rather suddenly and almost knocked me over. I'm a small, rather undersized man, as you can see. My hat—the same hat that I've put there on your desk—rolled into the gutter. But he was very apologetic and charming...It *was* the *Echo* you said, wasn't it?"

"Yes, sir—our notice appeared in the *Echo*."

"Good! Good! I must say that both my wife and I abominate that nasty cheap—"

"And what time would it be when you collided with this gentleman, Mr. Pillick?"

"Oh, late. Very late. Far *too* late. In fact it was very nearly twelve o'clock...er...that is to say, midnight. Most reprehensible. But as I was subsequently to explain to my wife—"

"He was coming away from the house?"

"Oh dear me, yes. In a great hurry. One might almost employ the phrase 'in a state of apparent agitation'. Most charming, though. Picked up my...profuse apologies...and drove off in his car."

"Can you recall the name or number of the house from which the gentleman had just come?"

"Most certainly. Both the name and the...Elysium—yes, that was the name. Elysium, number fourteen, Bindweed Crescent. I live at number twenty-two. It's a nice quiet—"

"I take it that this gentleman doesn't happen to *live* at number fourteen?"

"At number...? Oh, good gracious—no. As a matter of fact I happen to know who does live at...But perhaps you're not...Or *are* you?"

"Decidedly, Mr. Pillick. All evidence is grist to our mill, you know."

"Quite, quite. Very apt. Now let me see? Oh yes, of course, you want to know who...A most charming young lady by the name of...tut-tut!...it's on the tip of my...Of course, I remember now! I caught a quick glimpse of her that very evening before she shut the...Now let me see..."

"Well, Mr. Pillick?"

"Miss…Miss…I know it's an alliterative…Ah yes…dear, dear…tut-tut!…of course. Miss Penelope Parker!"

II

Mr. Pillick was not the only witness to come forward and give information about the Man in the Teddy-Bear Coat. A young operative at the Rollup Corset Factory, on his way to the fancy-dress dance, had noticed him changing a wheel of his car *at a spot directly opposite the main entrance to the works.* This was at seven-twenty, just before the dance was scheduled to begin. And finally, a member of the Hertfordshire County Police, patrolling a section of the Great North Road near Hitchin, had seen the fellow at the wheel of his car when held up by adverse traffic-lights at a cross-road. This was on Saturday night, some fifteen minutes after midnight. The car was heading in the direction of London. Unfortunately he had not noticed the registration number of the car.

"Now, what exactly," pondered Inspector Duffy, "can I deduce from these separate scraps of evidence?"

One factor impressed him immediately. All three witnesses claimed to have seen the man on the same day and all within a few hours of each other—that is to say, between seven-twenty and twelve-fifteen on Saturday night. The shots had been fired in Mayblossom Cut at (*circa*) eleven-ten. Drawing a sheet of paper on to his blotting-pad, Duffy wrote:

Seen changing wheel outside factory	7.20
Seen by Arkwright and girl outside factory	10.45
Shots fired in the Cut	11.10 (*circa*)
Seen by Pillick outside No. 14 Bindweed Crescent	12.0
Seen by constable on Great North Road	12.15

Studying this brief summary of the time-factor in the case, the inspector felt prepared to put forward a theory concerning the man's movements. In his opinion, the man, in the light of this fresh evidence, was *not* a citizen of the town. He had probably driven down from London just prior to the dance and driven back again after his unaccountable visit to Bindweed Crescent. Certain it was that this visit in no way precluded the assumption that he was the man who fired the shots at Arkwright. There would have been ample time for him to have dropped in at No. 14 after the incident in the Cut. It was equally certain that, after his collision with the scatter-brained Mr. Pillick, he had jumped into his car and headed directly for London. So much for his possible movements.

But what was the significance of his visit to this Miss Penelope Parker. Who *was* this Miss Parker? Had she any connection with Sid Arkwright?

Duffy rang for Sergeant Underwood who was on duty in the outer office that morning.

"Look here, Sergeant," he said, as the burly figure entered. "You're about the biggest gossip and scandalmonger in the station—what do you know of a Miss Penelope Parker? Anything worth-while?"

"Miss Parker of Bindweed Crescent?" Duffy nodded. "Well, sir, she's a good-looking party, in her late twenties, I should say. Well-breeched to judge from the establishment she manages to keep up. She's a pretty active member, too, of that queer sect in Carroway Road—that Temple of Osseris or whatever it's called."

Duffy gave a low whistle and nodded his satisfaction.

"Thanks, Sergeant. You've told me just what I wanted to know."

So Miss Parker, in a roundabout way, was connected with Sid Arkwright. And, of course, with Penpeti, since they were all members of the same faith. Umph!—a queer lot. First the mysterious disappearance of that Crux Something-or-other, and now this equally mysterious affair in Mayblossom Cut. But how did this tall, broad-shouldered Man in the Teddy-Bear Coat fit into the picture? Was *he* one of these high-faluting Children of Osiris? And if so, was there some sort of skullduggery going on inside the Movement?

Duffy jumped energetically to his feet and reached for his peaked cap. Well, it was no good sitting there asking himself a series of damfool questions to which he didn't know the answers. What was it his old Chief used to say? "Get out, get the evidence, and get on with the case." Exactly! And if he wanted further information, surely this Miss Penelope Parker was the one person who could supply it?

III

Penelope, swathed in pale heliotrope veiling, in a flowing gauzy dress with long filmy sleeves and a silver *uraeus* binding her long tresses, was seated on a high-backed chair with her eyes closed. Two joss-sticks burned on a coffee-table by her side. A large, tawny-eyed cat lay curled on an oriental cushion watching her with baleful rigidity. The room, although it was mid-morning, was submerged in a mellow and mystical twilight, for the heavy brocaded curtains had been drawn across the french-windows which led into the garden. The sole illumination, in fact, was diffused through the enormous amber eyes of a big bronze Anubis set in an alcove by the fireplace. The room was reminiscent of a cinema foyer that had been specially decorated to advertise such forthcoming attractions as *Ben Hur* or the *Birth of a Nation*.

Penelope, for the last twenty minutes, had been in a profound state of "non-being". She had, despite the vague repercussions of a large breakfast-plate of mashed banana and cream, succeeded in merging her Grosser Self into the Infinite. She had elevated herself on to this Higher Plane with the avowed intention of projecting a series of Beautiful

Thoughts towards her maid, who only two days before had been rude to her in the kitchen. But to her annoyance and dismay, no sooner was she well astride the Higher Plane, when she clean forgot what had originally prompted her to make this mystical ascent. She had, of course, two alternatives. Either she could go through the somewhat lengthy and arduous process of returning once more to the Finite Plane, there to pick up the lost thread, before clambering back laboriously on to her present exalted perch. Or she could stay where she was in a state of Absolute Nothingness. Being of an indolent nature. Penelope had no difficulty in making her choice. She just squatted up there on her Higher Plane and passed out into the realms of Nirvana.

Inspector Duffy's visit could scarcely have been more ill-timed, for the maid's entrance to announce his arrival suddenly jerked Penelope off her Higher Plane and back, with somewhat of a jar, into her Grosser Self. She eyed the servant in a dazed sort of fashion.

"Who?" she murmured.

"Inspector Duffy, ma'am."

"Very well, Hilda. Show him in."

Duffy came in smartly, hat under his arm, and gave a stiff little bow. Penelope waved a languid hand towards an imitation Hathor couch covered with a vegetarian leopard-skin and struggled hard to come to grips with the realities of the situation. A police inspector. But why? What did he want? She suddenly felt nervous and a little dizzy.

She said inanely: "You wish to see me about something?"

"A little routine matter. Perhaps you'd be good enough, madam, to answer a few simple questions."

"Of course...if I can."

"It concerns a gentleman whose movements and present whereabouts we're anxious to trace. Perhaps you've seen this week's edition of the *Echo*?"

"No. I only read the *Cabalist* and the *Mystic Times*. I don't find local journalism very elevating."

"Quite so." Duffy coughed uncomfortably. The glaring amber eyes of the bronze Anubis rather distracted him. "We have reason to believe that shortly before midnight last Saturday, the gentleman in question paid a visit to this house."

"I beg your pardon?" Duffy reiterated his statement. "To this house?" echoed Penelope. "But that's impossible! If he had visited this house I should certainly have been aware of it. I was alone at the time. Hilda, the parlour-maid, always spends Saturday night with her mother at St. Albans. And cook, as I happen to know, went up to bed before ten o'clock. So you see, Inspector…there's no question about it."

"But I have evidence, which I consider to be reliable, that this gentleman left your house about midnight and drove off in his car, which was parked outside your gate. You're quite sure of your facts, madam? It's easy to forget details, even in a few days. I repeat—this was last Saturday night."

Penelope's expression during the inspector's statement had undergone a curious and subtle change. It was obvious that she was now fully alive to the situation—no longer trailing clouds of glory, but alert, even watchful, gazing at the inspector through narrowed lids.

"But there must be some misunderstanding. No visitor came to this house on Saturday night."

"Not even for a brief visit?" Penelope shook her head. "Curious," muttered Duffy with a meaning glance. "Very curious. My witness was convinced that he saw you at the open door as the gentleman was leaving."

"Your witness, perhaps, mistook the…the number of the house."

"This is number fourteen Bindweed Crescent, isn't it?" Penelope inclined her sleek head. There was a long and awkward pause and then, with an abrupt change of tone, Duffy rapped out: "I must ask you to think again, Miss Parker, and think carefully. I've no need to tell you that it's a crime to withhold information from the police. I'll put the question to you once more. Did you or did you not receive a gentleman into this house shortly before midnight last Saturday?"

Penelope hesitated a moment, pursing her lips and half-closing her eyes in the face of the inspector's stern and piercing scrutiny. Then with a toss of her head, she said with a defiant air:

"No—I did not. I can't imagine how this mysterious rumour has reached you. It's very upsetting."

"Very well." The inspector rose. "I'm sorry to have taken up your time, Miss Parker. No—don't trouble to ring for the maid. I'll see myself out." He gave another stiff little bow. "And thank you."

As Duffy closed the front door, he heard the click of the garden-gate and turned to see a familiar figure advancing towards him. As they passed each other on the path, Duffy's eyebrows lifted quizzically, but he said affably enough:

"Good morning, Mr. Penpeti. Not quite so raw to-day."

"Exceptionally mild," beamed Penpeti. "At least, for the time of the year."

IV

This chance meeting was equally intriguing to both of the participants. In the amber twilight of Penelope's exotic drawing-room, Penpeti was demanding:

"But what was he doing here? What did he want? What exactly was he after?"

His extreme nervousness, coupled with his intense curiosity, rather surprised Penelope. But she said lightly:

"Oh, just a little private matter. Nothing of importance."

"You're sure?"

Penelope laughed gaily.

"My darling Peta—please!"

"You must excuse my anxiety. But the thought of you being badgered by the police…most repugnant to me. A small matter you say?" Penelope nodded, as she accepted a light for her herbal cigarette. "I only ask because they don't usually send a police inspector to deal with trivial matters. You're sure you're not hiding something from me, my dear?"

"Hiding something from *you*! But why should I?"

"Out of the kindness of your heart, chérie. To protect me from any hurt or humiliation, perhaps."

"I…I don't follow, my darling."

Penpeti seemed troubled by an unfamiliar embarrassment.

"I wondered if the inspector had been asking any questions…er…about me. If so, I think it only fair that you should tell me the truth."

"But why should he ask questions about you?" asked Penelope, bewildered.

"Oh, in a general sense, I mean. I haven't spoken to you about this before, but Inspector Duffy called on me after the Crux Ansata had been stolen. He left me with the impression that he thought *I* was the thief!" Penpeti's laugh was a trifle hollow. "Preposterous, you'll agree. But once these uniformed gentlemen get a bee in their bonnet…"

Penelope's arms slid gently round his neck as she drew him down on to the gilded Hathor couch.

"Now don't be a great stupid. It had nothing to do with you. As I said before, it was a private matter of no importance. Now let's forget all about the inspector's visit and…"

Penpeti, knowing well enough what was expected of him, seemed prepared to abandon the subject. But that morning Penelope noticed that his love-making was perfunctory and by no means up to standard. He seemed worried and absent-minded.

Duffy, too, was worried. He had suddenly run his head into a brick wall. It was the old cul-de-sac of conflicting evidence. Mr. Pillick's assertions versus Miss Parker's denials. What precisely did it mean? Had the Man in the Teddy-Bear Coat visited No. 14 last Saturday night or not? Duffy's inclination was to suspect that he *had,* and that for some reason Miss Parker was anxious to conceal the fact from the police. But why? Was she in any way connected with the attempt on Sid Arkwright's life?—an accessory, perhaps, both before and after the fact?

That the Man in the Teddy-Bear Coat knew something about the lay-out of Welworth was obvious. After all, if he *had* taken up his position in the Cut after overhearing the conversation between Arkwright and his girl, it meant very definite knowledge of the local topography. Either the fellow had at one time lived in the Garden City or else he had been a frequent visitor to the town. A frequent visitor to No. 14 Bindweed Crescent, perhaps?

Another significant point occurred to him. Miss Parker and Penpeti were acquainted. Nothing very surprising about that, since they were both members of that odd religious set-up in Carroway Road. On the other hand, it was on the cards that the would-be murderer had fired those shots at somebody he believed to be Penpeti. Surely there was a suggestive link-up here? Penpeti knew Miss Parker and Miss Parker knew the Man in the Teddy-Bear Coat. Was he, at last, on to a really plausible line of investigation? Did the motive for the attempted murder lie in the relationship between these three widely diverse personalities?

Chapter VIII

Near Miss

I

It was at this interesting point in his investigation that Inspector Duffy got bogged down. No fresh evidence, no unexpected clue, no further development. The mystery shooting in Mayblossom Cut was evidently destined to remain a mystery. Sid Arkwright was soon back at the wheel of Eustace's luxurious Daimler. Mr. Penpeti continued to parade about the Garden City in his bizarre *ensemble*. Duffy often saw Miss Penelope Parker out and about in the shopping centre. The Man in the Teddy-Bear Coat was not, as far as the inspector knew, seen again in Welworth.

The Garden City, in fact, seemed to settle down to its customary winter-time activities. There was the usual seasonal outburst of amateur theatricals, lectures, chamber-music, religious, political and educational meetings. There was the usual spate of head colds, chills, neuralgia, catarrh and laryngitis—striking impartially at meat-eater and vegetarian alike. There was the inescapable arctic wind blowing down Broadway, constant, penetrating, bitter, so that before March was out tempers were frayed and the lightest disagreement liable to break out into downright hostility.

Poor Eustace was miserable to a degree. The feeling that all was not well in the world of Cooism, deepened. Several ugly quarrels flared up between members of the Inmost Temple over trivial matters of procedure and dogma. Periodically Mrs. Hagge-Smith descended on Welworth from her country seat to attend these meetings, put several spokes in several wheels, issued a few high-handed manifestos concerning finance and publicity, paid a few lush compliments to her dear Mr. Penpeti and departed in a whirl of last-minute amendments and reminders. To Eustace she was polite rather than friendly, still angry over his refusal to produce *The Nine Gods of Heliopolis*. It was, in fact, a lonely and unhappy period for the High Prophet. Opposed by Alicia and Penpeti, seemingly abandoned by Hansford Boot, humoured like a small child by Penelope, high-hatted by his worthless offspring, he grew more and more morose. There were times when he wanted to run away from it all; to resign his high office and cut himself adrift for ever from the Movement he had originated. If it had not been for his pride and Penelope, perhaps he would have left the Garden City. Of late his letters had grown more passionate, more outspoken, more demanding, until, finally driven almost desperate by her detachment, he actually wrote and asked her to marry him. Penelope was very kind, very tactful, but very firm. She thought that, in the circumstances, it would be better if Eustace refrained from writing her in the future. She was sorry, but for his own sake…

Sadly Eustace took the hint and, from that day onward, continued to worship her, but only from afar.

II

During those winter months Penpeti realised that, from a financial point-of-view, he was sitting pretty. Hansford was disbursing with the regularity and efficiency of a ticket-machine. Yacob, aware that his own interests were being served by these extortions, remained comparatively tractable. Provided he got his rake-off from the blackmail, and occasional extra slices of "the necessary" (for what he termed his "running expenses") he was prepared to leave Penpeti, more or less, alone. On top of all this Penelope seemed not only ready to loosen her purse-strings, but to leave them permanently untied. Of course he had to work hard to retain her in this generous mood, but as Penpeti, since the age of sixteen, had taken to love-making as other boys to cricket, wood-carving or stamp-collecting, he was blessed with that facility of execution which accrues naturally from years of practice.

Yes—from the financial angle, Penpeti was satisfied that he was doing very well for himself. Yet his peace-of-mind was not without blemish. The shooting affair in Mayblossom Cut had not escaped his attention and he was fly enough to spot the joke that had been levelled at him by the ingenious Sid Arkwright. And the more he analysed the incident, the more certain he grew that he had been the intended victim of those shots in the dark. When Yacob next slipped up to Welworth and sidled in through his front door to collect "the necessary", Penpeti showed him the reports in the local papers. Yacob whistled.

"So it's like that is it? Dear! Dear! You don't suppose that—?"

"I've my own suspicions," broke in Penpeti. "That's why I showed you these cuttings. I want *your* opinion, Yacob."

"You're thinking of Gaussin, eh?"

Penpeti nodded solemnly.

"Naturally."

"But that's impossible!" exclaimed Yacob. "Out of the question. I happen to know that Pierre Gaussin's out of town. He's been out for some months now. Working the Côte D'Azur. The usual racket."

Penpeti breathed an audible sigh of relief.

"You're sure of your facts?"

"Certain! I've always made a point, a very *special* point, my dear fellow, of checking up on Pierre's movements. After all"—Yacob flashed Penpeti a quick, meaning smile—"you know I've always got your interests at heart. Oh no—you can't pin this on to Gaussin. He's a slippery customer, but he'd have to work darn fast to put anything across me." Yacob paused, lit a cigarette and suddenly observed: "There's another possibility, you know."

"Well?"

"Our mutual friend. The plump pigeon you're now picking."

"Sam Grew?" exclaimed Penpeti. "Confound it! I hadn't thought of him. But he wouldn't dare try anything as drastic as that."

"A cornered rat will dare anything," commented Yacob sagaciously. "If you'll take my advice, you'll watch your step with Mr. Sam Grew. You can leave Pierre out of it."

One dark night towards the end of March, Penpeti had good cause to remember Yacob's advice. He was just entering the house, when something whizzed by his left ear and thudded into the woodwork of the door. Even before it had stopped quivering, Penpeti had wrenched the object free and swung round on the gate. Unfortunately a large lilac bush afforded perfect cover and, by the time he had rushed into the roadway, he saw no more than a rapidly diminishing shape receding into the shadows. The sequence of events had been so rapid that Penpeti had difficulty in believing that they had really happened. But the long, wicked-looking knife in his hand proved unquestionably that they had!

Penpeti shuddered as he let himself into the house. He felt sick and dizzy. Another inch to the right and...he shuddered again. Like Eustace, he had grown acutely aware of the malignant forces abroad in the Garden City. Was Yacob right? Was it Sam Grew alias Hansford Boot who had thrown that knife? He doubted it. Hansford didn't strike him as the type of man to make a cold-blooded and calculating murderer. Too weak-kneed. Too imaginative. But if Pierre Gaussin were in the South of France...then who, who?

Thereafter, Penpeti never went out after dark. He pretended to Penelope that his eyesight was failing. But refusing to be diddled of his company during the long evenings, she finally persuaded him to stay the night. He bowed his head to the inevitable and, to prevent the domestics from gossiping, slunk away from Elysium before Hilda and the cook were awake.

He toyed with the idea of discarding his caftan and fez. But in the end he realised that such a move might prove dangerous. It might mean questions, awkward questions, and questions were something he was most anxious to avoid. For that same reason Penpeti never made any mention, save to Yacob, of the knife-throwing episode. He knew only too well that he was in no position to suffer the searching cross-examinations of a police enquiry.

III

And so it was, with all these unsolved enigmas hanging like a huge question-mark over the Cult of Coo, that the hierarchy of the Order, towards the end of May, made preparations for their imminent departure to Sussex.

Part II

Old Cowdene

Chapter IX

Sid Arkwright Listens In

I

Alicia Hagge-Smith's vision was already well on the way to becoming a reality. As she sat by the mullioned window of her boudoir—a severely Spartan room with no feminine non-sense about it—her somewhat beady eye raked the broad acres of the park and brightened with a gleam of satisfaction. Near and far, amidst the clumps of bosky elms, workmen were busy digging ditches, erecting tents, driving pegs, tying off guy-ropes, laying wires, water-pipes and cinder-tracks. The pink and white mayblossom was in full flower and a golden tide of buttercups seemed to sweep up to the outer confines of the manor garden and break in silence against the mellow brick walls. Under her window a motor-mower was buzzing like a trapped bee as the third-gardener moved up and down the gently-undulating lawns. The fourth-gardener was visible beyond the rose-walk, engaged in mulching the peony-beds with liquid manure. The fifth, no more than a dot at the far end of the kitchen-garden, was busy pricking out young lettuce plants. The second-gardener was not to be seen, since he was sitting on a barrow in the centre of a rhododendron clump enjoying a leisured pipe. The head-gardener, as befitted a man of such eminence, was taking a post-prandial nap in the potting-shed.

Mrs. Hagge-Smith was content. All was going well. Two days earlier the members of the Inmost Temple had arrived at Old Cowdene as an advance party to the flood of ordinary members who were due in about a week. Their distribution about the estate had now been completed, for it had been agreed that all the spare rooms in the manor should be reserved for the more enfeebled members of the Movement. Penelope, with Hilda and the cook, were now comfortably installed in the Dower House on the south fringe of the park. Eustace, with typical modesty, had claimed nothing more grandiose than a furnished lodge at the north entrance. Terence and the blonde housekeeper, Mrs. Summers, had travelled down in the Daimler with him. Sid Arkwright had taken up his quarters in a nearby barn where the car was to be garaged. Other members of the Inmost Temple, including Hansford Boot, had, at their own request, been accommodated in a cluster of bell-tents not far from the Chinese summer-house, which had been converted into a quiet and tasteful Temple of Meditation. Penpeti alone had refused to remain within the hallowed precincts of the estate. For reasons, upon which he was obviously not prepared to enlarge, he had engaged a couple of rooms at the local inn—The Leaning Man. Alicia was naturally shocked. It was infra dig, she felt, for a Prophet-in-Waiting to take up residence in a public-house. She begged him to change his mind, but Penpeti remained adamant. He spoke vaguely of that "isolation and detachment necessary to come to terms with one's Higher Self"; the need for a private retreat "away from the commendable hubbub of mass devotion". And as Alicia had no more idea of what he meant than Penpeti himself, she was forced to accept his explanation and leave it at that. She was disappointed, a little huffy, but resigned.

Once every twenty-four hours, at dinner, the members of the Inmost Temple foregathered at the manor and went into a huddle. For the remainder of the day they busied themselves about the thousand and one practical activities demanded by the impending conventicle. A casual onlooker might have supposed that a certain amount of the tension which had been so noticeable in Welworth had evaporated.

But beneath the crust of all this activity, the yeast of personal prejudices and problems was still working overtime. The "goodly apple", alas, was still thoroughly "rotten at the core".

II

For months Terence had been dreaming of this moment—dreams in superb technicolour, starring the one and only woman in his life…Denise Blake. Once at Old Cowdene he felt sure that he would be able to see Denise alone. It was an extensive estate and his father and the Blot could not possibly police all of it all of the time. True, Denise was tied to her job most of the day, but surely sometime, in the evening in the gloaming…? He had attended his first dinner-party at the manor in a whirl of excitement and anticipation. But, to his acute disappointment, Denise didn't show up. After all, how was Terence to know that Alicia and Eustace had laid their heads together and decided to do all in their power to keep the couple apart? Alicia because she didn't want to lose a good secretary: Eustace because he didn't want to lose his influence over his son.

Once Terence had glimpsed Denise in the distance—a sylph-like figure slipping through the rose-garden with a basket of flowers on her arm. Daring all, he had called her by name—an anguished, love-lorn bellow that echoed against the grey-stoned walls like a roll of thunder. The result had been disheartening—a collection of heads bobbing up from the most unexpected places, all staring in his direction. Gardeners peering over shrubs, maids from windows, workmen from holes in the ground; and, finally, like some outraged *diva,* Alicia Hagge-Smith herself, glaring at him from the terrace. Denise had fled into the house. Terence, flushing to the roots of his hair, had stumbled off across the park.

He was furious with his father, the Blot, himself, life, every damn thing! Any normal chap with a normal father would have been allowed to make contact with a decent, normal girl like Denise. It was sickening, vile! If he had to bottle himself up much longer, he'd…he'd…

But Terence wasn't sure just what he *would* do when the critical moment arrived. Something drastic and dramatic. Of that he was convinced!

III

Penelope had given instructions that Mr. Penpeti was to be admitted without question to the Dower House whenever he chanced to call. Now, more than ever, she needed a strong arm upon which to lean; a stimulating personality to revitalise her jaded nerves. For Penelope, after a lifetime of ease and security, suddenly found herself in a jam. Two days before leaving Welworth, like a bolt from the blue, she had received a letter from her broker in the City. Its contents left no room for doubt. Due to a totally unexpected fluctuation of certain shares, a large slice of Penelope's private income had, so to speak, vanished overnight. Retrenchment was now the order of the day—a cutting down here, a denial there, and so on. All unnecessary luxuries would have to go, including, of course, her little "loans" (as she optimistically liked to call them) to Peta. Penpeti was horror-struck when he learnt the news, for Yacob, as the result of a series of losses on the turf, had suddenly begun to tighten the screw. True, there was still Hansford Boot's fifty pounds a quarter, but without Penelope's extra disbursements it was going to be the very devil to keep Yacob sweet and reasonable.

But this financial set-back was as thistledown to the second worry which tormented Penelope. For weeks she had been wrestling with a new and terrifying complication, determined that Penpeti's life should not be darkened by her secret. But two days after her arrival in Sussex, she broke down and confessed everything.

"But good God!" cried Penpeti, shaken to the core. "It can't be true! It can't!"

"Oh, I've tried to persuade myself that I've been imagining things!" cried Penelope in stricken tones. "But I'm not, Peta. We've got to face up to it. I'm going to have a child— *your* child! It's terrible, I admit, but it's true!"

"But good heavens, don't you see?" blustered Penpeti. "If this leaks out, I'm ruined. Ruined! Imagine Alicia's reaction to the news. Me, the Prophet-in-Waiting, the father of—"

"Peta darling, we must keep our heads."

"Confound it—I'm trying to. But you must see it from my point-of-view. As Prophet-in-Waiting I receive certain emoluments that go with the office. What happens to my income if—?"

"Then Alicia *mustn't* find out!"

"Don't be absurd. How the devil can we prevent her? Unless," he added, suddenly brightening, "unless you're prepared to go away. Is that it? You're willing to go abroad, perhaps?"

Penelope shook her head.

"No, Peta. For one thing I couldn't afford it. For another, my darling, I just couldn't bear to be away from you at this awful moment. I just couldn't! Surely you see that?"

"Then how can we hoodwink Alicia, Eustace and all the rest of them? In a few more weeks your condition will be obvious to everybody. I tell you, Penelope, this will ruin me. I shall be done for in the Movement. Defrocked! Disgraced!" Penpeti threw his arms wide in a gesture of despair and began to pace rapidly up and down the room. "That this should happen now—*now,* when there's a strong possibility of my promotion. Only the other day, Alicia was hinting to me…there's a growing faction inside the Order who would like to see Eustace out of office. Too unenterprising. Too dogmatic. Too reactionary. I haven't spoken about this before, but Alicia's convinced that if the matter were put to a general vote…" He clasped his hands dramatically to his head. "And now it's hopeless, hopeless! This has finished me. I can be written off!"

He dropped into an armchair and lay back exhausted, scowling at the overcast sky beyond the window. All his plans thwarted. All his hopes dashed to the ground. Suddenly he was aware of Penelope's cool hand brushing over his cheek.

"Peta."

"Well?" He snatched aside her hand with a surly gesture and glared up at her with an expression of impatience.

"I want to show you something."

She went to a small antique bureau, unlocked the lid, picked up her letter-case, unlocked it in turn and took out a bundle of letters tied with ribbon.

"These," she murmured, handing the bundle to Penpeti. "Read them. I think they may interest you."

Penpeti briskly untied the ribbon, flattened out the first letter and began to read. He did so without comment. Then he took up a second epistle, then a third, and gradually his scowl evaporated. He leaned forward in his chair, stroking his beard, absorbed, devouring page after page of the closely-written sheets with unbridled attention.

Then: "Eustace!" he cried. "Good heavens, it's impossible!" He began to laugh softly, derisively. "Of all the damned hypocrites. I can't believe it. How long has this been going on?"

"Oh months," said Penelope. "Until I put a stop to it a few weeks ago…after he'd made me a proposal of marriage."

"A proposal?" shot out Penpeti. "Eustace?" He laughed again; then suddenly recalling the conversation which had led up to the revelation of these letters, he went on tartly: "This is all very amusing, I admit, but why show them to me now?"

"But, Peta, don't you see?"

He stared at her blankly.

"I haven't the—"

Penelope broke in tenderly.

"Do you think I want to spoil your career, my darling? Your chances of becoming High Prophet? Peta dear, don't be so obtuse. Surely you think a little more highly of your adoring Penelope than that? Don't you realise? I was wondering if Eustace, perhaps, wasn't the one person who could get us out of this dilemma."

"Eustace? But how?"

"Well," murmured Penelope, with a mystical expression. "Suppose I went to Alicia and…and told her *that Eustace was the father of the child I'm about to bear?*"

Dumbfounded, Penpeti sprang to his feet. He stared at Penelope as if he suspected her of having lost her reason. Then slowly a smile spread over his swarthy features.

"Eustace," he said softly. "Eustace, who has written you all these intimate little notes. Eustace, who has made you a proposal of marriage—a proposal *in writing*! My dear, but this is sheer inspiration. You're wonderful. And for my sake, you're prepared to suffer the inevitable scandal that will follow this dénouement?"

"For your sake, Peta," said Penelope with perfect simplicity, "you know I'm ready to do *anything*."

"But Eustace may deny the charge of paternity."

"What of it? It will be his word against mine. And when Alicia reads those letters...I've an idea that the office of High Prophet—"

Penpeti's dark eyes glittered.

"Mine!" he muttered. "This will set the seal on it. Good heavens! Penelope, you're incomparable! Superb!"

What did it matter now that Penelope's financial aid had dried up? If this scheme were successful, Eustace was finished, and he, Penpeti, would without any shadow of doubt, step into his shoes. And the office of High Prophet, as he often had good cause to remind himself, carried with it a salary of five thousand a year!

One thing alone perplexed him. Why hadn't Penelope used this contretemps as a lever to force him to marry her? There was nothing really standing in the way of such a union. Thank heaven, of course, that the idea *hadn't* occurred to her! For all that, it was a strange and puzzling omission.

IV

But in the first flush of his enthusiasm for a scheme that would whitewash his own character at the expense of a man who stood between him and five thousand a year, Penpeti forgot to make allowances for a possible nigger in the wood-pile. The conspiracy, as propounded by Penelope, seemed pretty well flawless, and perhaps it would have been if Sid Arkwright hadn't enjoyed an occasional half-pint of mild and bitter.

Sid was happy in his loft above the barn. He liked the free-and-easy rural atmosphere that reigned at Old

Cowdene. In point of fact he had little enough to do during that first week in Sussex, for his employer scarcely ever left the confines of the park. Occasionally he taxied the High Prophet from one corner of the estate to the other, for the park covered a surface of nearly nine square miles. But apart from these brief journeys, Sid was more or less left to his own devices.

Before leaving Welworth he had had just one helluva row with Violet Brett. Not that she hadn't good reasons for feeling annoyed, but Sid preferred to forget that. At first he had been depressed by the quarrel, but by now he was quite heart-free and ready to take up with any girl that chanced to take his eye. Hilda Shepstone, for example, Miss Parker's maid over at the Dower House. In Sid's opinion a bit of a high-stepper and well worth cultivating. Of course, Hilda wasn't always free in the evening, so Sid had dropped into the habit of taking a stroll up to The Leaning Man once he had deposited the Mildmanns at the manor. After dinner they usually walked back through the park, which gave Sid the rest of the evening to himself.

It was a Saturday night just after closing-time, when Sid first found himself involved in the secret machinations of his superiors. It happened quite by chance. Rounding a bend in the road at the end of the village on his way back to the park, he was suddenly aware of a figure preceding him down the moonlit lane. The man was moving swiftly, silently and, in Sid's opinion, furtively. He was continually stopping in his stride and looking back over his shoulder. His curiosity aroused, Sid moved on to the wide grass verge and proceeded to stalk this mysterious figure. There was deep shadow under the overhanging trees and, to judge by the man's behaviour, he had no idea that Sid was following him.

Presently the man drew into the side of the road and Sid heard more stealthy footsteps advancing, this time, up the lane. He crouched back under a tangle of briar and waited. In a short time the second figure became clearly visible in the moonlight and Sid gave a start of surprise. There was no mistaking the black-bearded features and the long black caftan. He noticed, however, that Mr. Penpeti was carrying his fez and it struck Sid that he had done this to make himself less conspicuous.

The man in the shadows gave a low whistle. Penpeti halted, looked cautiously up and down the lane, and joined the second figure under the overhanging branches of elm. Almost at once they broke into a brisk though muted conversation. With his curiosity now at fever heat, Sid withdrew gently up the lane to a point where he had previously noticed a stile that gave on to a field on the same side of the road as the two men. In a flash he was over the stile and creeping silently towards them on the far side of the hedge.

At a point some five yards away, which was as near as he dared to advance, Sid halted and listened. It was quite impossible to hear every word of their conversation. In fact it was only a few detached phrases of Penpeti's that he was able to isolate, for his companion was talking in a kind of harsh and throaty whisper. But what he *did* hear was sufficient to whet Sid's appetite to hear more. What did it mean? Why had Penpeti met this man so secretively in the lane? And who was his companion?

After a few seconds Sid realised that it was his employer they were discussing. He caught a series of broken phrases.

"…point is…Mildmann has been writing letters…long period of time…this woman in question…use these as a lever to…out of office…"

Then followed a few quick, inaudible comments by the second figure, terminating in a low, mirthless sort of chuckle. Again Penpeti took up the conversation.

"Awkward, I admit…Parker girl's all right, though…let me down…work it right…Mildmann will take the rap…I tell you…on to a dead cert…end of our friend Mildmann… kaput!"

There was another chuckle and further inaudible comments from the second man. Again Penpeti—this time with a persuasive note in his voice, rather anxious.

"But confound it…asking you to wait a few weeks…must have patience…pay you out then O.K…safe bet, I assure you…in clover if things go…"

But suddenly Penpeti dropped his voice to match the husky whisper of his fellow conspirator, and Sid was unable to isolate any further sequence of words. But what he had heard roused in him the wildest speculation. This was his chance, he realised, to make amends to his employer for his previous unkind behaviour. He had never forgotten Eustace's sympathy and generosity in the days following the shooting incident in the Cut. He had fussed over him during his convalescence as if Sid had been his own son. And if he had been wounded by Sid's rather cheap mockery of all that he held sacred, Eustace never revealed the fact. He said nothing, so that Sid, for the first time in his life, felt thoroughly ashamed of himself. From that day to this Sid had devoted himself with unswerving loyalty to his master's service. He still thought Cooism a bit of a "queer do", but he would have rather cut off his right hand than let his employer tumble to the fact.

He decided that he had nothing further to gain by waiting any longer behind the hedge. Stealthily he retraced his steps and, making a wide detour round the edge of the big meadow, entered the lane at a point some two hundred yards beyond the two men. Thereafter he quickened his pace until the North Lodge came in sight. A light was burning beyond one of the latticed windows. Sid did not hesitate. Instead of making for his loft in the nearby barn, he slipped through the wicket-gate of the drive entrance and pulled the wrought-iron bell under the clematis-covered porch of the front-door.

Chapter X

The Letters in the Case

I

Long after Sid had departed to the barn, Eustace sat in the softly-lit cosy little parlour of the lodge and pondered darkly. No longer were the malignant forces that had encompassed him relegated to some indeterminate background. In a flash, they had come sharply into focus. Quite suddenly Eustace could see with horrible clarity exactly where time and destiny had conspired to lead him. He was poised on the edge of an abyss. One false move now and he would be done for!

It had been an acutely difficult and embarrassing interview for both of them—for Sid because he had learnt something about his employer which his employer had obviously been anxious to conceal; for Eustace because he was naturally humiliated by Sid's discovery. It was not pleasant to reflect that he, the High Prophet of Coo, had been found out and found wanting by his own chauffeur. But in the perilous situation which had now arisen, he had been forced to discuss with Sid Arkwright the full details of what he had just overheard. Luckily Sid had a retentive memory and he had been able to put in, so to speak, a verbatim report. Eustace had carefully written down the phrases as Sid recalled them.

It was this sheet of paper he was now studying.

Three troubling facts were immediately evident to him; (*a*) that Penelope had kept the letters with which he had so foolishly bombarded her (*b*) that she had told Penpeti about these letters (*c*) that they obviously intended to use these letters to defame his good name inside the Movement. The motive for this unchristian desire was not far to seek. Hansford Boot's original reading of Penpeti's character had been correct. The man was ambitious, determined, relentless—no doubt about that. He was in league with Penelope and together they were conspiring to undermine his position as High Prophet. It was, perhaps, Penelope's attitude in this sorry affair that most upset him. He realised now that for all these months of apparent friendliness, Penelope had really been a snake in the grass. It was a sad and sobering thought!

And who was this man that Penpeti had met in the lane? How did he enter into this shabby conspiracy? Sid had been able to tell him little about this mysterious and furtive individual. He had described him as "about the same height and build as Mr. Penpeti, same dark sort of skin". Sid had not overheard a single word of what he had said and was thus unable to gauge the relationship existing between the two men. This much he *was* prepared to say: "Seems that Mr. Penpeti was sort of scared by the other chap—like as if he'd got some sort of hold over him." But this sort of vague generalisation, Eustace realised, did little to clarify the enigma of this clandestine meeting.

In any case, wasn't this a mere collateral to the single overwhelming fact that Penelope still possessed his letters and was threatening to show them to Alicia. And since Alicia was already furious with him for his refusal to sponsor a production of her *Nine Gods of Heliopolis*, once she'd read those letters he could expect no quarter. Only the letters mattered. By hook or by crook he must recover them. Somehow he must persuade Penelope to give them up. He must go to her without delay, appeal to her better nature and throw himself on her mercy. Humiliating but unavoidable. Once the letters were destroyed, Penpeti could do nothing.

"But what," thought Eustace in a panic, "if Penelope refuses to hand them over?"

He couldn't take them from her by force. For one thing he didn't know where she concealed them and, for another, she probably kept them under lock and key. And when he recalled some of the more impassioned interludes in the later notes, the complete verbal abandonment, the pleadings, the pledges, the avowals and compliments of his unbridled infatuation—yes, when he thought of all this he broke out into a cold sweat and closed his eyes against the dizziness which suddenly overpowered him.

"By Geb!" he thought, employing the single mild, yet satisfactory oath he allowed himself. "I've got to get them back! I've got to! I must see her at once. Yes, directly after breakfast to-morrow Sid must drive me over to the Dower House."

II

But poor Eustace at the very outset was destined to suffer an unexpected set-back. When he sent in his name via Hilda, the parlour-maid, she returned in a few seconds with the information that Miss Parker was sorry but she couldn't see him. Eustace blustered on the doorstep like a tongue-tied schoolboy. But it was impossible! He *must* see her. It concerned an important and urgent matter. Hilda must go to her mistress again and explain just how vital it was that he should see her. This time, to his enormous relief, Penelope consented to come down into the hall. But much to Eustace's chagrin she made no attempt to ask him into the house.

She asked in an uneasy voice:

"Good gracious, what *is* the matter, Eustace? An urgent and important matter, you say?"

"I must see you alone," exclaimed Eustace, adding meaningly: "It's not only urgent and important, but a highly delicate and private matter."

"We're quite private here. You can talk to me quite freely."

"I should prefer to come in."

"I'm sorry, Eustace. Please be good enough to tell me what you want here and now. I've a very busy day in front of me."

"You're sure we can't be overheard?"

"Quite sure."

Eustace took a quick look round and lowered his voice.

"It's about those letters," he said.

"Letters?"

"The letters I've been writing to you."

"Well, what of them?"

"I want them back. I must have them back. Please, Penelope. Every one of them. Now, at once!"

Penelope looked at him in amazement. The request had startled her considerably. How had Eustace found out about the letters?

"Really, Eustace—what *has* come over you? Why this sudden anxiety? Surely you're not ashamed of all the frank and charming compliments you've paid me? Oh I know I'm quite unworthy of—"

"It's something that I've heard," broke in Eustace sharply. "Something highly unpleasant. Something so disagreeable that I had the greatest difficulty in persuading myself that it was true."

"Something you've heard?" demanded Penelope with a flash of anxiety. "What exactly do you mean?"

"Something about you and Peta showing those letters to Alicia, with the deliberate intention of...of..."

"What ridiculous nonsense! I haven't even kept the letters. I destroyed them, one by one, as I received them."

"You've destroyed them?" gasped Eustace. "But...but..."

"And after such unforgivable innuendoes I should take it as a favour if you'd kindly stay away from the Dower House in the future. I can't imagine how this wicked rumour has reached your ears. Even less can I imagine how you came to believe it!"

"But...but..."

"I'd rather not hear any more about it, thank you." Her slim hand had already reached out for the ornate handle of the door. "I shall give the servants strict orders that you're not to be admitted—not on any account. Understand, Eustace?"

"Yes," he said meekly, his mind in a whirl.

"Then we'll consider this highly disagreeable interview as closed," rapped out Penelope. "And kindly don't refer to the matter again. It's upset me terribly. It's made me feel quite ill. I've never been so insulted in my life. Never! Never!"

And the next instant Mr. Mildmann found himself staring blankly at the massive oak door which Penelope, as a final expression of her indignation, had slammed tempestuously in his face.

III

Two minutes later Penelope was on the phone to The Leaning Man. Penpeti sounded annoyed.

"Indiscreet, my dear? Yes, I know it is, but I'm frantically worried. Something really extraordinary has happened. Eustace in some astounding manner has found out. No.

About the letters. Yes—that I've kept the letters. Oh, I can't possibly say. He was here just now. What? The use to which we were going to put them? That's just what I'm trying to say, my darling. He *knows* about it. No, of course not. I can't imagine how he…You'll come over at once? Yes, do. I shall feel much, much happier when we've had a little chat. Just walk in as usual. The servants know you've *carte blanche* to drop in just when you like. *Au revoir,* darling. And don't waste any time!"

Penpeti obeyed her injunctions to the letter. During his stay at The Leaning Man he had arranged for the garage opposite to have a car and driver always at his disposal. Fifteen minutes later, therefore, he was ringing the bell at the Dower House. Hilda let him in without comment and he raced upstairs to Penelope's private retiring room on the second floor. Glasses and sherry decanter were set ready on a small inlaid table. Penpeti's worried expression gave way to a gleam of approval.

"Most thoughtful. Most thoughtful," he said, giving her an absent-minded kiss. "I need a little stimulant. This news of yours is puzzling and upsetting, to say the least of it." He took up the decanter and held it with a look of enquiry over one of the glasses. Penelope nodded. "Personally, I think it must be mere guesswork. A shot in the dark on Eustace's part." He raised his glass to hers. "There's no need for undue alarm, my dear."

"Frankly, Peta, I'm frightened. How *could* this have leaked out? You haven't been talking out of turn, I trust?"

"Me? Don't be absurd! Of course not."

"You've never mentioned those letters to a soul?"

"Never!" he contested, with a bland expression.

After all, how could he tell her about his secret rendez-vous with the ubiquitous Yacob? What lay between him and Yacob was none of her business. And besides, how could his little talk with Yacob in the deserted lane have reached Eustace's ears. It was utterly impossible that the leakage had occurred then.

"Then, if you've said nothing," went on Penelope, bewildered, "how on earth has the wretch found out? It's queer."

"As I said before—a shot in the dark. He's probably been worrying about these letters for weeks and plucking up courage to come and ask for them back. Knowing damn well, my dear, that if Alicia or any other of the high-placed members of the Movement happened to see them, he'd be very much in the soup."

Penelope shook her corn-coloured head.

"I'm sure you're wrong about that. He expressly said that he'd *heard* you and I intended showing those letters to Alicia."

"Heavens above, but it's out of the question. Unless one of your staff overheard you talking in your sleep or something."

"Impossible. I sleep at one end of the house—my domestics at the other."

"You don't imagine that he suspects anything about—?"

"About the child?" Penpeti nodded. "No," went on Penelope. "At least he made no mention of the fact. Merely that we had the letters and were going to give them to Alicia." Penelope set down her sherry glass. Penpeti noticed that her hand was trembling. "It's uncanny, Peta. There's something very queer going on around us. I can sense it. Something strange and ominous." Adding with a look of remorse: "I rather wish now I hadn't thought of this horrid idea. But when one's in a tight corner, it's so easy to say the first thing that comes into one's head. I'm too impulsive, Peta. I didn't really stop to think about my suggestion."

Penpeti asked quickly:

"What did you tell Eustace?"

"I told him I'd destroyed the letters."

Penpeti nodded his approval.

"Splendid! Splendid! I knew I could rely on you to keep your head in an emergency." He drew her down on to the settee and went on earnestly: "Now listen—you've got to forget about Eustace and his visit this morning. Erase him from your mind entirely. Even if he had his suspicions, you've now probably convinced him that he was wrong, that the letters *have* actually been destroyed. In the meantime keep them safely locked away in your letter-case. Keep your bureau locked too. Don't let Eustace into the house. Keep an eye on him. Be very, very watchful. If you *haven't* convinced him he may try to do something desperate. He may even try to steal the letters or get somebody to do it for him. You follow?"

Penelope nodded.

"And you're still willing to go through with our scheme?"

She hesitated a moment, and then said in low quick tones:

"I don't know, Peta. When I come to think of it all in cold blood, it makes me feel rather ashamed of myself. Eustace's visit has worried me. I can't understand how he found out. You mustn't think me stupid or fanciful but...but I can't help wondering if…"

"Well?"

"If Eustace, perhaps, hasn't some…strange gift…some psychical power that enables him to pick up other people's thoughts. This unexplored realm of thought transmission… I'm convinced it's a reality, Peta. Only most of us haven't learnt how to use and control the gift."

"Oh poppycock!" snapped Penpeti, with a scowl of impatience. "I still think Eustace was prompted to ask for those letters because he has an uneasy conscience. You mustn't let your imagination run away with you."

"I know it's silly of me, but the whole affair has quite unnerved me. Do you really think we ought to go through with the scheme? Shan't we always have it on our conscience?"

Penpeti sprang up with a little cry of irritation.

"For heaven's sake, be logical! In the circumstances it's one or the other of us that will take the rap—either Eustace or me. Well, which is it to be? It's your choice, and out of fairness to me I should know your final answer."

Again Penelope seemed to be struggling with some inward uncertainty. Then suddenly she gave a little shiver, looked up at him and said quietly:

"I suppose there's no other way now, Peta. I shall just have to go through with it for your sake."

"Good!" said Penpeti.

But at that moment he realised that Penelope was in a queer, unreliable mood. Her conscience, confound it! Was on the prowl. It was on the cards that when the moment came for them to act, Penelope might well rat on him. It was a ticklish situation and would need very careful handling. Penpeti was worried.

IV

So was Sid Arkwright. He had not failed to register the little scene which had been enacted on the threshold of the Dower House. From where he sat waiting, like a graven image, in the car, he had not been able to hear what had transpired, but his employer's face, as he returned to the Daimler, had told him everything. When they reached the lodge, Sid had plucked up enough courage to ask a few discreet questions. His employer's answers had not been reassuring. Not for a single instant did Sid believe the Parker woman's story that the letters had been destroyed. The guv'nor, he thought, was too blooming ready to take people at their word.

"And now," thought Sid miserably, "he'll just swallow the yarn and let the matter drop. And before we can turn round that Parker girl will have shoved the damned letters

under old Haggie's nose. I wouldn't trust that Penpeti chap
further than I could kick him. Never have! He's out to nab
the position of High Prophet. I bet he's put the Parker wench
up to this. She's soft on him. No mistake about that!"

But how to find out if the letters were still in the Parker
woman's possession or not? Sid clicked his fingers. Of course!
He ought to have thought of it before. Hilda Shepstone—
she was the answer. He'd taken her over to the flicks at
Downchester on her half-day. Yes—Hilda would help him.
She was beginning to get a bit of a yen on him, eh? He'd nip
round to the kitchen door that evening, when everybody
was having dinner at the manor, and have a talk with her,
discreet like, about those blooming letters.

Sid did. And what he learnt completely justified his earlier suspicions. Luck was with him, for only that morning
Hilda, passing by the little upstairs sitting-room, had heard
her mistress make mention of the letters.

"That there creepy Mr. Penpeti was with her," said Hilda.
"Always in the house he is. Proper hot 'un, I reckon. Anyways, just as I went by the door, I heard him say 'And what
did you tell Eustace?' That'd be your guv'nor, of course.
And she said as she'd said she'd destroyed the letters. Then
I heard him—that's Mr. Penpeti—say as he could trust her
to keep her head in an emergency. All seemed a bit fishy to
me. Always laying their nappers together them two. Thick
as thieves."

"Swear you won't breath a word about me coming here,
Hilda." Sid winked. "There's things in the wind—see? Nasty
under'and things. Now tell me—where d'you think she
keeps these letters?"

"Can't say exactly. In her desk, I expect, up in her own
room."

"What time does she usually get back from the manor?"

"Never later than ten. Usually between 'arpas nine and ten."

Sid glanced at his watch. Eight-fifteen. He looked meaningly at Hilda, pointed to himself and jerked a thumb towards the upper part of the house.

"Safe, eh kiddo?"

"There's cook," breathed Hilda nervously. "She's in the kitchen. But if you sneak round to the front, I'll let you in through the french-windows of the big drawing-room."

"O.K.," said Sid.

Five minutes later, on tip-toes, he was following Hilda up the main staircase. Once on the landing, she paused and pointed to a door a little way down the spacious corridor.

"That's the room," she whispered. "I won't hang about in case cook gets nosey. Let yourself out the same way as you came in, Sid. I'll close the latch later. And hurry! Much as my job's worth if you was caught here."

Sid waited until the girl had regained the hall and vanished in the direction of the kitchen, before creeping softly towards the door she had indicated. Gently he turned the handle, opened the door and slipped into the room.

Then, with a stifled cry, he stopped dead. Seated in an armchair, directly facing him, was a man—a big, broad-shouldered man in a suit of plus-fours. He stared at Sid grimly.

"And what the hell may you want, eh?"

"Er…nothing…nothing," stammered Sid. "I…I was just looking for something."

"Didn't expect to find me here, I imagine?"

"Since you ask—I didn't."

The man rose, stalked to the door and cautiously closed it.

"Well, now you are here, you're going to tell me just who you are and what you're doing in Miss Parker's room." Sid remained obstinately silent. "So you're not going to talk, eh? Very well, I won't badger you with questions which you obviously can't answer. But before I let you go, understand this—if you breath a word to anybody about seeing me here, I'll…I'll break your confounded neck! Understand?"

"O.K.," said Sid, sidling gradually towards the little bureau which stood near the door. "I won't split on you if you won't split on me. Fair deal, eh?" His hand groped up behind his back, feeling for the handle of the desk. "Strikes me," he added, "that you were as startled to see me as I was to see you!" He tugged at the handle, but the lid of the bureau didn't budge an inch. It was obviously locked. "Right about that, sir, aren't I?"

The man ignored the query and jerked a hand towards the door.

"Go on! Clear out and stay out. And remember, unless you want to get yourself into trouble, you haven't seen me."

"O.K.," reiterated Sid with a grin. "O.K.!"

But once clear of the house, as he hurried through the chilly Maytime dusk that was descending like a miasma on the park, his mind began to work overtime. What the devil did it mean? Why was that big, broad-shouldered chap sitting in that armchair, obviously waiting for that Parker woman's arrival? And how was it that Hilda was unaware of his presence in the house? All these puzzling factors struck Sid as damnably fishy.

But there was something even more curious, a simple fact that remained diamond-sharp in his mind. It was something he had noticed just as he was leaving the room. On the arm of the settee was a brown tweed cap and, flung carelessly over the back of it, unmistakable, significant, arresting, was *an elegant coat fashioned of teddy-bear cloth!*

Chapter XI

The High Prophet Plans a Theft

I

In the few days that intervened before the arrival of the some six hundred members who were scheduled to attend the convention, there was an ominous lull in the progress of events at Old Cowdene. Penpeti was biding his time. His argument was logical. If the High Prophet were to be tumbled from his pedestal, it was far better that his fall should be witnessed by as many people as possible. The whole affair if allowed to come to a head when the convention was in full swing would be just twice as dramatic and effective. Granted Penpeti felt nervous in postponing the dénouement, for Penelope was becoming more jumpy and conscience-stricken at their every meeting. It was a case, Penpeti upheld, of weighing one advantage against another.

For Eustace it was a period of the deepest depression. He lived under the shadow of fateful and imminent happenings, uneasy with apprehension, taut-nerved, disillusioned and desperate. Sid had spoken to him quite frankly about his talk with Hilda at the Dower House. He had said nothing of his abortive attempt to recover the letters, however, or of his startling encounter with the Man in the Teddy-Bear Coat. But he left no doubt in Eustace's mind that the letters still existed; that Penelope had deliberately lied to him; that Penpeti's threat to show the letters to Alicia was no evil dream but a very present reality.

But how to counter this threat? Eustace felt himself already fast in the trap. No matter in which direction he looked there seemed to be no way out. In due course Alicia would read those passionate epistles, call together an extraordinary meeting of the Inmost Temple, who would most certainly pass a unanimous resolution that he was no longer worthy to hold the exalted position of High Prophet. He would be called before the Inmost Temple, arraigned, cross-questioned and, finally, judged. And to make matters even more hopeless, Eustace felt that once his infatuation for Penelope were common property he *would* be unworthy of his high office. Yes—even if they didn't turn him out, he'd be forced to resign.

And yet…?

Eustace's jaw tautened and a stubborn gleam illuminated his dark eyes. To let Penpeti into the High Prophetship…it was unthinkable! Penpeti, who for all these months had so obviously been conspiring to bring about his downfall. To hand over his robes of office to an ambitious opportunist; to a man whose ideas concerning the Judgment of the Dead were ethically unsound; to a man who refuted the powers of Am-mit as "Eater of the Dead", who expounded the heretical theory that Neb-er-tcher should take precedence over the great god Osiris himself, who denied that Apep was the arch-enemy of Horus—No! No! Never! To allow the High Prophetship to fall into such hands was to deny the infallibility of his own theological beliefs.

But how to arrest the impending debacle? There was only one way. He *must* recover the letters. Quite—but how? In the name of Geb, how? It was obvious Penelope would never give them up. He had now been refused admittance to the house. Impossible, therefore, to renew his pleadings. Penelope just wouldn't see him alone. Impossible to steal the letters for with the doors locked against him, how to place himself in a position to do so? At his age, quite apart from the undignified aspect of such a performance, one did not shin up drain-pipes or pick locks with pieces of bent wire. No, in every direction he faced despair and frustration. Every day he expected the bombshell to explode.

II

And then one evening, some three days before the opening of the convention, he was sitting with Terence in the lodge parlour, when Mrs. Summers entered with the information that Sid Arkwright wished to see him. Owing to a slight indisposition Eustace had decided not to attend the dinner-party over at the manor that evening. It was a tiny deviation from his usual routine but, in the light of subsequent events, a detail of enormous significance.

Sid, cap in hand, was waiting deferentially in the cramped little hall.

"Well, Arkwright?"

"I must see you, sir," said Sid with a hint of excitement in his voice. "Private like, if I may. And the sooner the better, sir, if it's convenient. I was wondering…?"

"Well?"

"If you could slip across with me to the barn, sir. We could talk there without interruption."

"All right—if it's really important."

"It's vital, sir," said Sid emphatically. "Vital!"

Reaching for his hat, Eustace followed Sid out of the door, across the drive and up the broad cinder-track that led to the barn. There, seating himself on a rough bench outside the big double-doors, Eustace waited. Sid took a quick look around and, satisfied that they were alone, said abruptly:

"I gotta idea, sir. Came to me only a moment back. About them letters."

"The letters, Arkwright?"

"Yes, sir. I've thought of a way in which you could get 'em back."

Eustace sprang up with a look of disbelief. It was his turn to rake the screening bushes with anxious eyes, before asking in tremulous tones:

"Are you serious about this?"

"Dead serious, sir. You can't afford to be pernickety, if I may say so. You're in a nasty jam, sir, and no mistake. I've been thinking of a dozen ways to get you out of this, but until this evening I was stuck for the right idea. Now, I reckon, I've got it!"

Eustace sat down again. Sid came closer.

"Well?" demanded Eustace.

"It's like this, sir," explained Sid. "You know well enough that Miss Parker's not going to cough up them letters just because you ask her to. She'll do what Mr. Penpeti tells her—you mark my words! But suppose you was to go to her and give her a bit of a fright—threaten her a mite, lay on a sort of a gangster act. I reckon she'd crumple up on the spot and hand over the letters without a murmur."

"I'm afraid I don't follow, Arkwright," said Eustace stiffly. "A gangster act? What exactly—?"

"My idea's dead simple, sir. I'm pretty slick with my hands and it wouldn't take me a brace of shakes to knock up something that looked like a revolver from a few bits of wood—see? Well, sir, if you waggled this thing at Miss Parker and talked a bit rough—"

"Are you suggesting," broke in Eustace in outraged tones, "that I terrorise Miss Parker into surrendering those letters?"

"Why not, sir? Think what's at stake! It's no time to act soft."

"But...but...how am I to get into the house? You know as well as I do, Arkwright, that Miss Parker has given strict orders to the servants that I'm not to be admitted. I can't *break* in, can I?"

"No, sir, you couldn't. But the point is—what *I* did you could do—see? A hundred times better, too. You've got the same sort of dark eyes and skin. Much of the same build, too. It's a cinch, sir!" added Sid with a sudden burst of enthusiasm. "An absolute cinch!"

"You mean...?" But Eustace could get no further. The wild audacity of the idea left him dumbfounded. Was Arkwright out of his senses?

"I mean just this, sir. If you'll give me permission to nip up to London, I'll hire the same set of things as I did for that dance—make-up, spirit-gum and all."

"But even then, Arkwright—?"

Sid went on smoothly:

"We'll fix on a suitable evening in the near future. You find some excuse for not going over to the manor that night. Get rid of Mr. Terence and Mrs. Summers somehow and leave me to doll you up over here in the barn. Miss Parker always gets back to the Dower House somewhere between nine-thirty and ten. I found that out from her maid. All I've got to do then is to drive you down to the Dower House and wait under those trees about half-way up the drive there. All you've gotta do, sir, is to ring the bell bold as brass, wait till the door's opened, nod casual like and go straight up to Miss Parker's room. Hilda tells me she's got orders to let

Mr. Penpeti into the place at any time of the night or day, so there won't be any need to do more than nod and go upstairs. I know just where Miss Parker's room is situated on the second floor. I'll draw you a plan so as you can't make any mistake. Once you're inside, close the door, pull out your wooden gun and talk rough. And if you're not back in the car inside five minutes *with the letters in your pocket*, sir, then my moniker's not Sid Arkwright. As I said before, it's a cinch. You can't put a foot wrong."

Eustace looked as if he had his doubts. The daring and originality of Sid's plan had left him temporarily flustered. On the other hand, the very simplicity of it made an instant appeal. After all the letters were his, and since they were going to be used as evidence against him, he had every right to try out any expedient to recover them. His mind ran rapidly over the salient points of Sid's suggestion. Already, recovering from the initial impact of the idea, he was re-gathering his wits. Were there any flaws in the plan? Any difficulties that might arise if he put it into execution? One problem occurred to him immediately.

He pointed out:

"But what if Mr. Penpeti happens to call at the Dower House that evening, Arkwright? He might walk back with Miss Parker after dinner at the manor. That would be embarrassing, to say the least of it."

"Quite so, sir. But I've thought of that, too, and it struck me that if you worked it so that you'd know exactly *where* Mr. Penpeti would be that evening—well, Bob's your uncle, sir!"

"But how on earth am I to do that?" asked Eustace, puzzled.

"I was thinking of that there roster you and Mr. Terence was drawing up—that Chain of Meditation idea, sir, that's to be put into operation the moment the convention opens. Mr. Terence happened to show me his typewritten list the other morning. I noticed that Mr. Penpeti was earmarked to attend several times during the first week—that is in the temple in that Chinese summer-house place."

"Quite true—he is," agreed Eustace, feeling in his breast-pocket. "I happen to have the original list on me." He spread out the folded sheet of paper and glanced at it closely. "Yes, here we are—Mr. Penpeti's agreed to attend for one hour every week-day. The times of his attendance vary of course to fit in with his other commitments. On Monday next—that is the opening day of the conference—I see he's down to attend from nine to ten in the morning. On Tuesday from two to three in the—"

"You'll pardon me, sir," broke in Sid deferentially. "All we need bother ourselves with are the times of his evening meditations. I seem to remember that on Thursday next—"

"Thursday!" exclaimed Eustace, running his finger down the list. "Yes—Thursday from nine to ten in the evening."

"Well, there you are, sir!" pointed out Sid triumphantly. "What could suit us better? That makes sure of Mr. Penpeti. All you've got to do now is to see that Mrs. Summers and Mr. Terence are also away from the lodge that evening. And that shouldn't be difficult, sir."

Eustace sighed.

"I'm afraid I'm no good as a conspirator, Arkwright. I haven't got the proper mental twist."

Sid grinned.

"How if you suggested she had the afternoon off, sir? They're showing a top-notch variety show over at the Downchester Palladium. You might suggest that Mr. Terence goes with her and that they both stay on and look into the show."

"Umph—it's a feasible idea. But do you really think this whole fantastic plan will work?"

"Certain of it, sir. If you're ready to carry it out just as we've arranged."

"Then you suggest next Thursday, eh, Arkwright?"

Sid nodded.

"Leaving the lodge somewhere about nine-thirty. That leaves us five days to attend to all the details and make sure we haven't tripped up anywhere. Agreed, sir?"

"Very well, Arkwright. I'm in your hands. I can't help feeling that it's all very melodramatic and undignified, but I can quite see that it's a moment for desperate measures. And please don't think I'm not grateful to you, Arkwright, for your sympathy and co-operation in this very distasteful matter. I *am*—exceedingly grateful. It's just that I can't see myself in the rôle you've allotted to me."

"Still…when the devil drives, sir…"

"Quite so, Arkwright, quite so."

And at that, their strange and clandestine discussion was concluded.

Poor Eustace felt somewhat hypocritical, however, when some ten minutes later Penpeti turned up at the lodge with a polite little note from Mrs. Hagge-Smith. She was sorry that he had been unable to come over to dinner and trusted that his indisposition was not of a serious nature. She was projecting kind thoughts in his direction.

III

During the afternoon of Saturday, June 1st, the first members began to silt into the park, where Hansford Boot (who was in charge of this part of the arrangements) detailed them to their various tents. Some came via the train and the station-bus, others in their own cars, some on bicycles, and some, from the nearer localities, on foot. Over the wrought-iron gates of the north and south entrances, Mrs. Hagge-Smith had ordered the gardeners to erect two banners—WELCOME TO OLD COWDENE. It was a happy touch that set the keynote to the opening phases of the convention. Everybody was a-glisten with good-will and good-humour, settling into their respective tents with much badinage and facetiousness, forgathering in the big marquee for their meals, chattering, laughing, renewing old friendships, making new ones. Yes, despite the somewhat chill and lowering skies, a heartening scene and one which grew more animated and boisterous with every fresh batch of arrivals.

By late Sunday evening the rally was complete and everything was set for the unfolding of the fortnight's programme, which was due to open with Alicia's speech of welcome in the lecture tent on the following morning. One odd incident occurred on Sunday afternoon over in the ladies' compound. Each bell-tent was scheduled to accommodate four members. It was quite understandable, therefore, that the inmates of Tent 6, Row D should go at once to Hansford Boot when they discovered a fifth and unrecognised member unpacking in their tent.

"But there must be some mistake," protested Hansford, scanning his official lists. "No tent is supposed to hold more than four. I'll come along at once."

He had no difficulty in settling the little dispute. The names of Barker, Wicksteed, Grant, and Hazlitt were clearly inscribed on his list. The name of Minnybell was *not*! In fact, the name of Miss Minnybell didn't appear on any official list, though to Hansford it had a ring of familiarity.

"Surely you're from Welworth?" he said. Miss Minnybell didn't deny it. "But I'd no idea you were a member of our Garden City group," went on Hansford, suddenly recalling the gossip he had heard about Miss Minnybell's reputed strangeness. "I never recall seeing you at any of our Carroway Road services."

"Oh dear me, no!" smiled Miss Minnybell, sweetly. "I only applied for membership five days ago."

"But we closed our list of convention members nearly six weeks ago. I'm afraid, Miss Minnybell, that in the circumstances we've made no provision for your accommodation."

"Oh please don't apologise," beamed Miss Minnybell. "I know how busy you must have been. I really don't mind where you put me. A simple palliasse in the open-air will do. That is," she added slyly, "if it doesn't rain. You can't possibly be so unkind as to send me away."

Hansford metaphorically scratched his head. Miss Minnybell had set him a teaser. Such wholehearted enthusiasm was praiseworthy and the poor soul seemed so helpless and vague that it would be a crime to deny her the spiritual feasts that were in store. He consulted his lists again, whilst Miss Minnybell stood patiently by his side, staring up at him with the eyes of an expectant spaniel.

"Well, Miss Minnybell, if you'll come with me," he said at length, "I'll see what I can do for you. I think there's a vacancy in Tent 12 Row H—a member from Manchester suddenly taken ill with appendicitis. It's all rather irregular, you know, but in the circumstances…"

Miss Minnybell trotted happily in his wake and, after consultation with two other officials in the Camp Commandant's office, it was decided that Miss Minnybell should be offered the vacancy that had occurred.

For the second time Miss Minnybell unpacked her meagre suitcase, whilst she affably engaged the rest of the tent in an interminable and one-sided conversation. She was well satisfied with the results of her scheming, for Mr. Penpeti's sudden disappearance from the Garden City had left her profoundly uneasy. She was quite certain that he had gone away to make final secret plans for her decimation. He was probably gathering around him a group of fellow-conspirators. Miss Minnybell did not hesitate. She learnt exactly where Mr. Penpeti had gone, filled in her membership form as a Child of Osiris and travelled down to Sussex. Now she was happy again. Once more she was in a position to keep an eye on him and thwart his evil machinations. She was determined, as far as circumstances permitted, to stick to Mr. Penpeti like a leech.

IV

It was on Tuesday at the breakfast-table that Eustace looked up from his poached egg on boiled lettuce and said with a nice air of sympathy:

"You're looking tired, Mrs. Summers. I trust you haven't been overdoing things down here. Without the domestic amenities with which we were blessed at Tranquilla, I'm afraid you may have found everything rather difficult."

"Well, it's not easy, Mr. Mildmann," replied Mrs. Summers with a martyred air. "But one has to carry on and make the most of it."

"Quite! Quite!" Eustace took a sip of his milkless green tea and went on: "I was wondering if you'd care to have a half-day off—say, next Thursday. I understand that Downchester is a very good shopping and entertainments centre."

"It would certainly make a nice change, Mr. Mildmann."

"Then we'll take that as settled," smiled Eustace with an inward sigh of relief. "Er...perhaps you'd care to have Terence as an escort. I imagine you may want to go to the evening performance at the theatre and return by the late bus. I should feel happier if he were with you."

"It would be nice to have company," agreed Mrs. Summers, "if Terence would like to come."

"I'm sure he'd like to—eh Terence?"

Terence looked up from his plate and grunted. It was obvious that his thoughts had been far afield. Mr. Mildmann repeated his suggestion.

"All right," muttered Terence ungraciously. "I'll go if you want me to. No option anyway."

And at that Eustace tactfully dropped the subject, only too thankful to find that this part of the conspiracy, at least, had been far easier than he had anticipated.

Chapter XII

Overture to Murder

I

By the morning of Thursday, June 6th, the cheerful bonhomie which had marked the inauguration of the conference had undergone a sad modification. It was raining—a light chill, weeping rain that went on and on, gently yet maliciously. It had been raining for forty-eight hours. It looked like raining for another week. Even Hansford Boot, oppressed as he was by Penpeti's constant threat of exposure, felt a warm surge of self-satisfaction course through his veins on finding his dour prophecy so amply fulfilled. The park was dismal with the slop and squelch of innumerable overboots and soggy sandals. Every tent was thick with the effluvia of damp tweeds. Every tree glistened and dripped and sulked behind a grey mist of rain. The Children of Osiris scuttled about the park with the aimless frenzy of disturbed ants; from bell-tent to lecture, from lecture to meal, from meal to meditation, from meditation to the dubious comfort of their camp-beds.

They made every effort to preserve their initial enthusiasm, but even the most fanatic found it difficult to con-
centrate on such lecture subjects as "The Triune God of the
Resurrection" or "The Inner Symbolism of Thoth" when
they were made uncomfortably aware of hard benches, wet
socks, damp underclothes, and the evil odour of massed
mackintoshes. Eustace did his utmost to whip up an interest
in the niceties of dogma but it was uphill work. He himself,
at the mercy of his personal troubles, was in exceptionally
bad form. Twice in one lecture members at the back of the
marquee were forced to ask him to speak up as they couldn't
hear a single word he was saying. Twice Eustace tried to
oblige them, only to find his voice issuing from him in a
quavering falsetto. People began to cough and fidget and
rustle their papers.

It was Penpeti who really rescued the convention from the
doldrums. He was here, there and everywhere, his magnetic
eyes flashing, his rich oriental voice upraised in greeting, his
oddly-garbed figure striding through the rain with Jehovah-
like indifference. His lectures were evangelical in their thun-
der-and-lightning intensity. Penpeti ignored the intellect and
concentrated on the emotions of his rain-sodden audiences.
His panegyric on the "Significance of Set, the Evil one" was
applauded as a masterpiece of didacticism. He made them
wriggle on their benches under the lash of his sarcasm. He
filled them with remorse and a desire for repentance. He
left them exalted in a whirl of mystical excitement, so that
many, quite unconscious of their surroundings, passed out
there and then into a state of "non-being".

Miss Minnybell alone remained totally unmoved. From
the middle of the third row she just sat there and stared at
Penpeti with watchful and suspicious eyes. She noted his
every gesture. Every detail of his person. And towards him
she projected a stream of enmity. More than ever she was

convinced that Penpeti was plotting to waylay her in some dark corner of the park in order to liquidate her. Her obsession had never been more virulent.

II

It was with a sigh of relief that Eustace watched Terence and Mrs. Summers depart for Downchester shortly after lunch on Thursday. Now that the critical hour was approaching his nervousness was at fever-heat. Sid had slipped up to London on Monday and returned with the complete "Penpeti" outfit, which he had concealed in the loft. Three times he had rehearsed Mr. Mildmann in the part he was to play. Together they had pored over Sid's simple plan of the Dower House. The dummy revolver was ready and waiting. Sid had even coached his employer in the kind of dialogue that might prove effective, forcing him to transmute his gentle tones into a kind of staccato bark; an ordeal that caused poor Eustace to squirm with embarrassment. In Sid's opinion nothing could go wrong. Eustace had already told Alicia that he would not be over to dinner at the manor that evening, owing to pressure of work. The Daimler was ready primed to rush him to the Dower House and back. Even the weather, Sid claimed, was in their favour, for the low rain-clouds would certainly mean a premature dusk. By the time Eustace was scheduled to approach the Dower House it would be almost dark.

For all that, as the afternoon wore slowly to a close, Eustace was filled with apprehension. He had a hasty cup of tea with his flock in the crowded mess-tent, slipped away unobtrusively, climbed into his waiting car and returned to the North Lodge. In about three hours' time he was due to go over to the barn and "doll himself up", as Sid put it. He spent the time in quiet meditation, alternating with periods of cold panic and a very natural impatience. If he succeeded in his quest he was quite sure that Penelope would never speak to him again. On the other hand, if he failed…

Closing his eyes against the possibility and dire consequences of failure, Mr. Mildmann screwed himself up to the sticking-point. The clock on the mantelshelf ticked relentlessly, throwing the minutes with gleeful indifference over its shoulder!

Chapter XIII

Inspector Meredith Gets Cracking

I

Inspector Meredith mounted the steps of New Scotland Yard with his customary springy step, issued a nod, a grin and a brisk salute to the commissionaire at the door and went through to his office. For the last six weeks he had been investigating a particularly dull and unenterprising forgery case in Finchley and he was feeling, to use his own phrase, "about as lively as a Welsh evangelist on a wet sabbath in Swansea." It was one of those cases calling for tremendous patience, a relentless attention to detail and a strict adherence to an unswerving routine. In short, it was typical of the ninety-nine out of a hundred jobs that the average C.I.D. man is called upon to tackle. And from Meredith's jaundiced point-of-view the case looked like stretching itself out for another six weary weeks. He stuck his lanky legs under his desk, sighed deeply and began to collate material from a number of depositions he had recently placed on file.

Barely had he got down to work, however, when the buzzer of the internal telephone sounded at his elbow. Meredith took up the receiver.

"Hullo? Yes—speaking. What? Immediately? O.K. I'll be right along."

As he wended his way along the corridors he wondered what was in the wind. The call had been put through by the Chief's private secretary. The Chief wanted to see him without delay. Why?

Meredith didn't have to wait long for his answer. The Chief, as usual, wasted no time in preliminaries.

"Morning, Meredith," he barked. "Seen the morning editions of the papers?"

"I just had time to skim the headlines over a bolted breakfast, sir—nothing more."

"Then you obviously didn't spot this item in the stop-press. Take a look at it."

The Chief handed over a copy of the *London Daily Echo*. Meredith read:

> *Mystery death of two well-known members of religious sect known as Children of Osiris was reported late last night. Tragedy occurred at Old Cowdene Park, Sussex, where Summer Convention of movement is now taking place. Police called in.*

As he handed back the newspaper, Meredith asked:

"And what exactly has this got to do with me, sir?"

"At the moment…nothing. In the future…toil, tears and sweat, Meredith. At least, that's what I suspect. Chief of the West Sussex County rang through from Chichester this morning. Old friend of mine. Wants a Yard man to go down at once and take over the case. It seems that there's more to it than meets the eye. What are you on at the moment?"

"That Finchley forgery case, sir."

"Who's working with you?"

"Haddon, sir."

"Then Haddon had better take over entirely. I want you to take the first train down to Tappin Mallet—that's the village adjacent to Old Cowdene. Ring Chichester and let them know when you'll be arriving. They've promised to send over a Superintendent to meet you."

"Right, sir."

"Oh, and you'd better ring your wife to pack a grip and be prepared to do without you for a few days. You'll have to be on the spot. You ought to find accommodation in Tappin Mallet. All clear, Meredith?"

"Yes, sir."

"Good!"

II

Superintendent Rokeby was on the platform at Tappin Mallet station when Meredith, in plain-clothes, stepped off the London train. Rokeby had no difficulty in spotting his man, for the lean wiry frame and aquiline features had been reproduced a dozen times in the press. He shook hands warmly.

"Glad you've been detailed, Inspector. We've never met before, but I know you well enough by reputation."

"Thanks," smiled Meredith.

"I've a car outside," went on the superintendent. "I suggest I run you along to The Leaning Man and see if they can fix you up. Then we might have a pint in a quiet corner while I give you the low-down on the affair. After that we'll slip over to Old Cowdene."

Twenty minutes later Meredith had arranged for accommodation at the inn, and the two men were seated in a corner of the deserted saloon-bar over a couple of pints of bitter. Rokeby set out the main details without delay.

"We were called in late last night, so naturally I've had no time to investigate. But the set-up is roughly this—a Miss Penelope Parker found dead in an upstairs sitting-room of the Dower House—that's a smaller establishment south of the actual manor but inside the boundaries of the park. Cause of death—poison. A cerebral depressant. Suspected prussic acid. The girl was seated in an armchair. Tray of drinks nearby. So far so good. All straightforward, eh?"

"Well it's homicide or suicide cut-to-pattern, if that's what you mean," admitted Meredith.

"Quite—but now comes the twist. Shortly before this Miss Parker was found dead in her sitting-room, she'd been visited by a man. It appears that he'd been driven over to the Dower House by his chauffeur, who waited outside for him in the car. By the way, this man is news, Meredith. He happens to be the founder of this Children of Osiris cult—a decent respected sort of cove, as far as I've been able to gather. Name of Mildmann—Eustace Mildmann." Rokeby took a pull at his tankard and nodded his satisfaction. "Landlord knows how to keep his beer here, eh? Clear and cool. Well, Mildmann was in the house for about ten minutes accord-ing to his chauffeur, when he suddenly staggers out gasping that he's ill, scrambles into the car and tells his man to drive like hell for the North Lodge—that's where he was staying during this convention. Point is this, when the chauffeur goes to help him out of the car, he finds the poor chap slump-ing back in the seat dead as a door-nail. Maxton, the police surgeon, went over with me from Chichester last night. He has no doubt that Mildmann had also been poisoned. Same cerebral depressant. A few facial contusions and a broken tooth in his upper denture. In Maxton's opinion probably the result of convulsions prior to his collapse. Well, there's the bare bones of the case. Interesting, eh?"

"Very," agreed Meredith dryly.

"Now for a rather curious complication. When Mild-mann called on Miss Parker he was disguised—very cleverly and completely too."

"As anybody in particular or just…disguised?"

"No—that's the odd point. He had got himself up to look like his second-in-command of this hazy-dazy religious order. A certain foreign-looking fellow by the name of Penpeti."

"Umph," mused Meredith. "Puzzling. This fellow Mild-mann—is he married?"

"Widower—one son."

"And Penpeti?"

"Bachelor."

"I see." Meredith drained his tankard, set it down smartly on the glass-topped table and picked up his hat. "Tell me, Rokeby, anything moved in the room where the girl was found dead?"

"Nothing. Door's been locked since I left last night. Local constable on duty at the Dower House."

"Good." Meredith got briskly to his feet. "Suppose you drive me to the Dower House first. After that I'll take a look at the other body at this North Lodge you mentioned. All set?"

"Let's go," said Rokeby.

III

Once Meredith was inside that room he ignored every-thing except the set-up of the crime. Rokeby posed one or two trite questions, but when he received no more than absent-minded grunts in reply, he sensibly held his tongue. He watched Meredith's approach to the lay-out with ever-increasing admiration. The inspector examined everything but touched nothing. He dealt methodically with every detail that caught his eye, without haste, without comment.

At the end of twenty minutes, he straightened up, drew on a pair of rubber gloves and moved to the inlaid table on which was set a sherry decanter and a set of glasses. Meredith had already noticed that two of the glasses had been used. One by one he picked them up between his finger and thumb, sniffed at them, then at the contents of the decanter. He turned to the superintendent.

"Well, Rokeby, that solves one little point at once. Both these glasses were filled from the decanter without a doubt and that decanter has been tampered with." He took it up again, removed the glass stopper and held it under Rokeby's nose. "Take a sniff!"

"Umph—bitter almonds," commented Rokeby. "That's prussic acid right enough. Maxton and I guessed as much last night. But it wasn't for me to put preconceived ideas into your head, was it?"

"But you see what it suggests?"

"You mean that Mildmann—?"

"—poisoned the girl and then poisoned himself," rapped out Meredith.

"So it's either a suicide pact or homicide plus suicide, eh?"

"I think we can fairly assume that," replied Meredith cautiously.

"So it looks as if we've got you down here on false pretences. Mildmann murdered the girl and then took his own life."

"Whoa! Whoa!" cried Meredith, amused. "Not so fast. I said we could *assume* the fact. But we can't be sure. There's the disguise factor to consider. And also," Meredith crossed quickly to the bureau by the door, "*this!* Note the splintered woodwork round the lock. The lid of this thing's been forced and recently, too. No assumption about that. Something's evidently been taken from this desk and, in the circumstances, I imagine Mildmann must have been the thief."

"Do you think he adopted that disguise in an attempt to pin the murder on to this Penpeti fellow?"

"No I don't," replied Meredith abruptly. "If he were all set to commit suicide then he certainly had no intention of trying to conceal his guilt. He would have realised that the moment he was dead his body would be subjected to a pretty detailed examination. And his disguise wouldn't stand up to a proper once-over, would it?"

"Then why the disguise?"

"Exactly. That's one of the points we've got to elucidate. And now," added Meredith, "let's see if we can isolate any prints. Either on these glasses or the decanter. I take it that none of these exhibits has been handled?"

Rokeby grinned.

"Is that a slam at the poor old County Police? Even we provincial flatfeet are familiar with our alphabet!"

Meredith chuckled and, taking out a small bottle of grey powder, he got down to work. At the end of half-an-hour, during which he made constant use of his magnifying-glass he said rather sourly:

"I'm afraid we're off to a bad start. One set of recent prints on one of the glasses. None on the other and none, confound it, on the decanter. What do you make of that?"

"Simple. Mildmann must have worn gloves."

"But *did* he?"

"Well, he was gloveless when I examined the body last night. But that means little enough."

"For all that, it's something we've got to find out. Was he wearing gloves when he entered the house? Had he a pair of gloves on his person? Why did he trouble to conceal his finger-prints—if indeed that was his idea—when he knew he was going to commit suicide?"

Meredith turned to the dead girl. She presented a gruesome sight as she slumped back in her chair, one bare slender arm dangling over the side, her stiffened fingers touching the carpet. Her head was canted over on to one shoulder as if she were listening acutely to something that she alone could detect in the deathly silence of the room. To a layman it would have proved a horrible and distracting spectacle, but to Meredith, inured by years of hard experience, this was but the centre-piece of yet another major crime.

Taking out a small ink-pad and official f-p form from his well-worn attaché-case, Meredith deftly took the necessary specimens of the dead girl's finger-prints. These he examined carefully through his magnifying-glass, at the same time comparing them with the excellent prints he had developed on one of the two recently used sherry glasses. He turned back to the waiting Rokeby.

"These are the girl's prints all right—just as I imagined. I see no reason now why the body shouldn't be moved. Maxton was quite satisfied that poison was the *prima facie* cause of death?"

"Completely satisfied."

"Then the constable had better get some help and have the body laid out properly in the bedroom. By the way, what about the domestic staff?"

"A parlour-maid and a cook, as far as I can gather. There's also a man for the outdoor work—a local chap working for the owner of the estate."

"Right! I'll cross-question them later. Before I do, I'd like you to drive me to the North Lodge." Meredith's grey eyes twinkled. "I prefer to work to a proper interrogatory sequence."

"Sounds impressive!" chuckled Rokeby.

IV

The High Prophet of Coo, mantled by a sheet twisted yet untroubled, lay on the bed in the humble, homely little room. Death, coming sooner than later, had solved his earthly problems. His spirit was now sojourning among the manifold gods of his faith.

Meredith noticed as he pulled down the sheet that he was still garbed in his disguise, even to the lifelike black beard that fringed his rigid jaw. His convulsed attitude was typical of the post-mortem appearance of a man who has died by a fatal dose of prussic acid. Quickly Meredith took a complete set of the finger-prints; then, drawing on his gloves, he carefully went through the dead man's pockets. To his surprise he found nothing. Every pocket in the trousers and long semetic caftan was empty. He drew Rokeby's attention to the fact.

"I'm not sure if it means very much," pointed out Rokeby. "He probably put on these clothes just before he was driven over to the Dower House. As you can see from that tab on the hem, they were hired from a London theatrical costumiers in Panton Street. The pockets would naturally be empty."

"But what about those gloves? If he wore them over at the Dower House, as the f-p evidence suggests, he must have disposed of them somewhere."

"What about the car?"

"Yes, I'd like to take a dekko at the car *and* the fellow that drove it. But before I do, we'll have a word with that lad of his."

Terence, looking pale and heavy-eyed, received the two officials in the parlour. Meredith cross-questioned him, quietly yet efficiently. What had been his father's relationship with the dead woman? Terence didn't know. Why had his father disguised himself as Penpeti in order to visit the dead woman? Terence hadn't the faintest idea. Was he at the North Lodge when his father set out? No, explained Terence, he'd left for Downchester with the housekeeper shortly after lunch and not returned until after eleven o'clock. In brief,

Terence had little worthwhile information to hand over to the inspector. As a witness he was a broken reed.

Sid Arkwright, however, proved to be a very different cup of tea. For the first time Meredith found himself harvesting data that really threw some light on the strange events of the previous night. Once inside the barn, he set the ball rolling by asking Sid the all-important question:

"Why had Mr. Mildmann disguised himself to resemble this Mr. Penpeti?"

Thereafter Sid had talked and talked a lot. Meredith barely had time to jot down a summary of this expansive deposition. He told the inspector everything he knew—the reason for the disguise, the reason for the visit, the threat that had been held over his employer's head by Miss Parker and Penpeti. Meredith listened with ever-increasing interest.

"But this much I *do* know!" cried Sid in conclusion, "the guv'nor never killed Miss Parker! I tell you straight, the guv'nor wouldn't have harmed a fly, the guv'nor wouldn't. Timid, kind-hearted chap he was—always out to do the decent thing by everybody. Why he should have killed 'isself, the Lord only knows, Inspector. Looks bad, I admit, but maybe it was the thought of terrifying Miss Parker into handing over them letters what made him do it. Sort of ashamed of 'isself. Acted on the spur of the moment like. And if you want my opinion, which I daresay you don't, I reckon Miss Parker was given the works *after* the guv'nor had left!"

Meredith shook his head.

"I'm afraid you're wrong there. For one thing Mr. Mildmann *didn't* frighten Miss Parker into handing over those letters. In order to recover them he was forced to break open the lid of her bureau. And for another, I can't help feeling that Mr. Mildmann went to the Dower House with the *deliberate* intention of murdering Miss Parker. You see, Arkwright, even if a man decides on the spur of the moment to take his own life, he wouldn't have made provision for carrying out his intention. Get the point? When your employer entered the Dower House the poison must have been on his person. And surely, if he had provided himself with the poison, it suggests that he *meant* to murder Miss Parker."

"But why, sir?" gasped Sid, perplexed. "Why did he murder her?"

"Presumably because she refused to hand over those letters." But despite Meredith's deadly logic, Sid seemed unconvinced. Meredith went on: "By the way, where *are* the letters? They weren't on Mr. Mildmann's person."

"They're here, sir," explained Sid. "In the back of the car—just where the guv'nor must have placed 'em last night. I naturally haven't touched a thing in the back of the car because the Sooper here locked the doors last night and took the key."

"Quite right," said Rokeby, drawing out his key-ring. "Arkwright merely got the body out of the car and into the lodge. In fact, he didn't garage the car until after we arrived."

As Rokeby unlocked one of the sleek, shiny doors, Meredith once again drew on his rubber gloves. Prominent on the spacious back seat of the Daimler was a sleek red leather letter-case. In a matter of seconds Meredith was dusting it over for the development of latent prints. The result was perplexing.

"Good God! Rokeby, what do you make of this? Again there's only one set of prints decipherable—prints that match up perfectly with those of the dead girl. Mildmann's are again absent." He turned to Arkwright. "Tell me, when your employer entered the house was he wearing gloves?"

"As far as I remember—no, sir."

"And when he came out?"

Sid reflected for an instant and then shot out excitedly:

"Well, I'll be—! Funny about that. I hadn't thought about it afore. When he came out of the house he *was* wearing gloves—sorta dark leather gloves."

"And he was carrying the letter-case?"

"Yes—I noticed that particular, seeing as that was what he'd gone for to the Dower House."

"And when you got the body out of the car, did you notice if Mr. Mildmann was still wearing his gloves?"

"No, sir," said Sid emphatically. "I'm darn sure he wasn't."

"Then he must have pulled them off in the car." Quickly Meredith entered the back of the car and made a thorough search. There was no sign of gloves! He turned again to Sid. "Were the back windows of the car open or shut?"

"Shut as you see them now, sir. As you may recall it was raining."

"Curious," muttered Meredith.

"Isn't it possible that he opened one of the windows, threw away the gloves and closed the window again?" asked Rokeby.

"Possible," admitted Meredith, "but not probable. Think of the circumstances, Rokeby! Here was a man in a state of convulsions just prior to his death from a killing dose of prussic acid. Would you be strong-willed enough to go through such a complicated performance? And, in any case, what was the point? Why get rid of the gloves?"

"Exactly," agreed Rokeby. "Why? In the circumstances, utterly senseless. Yet somehow he must have disposed of them."

Meredith again concentrated on Sid.

"When your master came out of the house what exactly did he say?"

"Little enough, sir. He just managed to gasp out in a wheezy sort of voice 'Drive home quickly—I'm ill!'"

"He appeared to be in a pretty bad state?"

Sid nodded.

"I was waiting behind a clump of trees on a bend of the drive so naturally I didn't see anything of him until he'd more or less reached the car. Before I could get down and give him a hand, poor chap, he'd wrenched open the door and more or less gone flat out on the back seat. I could see by the way he staggered that he was in pain."

"You then drove all out to the North Lodge?"

"More or less, sir. I had to nip out and open the gate of the Dower House drive. You see, they have to keep it shut because there's often sheep grazing in the park. Otherwise I drove as fast as I dared."

"Mr. Mildmann was dead when you arrived back here?"

"Yessir."

"Who else knew about the existence of these letters?"

"As far as I know, sir, only Mr. Penpeti."

"I see. Well, Arkwright, that's all for the present. You'll be served with a subpoena to attend the inquest. And even if the news-hounds get after you, keep your mouth closed. Understand?"

"O.K., sir."

Meredith turned to Rokeby.

"And now what about returning to the Dower House and having a word with the servants there?"

Chapter XIV

Unknown Visitor

I

Once back at the Dower House Meredith sensibly devoted the major part of his cross-examination to Hilda. After all, the parlour-maid would be in a far better position to give information than Mrs. Lundy, the cook, who was more or less relegated by her duties to the kitchen. He interviewed the girl in the big downstairs sitting-room, where there was nothing to remind her of the tragedy that had so suddenly darkened her young life. Hilda was in a bad state of nerves, pale and red-eyed from weeping. But after a few minutes of the inspector's quiet, casual questioning, she seemed to recover a little.

From the start, however, her evidence was surprisingly clear and concise. Meredith swiftly elucidated the following facts. Her mistress had returned from the Manor shortly before nine-thirty and gone straight upstairs as usual to the small sitting-room. She appeared to be in a perfectly normal state. About fifteen minutes later Hilda had answered a ring at the front-door and admitted Mr. Penpeti. He had gone straight upstairs to Miss Parker's room.

"You're sure it *was* Mr. Penpeti?" asked Meredith.

"Oh quite sure, sir. He's not an easy one to mistake, him dressing so odd."

"Did he speak to you?"

"Well, he just murmured 'Good evening' and nodded, sir, if you can call that speaking."

Meredith thought: "So even now she doesn't suspect that her Mr. Penpeti was really Mildmann. It's obvious she hasn't yet learnt the full details of the tragedy." Aloud he said: "I see, young lady. Well, go on."

"Well, sir," said Hilda, "there isn't much more to tell. About ten minutes later I heard somebody come rather heavily down the stairs and then the slam of the front-door. Naturally I guessed that it was Mr. Penpeti leaving. About arpas ten I usually take a cup of Horlicks up to my mistress as it helps her to sleep like. So I knocks on her door and walks in and...and..."

"All right," broke in Meredith tactfully. "I can guess the rest for myself. You rang the Manor, I understand?"

"That's right, sir, and Mrs. Hagge-Smith got through at once to the pleece before she come over here."

"When you entered the room, apart from the body of your mistress, was there anything else that particularly caught your attention?"

"I...I..." Hilda gulped rapidly and drew out a grubby-looking handkerchief. "Coo! It was that horrible, sir, I can't bear to think of it. Straight I can't!"

"But you must help us all you can, young lady."

Hilda took a grip on herself and blurted out:

"I was that put about...it ain't easy to get things straight. No, sir, I don't think there was much else I noticed except a strong smell of cigar-smoke."

Meredith looked up sharply.

"Really? Does Mr. Penpeti smoke cigars?"

"Come to think of it—he don't, sir. Leastways I've never seen him. Just a cigarette sometimes, as far as I can recall."

"What about Mr. Mildmann, does he smoke cigars?"

Hilda looked bewildered.

"But what's he got to do with it, sir?"

Meredith smiled.

"It's your job to answer questions, not ask them, you know."

"Sorry, sir. Mr. Mildmann? Lor' no, he's a non-smoker and non-drinker is Mr. Mildmann. Real saint he is…that is, *was!*" corrected Hilda with a series of gulps.

"Non-drinker!" exclaimed Meredith, exchanging a quick glance with Rokeby. "You mean, of course, that he doesn't touch alcohol?"

"That's right, sir."

Meredith was puzzled. Then how was it Mildmann had joined Miss Parker in a glass of sherry? And the cigar-smoke? How did that enter in? Surely the dead woman was not a cigar addict? He posed the question, but Hilda was emphatic. Her mistress *did* smoke but only queer sort of cigarettes that smelt like burning hay. Then how was it Hilda had smelt this very distinctive odour in the room?

"Now tell me," he went on, "did you hear any unusual noises coming from Miss Parker's room at any time during the evening?"

Hilda goggled at the inspector as if he were a magician.

"Lor' if that isn't funny! I mean, you asking that. I was going to tell you about it. But just after the mistress come in I did hear a sort of thumping noise coming from her room. Like thumping feet it was—heavy feet. Like as if somebody was walking up and down the room in a temper. I had to come through the hall to fetch something from the dining-room. Course I didn't think much about it at the time. I thought perhaps the mistress was doing her Sweden exercises or something. But seeing what has happened since—"

"What time was this exactly?"

"No more than a minute or so after Miss Parker come in."

"And you heard nothing further?"

"Well, I *thought* I did, but by then I was back in the kitchen. So I couldn't be sure about this."

"And what did you *imagine* you heard?"

"Something overturned or knocked against downstairs in the hall. Just a second or two before Mr. Penpeti rang the bell. But cook says I'm always imagining noises that aren't there. So maybe it was just fancy." Hilda paused, sniffed and added defiantly: "But even cook can't say as there wasn't something odd I spotted about the french-windows over there. Even if my ears play tricks, my eyes don't. You see, Inspector, I could have sworn that those windows were shut and properly latched when I went into the room about arpas seven. But when I went round the ground floor sometime after ten to see that everything was locked up for the night, the windows were ajar. No fancy about *that*! Strikes me," added Hilda on a solemn note, "that some queer things happened in this house last night. To my way of thinking somebody crepp into the place while the mistress was over at the Manor and crepp out again through those french-windows later that evening. It was them that I heard in the hall. But 'oo they was and what they was up to…well, you can ask me another!"

Meredith was patently interested.

"You're suggesting that while Miss Parker was having dinner over at the Manor, some unknown person managed to get into the Dower House and find their way up to Miss Parker's private room? And that, later, after Miss Parker had come in, they crept downstairs and left by the french-windows over there?"

"That's the ticket, sir!"

"You're suggesting that Miss Parker *met* this person before Mr. Penpeti arrived?"

"Well, that's my belief like."

"But could anybody have got into the house while Miss Parker was at the Manor without you realising it?"

"Oh easy, sir. Cook and me always has a bite of supper once the mistress has left. That means we was in the kitchen-wing, and if he come in quiet we wouldn't be none the wiser, would we?"

"But surely the front-door was closed and locked? I noticed that it had a Yale lock."

"Oh, I don't mean he come in through the front-door. Two of the hall windows was part open. If he was slippy enough he could have sneaked in that way."

"Then why didn't he leave the *same* way?" asked Meredith sharply, half-convinced that the girl had allowed her imagination to run away with her.

Hilda considered this point and then said with a bright smile:

"Well, sir, if he saw Mr. Penpeti coming up the drive, perhaps he wasn't so anxious to meet him. So he went out through the french-windows here at the side of the house. Natural like, isn't it?"

Meredith nodded.

"I think you've probably got something there." He turned to Rokeby. "Interesting, eh? Interesting and rather curious. A definite complication." He turned back to Hilda and patted her paternally on the shoulder. "All right, young lady, we shan't want you any more. You've been very frank and help-ful. I shall want you to make a signed statement about this later. But we'll see to all that in due course."

II

"And what now?" asked Rokeby, when the girl had been dismissed.

Meredith glanced at his watch.

"You may think this damned unaccommodating of me, but I suggest you go ahead in the car and order lunch at The Leaning Man. I'd like to follow on foot. Reason—a long, solitary bout of hard thinking. Any objections?"

"I was never the man to prevent anybody else from thinking," chuckled Rokeby. "I've heard that it's an excellent exercise for other people's minds! And by the look of it, you've certainly got plenty to think about!"

Once Rokeby had droned off down the Dower House drive, Meredith lit his pipe and began his trudge across the park to the north entrance, which would lead him on to the Tappin Mallet road. He purposely chose a route which would steer him clear of the tents, for he was anxious to avoid all distractions. Already he was convinced that the case was not quite as simple as it appeared to be on the surface. It was in fact bristling with oddities and perplexities of a peculiarly tricky nature. A stream of pertinent questions began to race through his brain, but with a disciplined will Meredith checked the flow and began to isolate and pigeon-hole the more outstanding of these problems. If he were to get results then it was essential to deal with the various problems one by one.

Hilda's evidence formed a natural starting-point for an analysis of the facts. Had somebody (other than Mildmann-cum-Penpeti) made contact with Penelope Parker just before her death? Certainly the girl's information seemed to suggest this. Hilda had spoken of this possible visitor as "he"—but that was a mere figure of speech. It might just as well have been a woman, though the odour of cigar-smoke noticed by Hilda suggested the male sex. At the moment the sex of the intruder was of little account. The important fact was that somebody had possibly entered the Dower House when Hilda and the cook were at supper, crept up to Penelope's room, had a brief conversation with her and attempted to leave the house just as Mildmann was approaching the front-door. This had forced the intruder to leave by means of the french-windows, which it was impossible to latch from the outside. Accepting these bare facts what could one deduce? That this unknown person *must* have been familiar (*a*) with Penelope's routine, (*b*) with that of the domestic staff, (*c*) with the lay-out of the house. In brief it must have been somebody with whom the dead girl was well acquainted. If so, why the stealthy entry and exit? Obviously to conceal the fact that the visit had been made. Which immediately suggested that the visit had been made with a criminal intention. But what criminal intention? Was it on the cards that the answer to this question was quite simply...murder?

In brief, *was Penelope Parker already dead when the cloaked and bearded Mildmann entered her room?*

Meredith was assailed by a brisk tingle of excitement. Assume this somewhat startling fact and then what? Mildmann had walked into that room and received a sudden and horrifying shock. Dead in the chair before him was the woman with whom he had been violently in love; with whom, perhaps, he was *still* in love, despite her unsavoury threat in respect of his impulsive billets-doux. From all accounts Mildmann was sensitive and highly-strung. Wasn't it possible that he had, in a moment of mental aberration, decided to take his own life? The poisoned sherry was at hand. He might well have noticed the odour of bitter almonds and realised, at once, how Penelope had met her death. Here, he decided, was an opportune means to end his own life.

"Umph," mused Meredith. "Neat but a trifle gaudy. Must consider the objections to this theory. An outsize one occurs to me at once. If Mildmann had committed suicide, why had he troubled to break into the desk and recover the letters? Illogical, of course. He must have known there was no possible chance of destroying them before he collapsed and died. And even if Mildmann murdered the girl himself before committing suicide, this is still a bewildering aspect of the case."

Objection Two was this—unless Mildmann had murdered the girl, why was he wearing gloves? According to Arkwright, when his employer entered the Dower House he was *not* wearing gloves. When he came out he *was*. In other words Mildmann must have put on his gloves once he was inside the house. And unless Mildmann was to be accepted as the murderer, this was a strange and senseless thing to do.

So what? Was the girl dead before Mildmann entered her room or was he responsible for the poisoning? Umph! A delicate point to decide and one that, for the moment, would have to be left in abeyance.

Meredith switched his mind on to the *modus operandi* of the murder. The exhibits were: (*a*) a cut-glass decanter containing the poisoned sherry and bearing no sign of recent finger-prints, (*b*) a used glass, smelling of bitter almonds, and bearing the finger-prints of the dead girl, (*c*) another used glass, also smelling of bitter almonds, but devoid of recent prints. The obvious conclusion was that the murderer had doctored the sherry in the decanter with the prussic acid and later poured it into the two glasses. Now the acid, thought Meredith, had probably been sealed in a small glass phial—either in the form of the ordinary Acidum Hydrocyanicum Dilutum with two per cent of the anhydrous acid or in a Scheele's solution of four per cent. Surely it was an unaccountable fact that the murderer had elected to smuggle the contents of his phial into the decanter instead of direct into the glasses? For one thing the decanter would have to be unstoppered and the neck, as Meredith recalled, was extremely slender. And for another, the murderer could have been more certain of an instantaneous effect if he had doped the glasses, since the prussic acid would have been far less diluted. Surely a peculiar and, at the moment, inexplicable eccentricity on the part of the murderer?

This naturally led Meredith to a second point in connection with the poisoned drink. If the liquid had been poured into the glasses from the decanter then both Mildmann and the dead girl would have swallowed a similar amount of the acid in solution. It could be reasonably assumed that the girl was dead before Mildmann left the room, since he would naturally desire to make sure of its lethal effect before taking the poison himself. According to Hilda's evidence, Mildmann had been upstairs in her mistress' room for about ten minutes. Certain it was that if Mildmann were the murderer he couldn't have led the girl to drink the poisoned sherry immediately. A certain amount of conversation must have preceded the fatal act. In short, it was logical to suppose that the girl's death had been, to all intents and purposes, instantaneous. Yet what had been the effect on Mildmann of an equal dose? He had walked downstairs, out of the house, staggered a good few yards down the drive and climbed into his car unaided. Death had not intervened until some time on the journey back to the North Lodge.

Granted that the effect of most poisons on different individuals is not necessarily identical. Some constitutions have a greater power of resistance. But in this case the discrepancy was sufficient to demand a close analysis of the facts. In other words, was the dose given to the girl equivalent in strength to that imbibed by the murderer? Mildmann could, of course, have poured himself out a smaller amount of the doped sherry. But why? If he were out to commit suicide then surely he would prefer to go out quickly rather than slowly?

One thing was essential. He must get Maxton, the police surgeon, to come over that afternoon to make a second medical examination of the two corpses. It was on the cards that when confronted with the direct query he would be able to state whether Penelope Parker had died instantly or not. As a corollary to this angle of the case, a careful analysis would have to be made of (*a*) the poisoned sherry left in the decanter (*b*) the residual drops of the liquid left in the bottom of the two used glasses.

And beyond that? Meredith pulled harder on his pipe. Sufficient unto the day was the evidence thereof. In his opinion there was only one thing more obstructive than a paucity of evidence, and that was a surfeit. He liked, if possible, to solve one set of problems before passing on to another; to tie up the loose threads as he went long.

That was what he preferred. But Fate has a habit of ignoring human preferences and bull-dozing ahead in its own pig-headed way. And, at that moment, although Meredith didn't know it, Fate was bracing its muscles to upset his neatly-loaded apple-cart.

Chapter XV

Fatal Effect

I

The repercussions of the double tragedy on the Summer Convention of the Children of Osiris can well be imagined. Granted it had stopped raining the day after the gruesome events at the Dower House had transpired. Granted the sun tried to break through a patina of watery cloud. But the shock of losing, at one foul swoop, a High Prophet and a well-loved member of the Inmost Temple left the members of the Movement depressed and horrified. Discussions concerning the mystic symbolism of the Ka and the Ba and the Ab no longer evoked the customary zealous interest. Many of the most fanatical Coo-ites no longer gave a damn whether the Sahu *did* possess an Aakhu or not, which merely goes to show how violent was the impact of the news on their imaginations.

Outside the lecture tent there was only one subject worthy of discussion…the Tragedy!

There was, of course, a stern refutation of the rumour that Mr. Mildmann had murdered Penelope Parker and then taken his own life. The general belief was that the poison had been planted by a third person who had a grudge against the High Prophet and his charming acolyte. So far, the fact that Mr. Mildmann had paid his last visit to the Dower House in the guise of Mr. Penpeti had not leaked out. The crux of every argument concerning the case was this: Had any member seen anybody suspicious hanging about near the Dower House just prior to the tragedy? If so, they upheld, it was the duty of such a member to go at once to the police. It was in this manner that Mr. Menthu-Mut (the only *proven* Egyptian in the Movement) came to meet Inspector Meredith.

Mr. Menthu-Mut had three large passions in life— Ancient Egyptology, Pasteurised Milk, and Moths. To the first and the third he devoted much time and study. On the second he more or less existed. He was, if one may use the expression, a milk addict, an incurable toper of milk. Provided, of course, that it was pasteurised. His pride in the magnificent civilisation of his forebears had brought him into the orbit of Cooism. His activity as a lepidopterist had brought him on the evening of Thursday, June 6th, to the edge of the lily-pond, some four or five hundred yards southwest of the Dower House.

During his few days at Old Cowdene, Menthu-Mut had already captured a good few specimens—including two flawless *Rostralis,* a female *Tortrices Sorbiana,* and an undersized *Furcula Cuspidates.* This was all well and good, but his immediate concern was to net a *Stagnalis Pyralides,* a moth that was only to be found near stagnant water. Shortly before dusk, therefore, Menthu-Mut had set out, with his lantern, net and specimen-case, across the park to the lily-pond. The drizzle in no way discouraged him, for long experience had taught him that such meteorological conditions were perfect for a moth-hunt. He trod softly in his goloshes, his lantern shuttered, until he came to the broad ring of sallow trees that bordered the pond. There, abruptly, he unshuttered his lamp and sent its beam playing over the foliage, already a pearly-grey in the fading light. The result of this action startled him, for, almost at his feet, the figure of a man sprang up and dived deeper into the bushes.

"Who goes?" cried Menthu-Mut in alarm. "Please to speak up yourself and reveal, I beg. Who is?"

Silence, save for the gentle drip of rain-drops on to the still surface of the pond. Menthu-Mut was puzzled and a little frightened, but for all that he plunged deeper into the tangled undergrowth below the sallows, the beam of his light roving about in the darkness like a prying eye. Then for the second time he disturbed the prowling figure, which on this occasion broke clear of the trees and dashed round to the far side of the pond. Menthu-Mut attempted to follow, tripped, fell, and shattered the bulb of his electric-lamp. But, in the brief instant before the figure had disappeared, Menthu-Mut had noticed two things—the man was wearing a belted rain-coat and he was hatless. Of his features he had seen nothing.

At the time, of course, although perplexed, Menthu-Mut had not valued the full significance of the event. It was only the next day when the news of the double tragedy "broke" that Menthu-Mut's public-spirited tent-mates urged him to go to the police.

It was through Mrs. Hagge-Smith that Menthu-Mut learnt that Inspector Meredith had made his headquarters at The Leaning Man in Tappin Mallet. Shortly after lunch in the big marquee, therefore, Menthu-Mut borrowed a bicycle and rode over to the inn. Luckily Meredith, who had been discussing the case with Rokeby over their meal, had not yet left the place to continue his investigations. He arranged with the landlord for a private parlour to be put at his disposal. And it was amid the potted ferns, red-plush, and Toby-jugs of mine host's own sitting-room that Meredith learnt of yet another complication in the case.

Menthu-Mut, despite his inadequate mastery of the English tongue, was voluble. In a few minutes Meredith had jotted down the salient points of his evidence and started his cross-examination.

"What time did you reach the lily-pond?"

"About sometime not more beyond nine o'clock than a little," he said neatly.

"It was quite dark when you reached the spot?"

"Not complete. There was light of a small quantity but not much. I have my lantern for the moths which make me see a little more than otherwise."

"You say this man was crouching under the trees?"

"So it has the appearance of."

"You had the impression that he was anxious to avoid you—that he wanted to conceal his identity?"

"Indeed so!" exclaimed Menthu-Mut brightly. "If not so why make no answer when I make the question of him 'Who goes?' and 'Who is?' To which he replies not at all but bounds only away and into the dark disappears."

"You say you were unable to catch a glimpse of his features, Mr. Mut. What of his build and height? Any idea?"

"Oh, of big size. Much muscular build. Very high as it goes among the average. Perhaps six foots or there around."

"In a belted rain-coat but hatless, you said. What was the colour of his hair—fair or dark?"

"In the light of my lantern it was difficult. But more of the fair than of the dark, I would have it."

"When he slipped away the second time you made no further attempt to follow him?"

"No. It was then much more dark than it was. Without my lantern I was no good to follow. I have very bad eyes to see in the dark." Mr. Menthu-Mut paused and added with a shamefaced little smile: "Beside I am small built and I had a little fear as you will understand me. The pond is much alone in the dark—far from everywhere else. You have seen, perhaps?"

"No," admitted Meredith, "not yet. But I intend to take a look round there this afternoon. Suppose you meet me there in an hour's time, Mr. Mut. Is that convenient?"

"I have much pleasure," said Menthu-Mut with a little bow.

"Good!" concluded Meredith.

II

No sooner had Mr. Menthu-Mut departed on his bicycle, when Meredith was discussing the implication of this fresh evidence with Rokeby. He was irritated by this introduction of a new line of investigation when he already had a number of unsolved problems on his mind.

"You see," he observed with a disgruntled expression to Rokeby, as they finished their pipes in the landlord's over-crowded little parlour, "we're already far from your original belief that this was a cut-to-pattern case. The pith of the main problem is this—did Mildmann kill the Parker girl and then take his own life? Or did he commit suicide because he found her dead when he entered the room? Or is it within the bounds of possibility that *both* Mildmann and the girl were murdered by a third person?"

"It's no good looking at me!" chuckled Rokeby. "As far as I'm concerned, one bet seems as good as another."

Meredith went on:

"This much we can fairly assume, however—somebody entered that upstairs sitting-room before the girl returned from the Manor. Now the question is, was this 'somebody' the same person that our friend Mr. Mut disturbed near the pond?"

"What about the time-factor?" asked Rokeby.

"Not very illuminating. You see, we don't happen to know what time the unknown person sneaked into the Dower House. It was not until nine thirty-five that Hilda heard those strange thumping noises up in the girl's room. Mut arrived at the pond somewhere about nine o'clock."

"Which means that the man seen by Mut and the man heard by Hilda could well be one and the same person?"

"Undoubtedly."

"And if the fellow wanted to slip into the Dower House just before the Parker girl returned from dinner, surely that ring of trees round the pond was the ideal place in which to wait?"

"But why wait?"

"Eh?"

"I said—why wait? Why not arrange matters to arrive at the Dower House at the time he considered most suitable? After all, to hang about in the vicinity was to take an unnecessary risk. As it was, he only escaped identification by the skin of his teeth. If Mut had been able to see his features, we should probably have no difficulty in tracing him. As it is…" Meredith lifted his shoulders. "Tall, broad-shouldered, fair-haired—not much to go on, is it?"

Rokeby shook his head with an absent-minded expression. He appeared to be following some line of thought unconnected with the inspector's statement. Suddenly he glanced up.

"You realise that prussic acid is a convulsant?"

"What of it?"

"That thumping noise heard by the maid."

"Well?"

"It might have been the girl in her death throes. An unpleasant thought but logical."

Meredith objected.

"But Hilda said it was like heavy footsteps. That suggests a certain regularity of rhythm. My personal opinion is that it *was* footsteps."

"Any particular reason?"

"A very definite one. Hilda said she heard the thumping noise 'a minute or so' after her mistress came in. And I just don't think it possible that the moment the girl entered the room, she was tricked into taking a glass of that poisoned sherry."

"But why not?" argued Rokeby. "The very fact that the girl didn't call out or scream rather suggests that she was not surprised to find this man in her room. Or, to put it another way, she may have been surprised to find him there at that particular moment but was not in any way frightened because the fellow was familiar to her. And if familiar, what more natural that the man should pour her a glass of sherry a minute or so after she came into the room?"

"Quite a neat little assumption," admitted Meredith. "But surely this friend would have joined her in a drink? And we know he couldn't have done so because some time later he slipped out of the house via the french-windows. And he couldn't have poured himself out an unpoisoned glass because it was the decanter which had been tampered with. Moreover, only two glasses were used and the second we know must have been used by Mildmann."

"My dear fellow," laughed Rokeby, "do you know anything about this Osiris gang? I bet a good fifty per cent of 'em are T.T. This chap may have been one of the fifty per cent."

"So you think it was this interloper and *not* Mildmann who murdered the girl?"

Rokeby nodded.

"Quite frankly, I do."

"And Mildmann?"

"Well, as you said, he may have found the girl dead and committed suicide. On the other hand…"

"Well?"

"What about accident?"

"Accident?"

"Exactly," smiled Rokeby. "Mildmann may have been so overcome by the sight of the dead girl that he felt faint. What more natural than to turn to the sherry decanter? The point being that *he didn't know it was poisoned!*"

"It's a possibility, of course." Meredith considered the new theory for a moment and then went on: "But if so, Rokeby, why the devil did Mildmann put on his gloves before pouring out the sherry? Strange, eh?"

"Good God!" exclaimed Rokeby. "I was forgetting all about those darned gloves. Not wearing them when he entered the house, but definitely wearing 'em when he came out. It's a teaser!"

"I *could* use a more graphic word, but I won't!" grinned Meredith. "You see, my dear chap, we're in a very unsatisfactory position. We can put up between us quite a nice little collection of sound little theories. And we can just as easily bowl 'em over." Meredith rose, knocked out his pipe in the glossy little grate and took up his hat. "And now, before we keep our *rendezvous* with Mr. Menthu-Mut, could you phone Maxton and ask him to come over this afternoon? I want a few more details of the medical evidence. In the meantime I'd like a despatch-rider from your H.Q. to run up to the Yard with some exhibits."

"You mean?"

"The sherry decanter and those two glasses. I want an analysis made of the liquid residue in all three. If Mildmann and the girl drank that sherry at one and the same time, I still can't see why there was such a time-lag before Mildmann actually passed out."

"You think the girl died instantaneously?"

"Yes—more or less. If not, my dear fellow, surely she could have got to the door after Mildmann left and called for help? That's one of the reasons why I want Maxton to make a more thorough post-mortem."

III

Mr. Menthu-Mut was waiting for them near the lily-pond. He enacted with considerable histrionic ability the events of the previous night, pointing out where he had first made contact with the unknown prowler and so on. Snatching out his notebook Meredith made a rough sketch-map of the locality which, later that day, he expanded into a more comprehensive map of the Old Cowdene estate. He judged the pond to be about four hundred yards from the boundary fence of the Dower House. Although the immediate environs of the pond offered excellent cover, the ground between it and the house was more or less flat and open. A vague path meandered by the pond and terminated somewhere round the back of the Dower House. This path Meredith determined to investigate.

But before leaving the pond he closely examined the spot where Menthu-Mut claimed the man had been crouching. Although the ground was still somewhat soggy after the rain, no footprints were visible, for the weeds and grass were too lush and springy to accept any clearly-defined print. Certain it was that the grass and undergrowth at this point had been trampled underfoot, suggesting that the man's wait under the sallow trees had been prolonged. Furthermore, to lend emphasis to this assumption, Meredith collected no less than four apple cores from the ground.

"Curious," he observed to Rokeby.

"Why?"

"Because when a man's keyed-up and waiting for zero-hour, his normal comfort is a smoke."

"He may have been a non-smoker."

"Impossible, if we accept Hilda's evidence. Remember what she said about the smell of cigar smoke?" He turned to Menthu-Mut, who was standing discreetly in the background. "We needn't bother you any more, Mr. Mut—thanks." He swung round again on Rokeby. "Now let's follow this path to the house."

A minute or so later they discovered an interesting fact. The path led to a low gate let into a fence of the kitchen-garden, and just beyond it, half concealed by a clump of spruce trees, was a small thatched cottage.

"Hullo!" exclaimed Meredith. "This may prove useful. Let's see if there's anybody around."

His knock was answered by a fresh-complexioned buxom young woman who, on seeing Rokeby's uniform, looked a trifle worried. Meredith, catching her glance, reassured her.

"It's all right, young lady. I just want to ask you a few questions. You can guess what it's all about, eh?"

"That affair over at the Dower House, I reckon."

"Exactly. What's your position on the estate?"

"My man's gardener here—employed by Mrs. Hagge-Smith at the Manor. You'll be wanting to see him, maybe?"

"Possibly. But first let's see if you can help us. We rather suspect that somebody came through this gate shortly before nine-thirty last night. And we think there's a possibility that he left the place the same way some fifteen or twenty minutes later. Now I suppose you didn't—?"

"Just listen to that now! My man's been troubled about this ever since we heard what had happened to that poor Miss Parker. Only this morning he said to me, 'Ruth,' he said, 'there may be something in this and I reckon I ought to tell the pleece about it.'"

"About what?" snapped Meredith eagerly.

"About what him and me saw last night. Just before ten it was. Herbie and me was sitting in the parlour when Dandy—that's our terrier—started barking like he was gone mad. 'Ruth,' says Herbie, 'there's somebody out there, or the face in the mirror ain't mine!' he says. Well, the curtains of the window was undrawn and the light was shining out across the path." The young woman swung round on the steps to face the cottage. "It's that window there, see? Well, both Herbie and me turned naturally to look out of the window and, as we did so, we saw somebody slip by towards the gate. Proper caught in the light he was for the moment. Gave us a rare turn it did, too!"

"You noticed the man's features?"

"Well, not as you might say in detail. Middlin' old we reckoned—clean-shaven—'bout forty, maybe."

"Wearing a belted rain-coat and no hat?" rapped out Meredith. "Tall, broad-shouldered, eh?"

"He was a tall, well-set-up sort of chap—that much I will say," said Ruth in measured tones. "But he was wearing a hat all right. One of them soft tweed hats what gentlemen wear out shooting. And he certainly wasn't wearing a coat, which we thought odd, seeing as that it was raining. I should say it was a sort of tweed suit he'd got on but I can't properly swear to it. A gentlemanly chap, Herbie reckoned he was, to judge from his clothes, but neither of us could be sure about that as it all happened so quick. It was certainly nobody we reckernised. Nobody local, that is."

"Is your husband anywhere about?" asked Meredith, puzzled and deflated.

"Down in the potting-shed beyond the asparagus-bed— over there, see?"

"Thanks," said Meredith. "I'll just go and have a word with him. And thanks for your information, young woman."

They had no difficulty in running the gardener to earth. He was pricking out dahlia plants in the musty gloom of his potting-shed. But at the end of five minutes Meredith realised that, although he had fully corroborated his wife's statement, he had no fresh evidence to offer.

As they walked slowly towards the Dower House, Rokeby observed sarcastically:

"A quick-change artist, eh?"

Meredith's laugh was a trifle hollow.

"Damn it, Rokeby! What the devil *was* happening around here last night? You know now as well as I do that the man lurking near the pond was not the same man that slipped out of the garden just before ten o'clock. But I'm ready to swear that the man who sneaked out of the Dower House via the french-windows *was* the gentleman in the shooting-hat seen by the couple in the cottage."

"Perhaps the chap by the pond was a confederate," suggested Rokeby.

"Umph—it's possible." Meredith glanced at his watch. "What time did you say Maxton would arrive?"

"About three o'clock."

"In about ten minutes, eh? Good. Suppose we go up to the girl's room and wait for him."

IV

It was actually some twenty minutes later when Maxton, the police surgeon, arrived in his car, escorted by the despatch-rider from County H.Q. In the interim Meredith and Rokeby had borrowed string and paper and cotton-wool and carefully packed the sherry decanter and two glasses. Before Meredith went into a huddle with Maxton, he wrote a note to Luke Spears, the chief analyst at the Yard, explaining exactly what he wanted. This note and the parcel he handed over to the despatch-rider.

"You'd better stay the night in Town and bring back the analyst's report to-morrow. And for God's sake, don't bump the exhibits! This way up, fragile, glass with care! Remember that and go easy on the acceleration!"

The constable grinned, saluted and drove off soberly round the bend in the drive. Meredith returned upstairs to Maxton and Rokeby.

"Good of you to come over so quickly," said Meredith. "But I want to bring myself into line with the detailed medical evidence. There's no question about the poison being prussic acid, I take it?"

"None whatsoever," said Maxton emphatically.

"And in the case of the girl—what's your frank opinion— was death instantaneous?"

Maxton reflected for a moment and then said with professional caution:

"I can't be absolutely sure about that at present. When your analyst has determined the exact concentration of the poison in the residue left in the glass handled by the girl, it will be easier for me to give a more exact answer. All the symptoms *suggest* that the girl died, more or less, instantaneously." Maxton smiled. "You'll say that the expression 'more or less instantaneously' is a paradox, eh Meredith? And as a purist I'd be inclined to agree with you. But medically the term 'instantaneous death' is rather more elastic than it suggests. Take the case of a person who swallows a concentrated dose of prussic acid. Death has been known to intervene within two minutes which, from a coroner's point-of-view, could be described as instantaneous. In many cases where the acid has been drunk from a bottle, the victim has not only replaced the cork but put the bottle back on a shelf before the fatal collapse occurred. In other cases a person's senses may be atrophied at once, though the victim is not actually dead."

"And in this case?" asked Meredith.

"As far as I can judge from the post-mortem symptoms, the girl was instantly affected by the poison and probably only lingered on for a very few minutes."

"Then can you explain why Mildmann, who presumably swallowed a solution of the acid equal in concentration to that swallowed by the girl, was able to open the door, walk down the stairs, let himself out of the house, walk twenty yards or more down the drive to where his car was parked, climb into it and, apparently, not collapse until the car was on the move?"

Maxton shook his head.

"Most emphatically—I can't. Naturally I was unaware of these more detailed facts when I made my initial examination last night. Mind you, different constitutions suffer different reactions to equal doses of a poison. That's a medical fact. But in this case…no, I'm damned if that can be the whole answer! The discrepancy between the times of the fatal effect is too great."

"When you examined Mildmann's remains, what was your opinion then?" persisted Meredith.

"My superficial examination led me to believe that, like the girl, death had intervened within a minute or two of taking the poison. The post-mortem appearance was identical."

"Is there any way we can check up on your assumptions?" asked Meredith anxiously. "Confound it, Maxton, this sounds damned rude of me, but it's a devilish important aspect of the case."

"Oh, you needn't study my professional feelings," laughed Maxton. "I'm a pachyderm and don't you forget it! And let me reassure you—we have two very good checks! First, an analysis of the liquid residue in the two glasses, as I mentioned before. Secondly, we could have an autopsy on both Mildmann and the girl with a subsequent analysis of the stomach content. And once we're convinced that they drank a poisoned solution of equal strength, then we can fairly assume that they would have died within a minute of each other."

Meredith turned to Rokeby.

"What's your opinion, Rokeby?"

"I think we should press for an autopsy in both cases. If you like, and Maxton's agreeable, I'll get in touch with the coroner at once and arrange for the police ambulance to take the bodies to the mortuary."

"I should feel happier about my findings *after* an autopsy," said Maxton.

Meredith rose.

"Good. That's settled then. I'll leave you to make the arrangements. As a matter of fact, Rokeby, I don't think it's fair of me to take up any more of your time. If you can send me over a good sergeant with local knowledge and a police car from County H.Q. to-morrow, that's all the help I shall need at present. Can do?" Rokeby nodded. "Right! Tell him to report at The Leaning Man. Nine o'clock on the dot!"

Chapter XVI

Terence Through the Hoop

I

When Rokeby and the police surgeon had left, Meredith sat for a good ten minutes without the movement of an eyelid. He looked as if he were asleep. But mentally he had never been more alert. The case both interested and irritated him. Interested him because it was complex and shot through with unexpected twists—irritated him because the evidence, most of it conflicting, was coming in faster than he could comfortably deal with it. From the easy assumption that Mildmann had murdered the girl and then committed suicide, he had now passed on to the indisputable fact that any one of three people might have committed the murder—Mildmann, the man who slipped out of the french-windows, the man seen by Menthu-Mut.

His mind naturally turned once more to finger-prints. Mildmann's he had been unable to isolate because he had undoubtedly worn gloves. But what of the man Hilda claimed to have heard leaving the house just before

Mildmann arrived? Granted there were no recent finger-prints on either the decanter or the two glasses, save several clearly-defined specimens left by the girl on the particular glass she had used. But that did not mean Penelope Parker's first visitor had also worn gloves.

Meredith considered the facts. The man arrived in the room before the Parker girl returned from the Manor. He was in a position, therefore, to doctor the sherry without secrecy or haste. To do this it was only necessary for him to withdraw the stopper from the decanter and pour in the solution of prussic acid. This theory would at once dispose of the problem as to why the acid had not been poured direct into the glasses—all in all, a far more effec-tive method. Time and secrecy being at a discount, it would be just as easy to pour the poison into the decanter. Immediate objection—the glass stopper had surrendered no finger-prints. Quite. But suppose the visitor merely covered the knob of the stopper with a handkerchief whilst withdrawing and replacing it? That disposed of *that*! But what about the other objects in the room that the man might have inadvertently handled?

The tumbler switch? The door handle? Of no use. A dozen different people's prints would have been left on both. Meredith's keen eye roved round the room and suddenly came to rest on the mantelpiece, where he spotted a small beaten-silver ash-tray. Lying in the ash-tray, in splendid isola-tion, *was a cigar-butt!* Damn it! He ought to have noticed that before. In a flash Meredith drew on his rubber-gloves, picked up the butt and examined it. One point struck him at once. The cigar had not burnt out. It had been crushed out—quite obviously against the bottom of the ash-tray. (So Hilda's nose had *not* let her down!) But how did this help from the finger-print angle? The cigar-leaf offered a very poor surface from which to "lift" a print. But hang on! Wasn't the ash-tray of a very light and flimsy design? What would be a man's instinctive gesture when crushing out the butt? *Surely to steady the ash-tray with the other hand?*

Three minutes later Meredith knew he had rung the bell. Several flawless prints were clearly visible after dusting over the highly-polished surface of the silver. And since the cigar-butt was the only object in the ash-tray, it was reasonable to suppose that these were the prints of Penelope Parker's first visitor. Cautiously Meredith wrapped up the ash-tray in a clean piece of cloth, which he kept for such purposes in his attaché-case. Five minutes after that he had taken specimen prints from Hilda and the cook. Then, from the domestic quarters, he went straight through to the big downstairs sitting-room.

He did not have much difficulty in finding just what he was after. On one of the glass panes, near the swivel-handle of the french-windows, he developed two or three prints, which under his magnifying-glass proved to be identical with those on the ash-tray! With a glow of satisfaction he turned back into the hall.

As he did so there was a prolonged peal on the front-door bell. Without waiting for Hilda, Meredith decided to take matters into his own hands and open up. There was a momentary pause as the visitor looked him over with a fierce and beady eye, then a booming voice demanding:

"You're the man from Scotland Yard, aren't you? No need to tell me. It sticks out a mile. You're just the person I want to see." Then over Meredith's shoulder: "No, no, Hilda. Run along! I wish to speak with this gentleman in private." Then as Hilda, bolt-eyed and a little dazed, scampered off, she added: "I'm Mrs. Hagge-Smith. I own Old Cowdene. Suppose we go into that room and have a long heart-to-heart talk about this terrible contretemps."

II

Ten minutes later Meredith was also bolt-eyed and a little dazed. The forceful tide of Mrs. Hagge-Smith's monologue broke over him and took his breath away. He sensed his peril at once. He was up against a woman possessed of that awful virtue, "a strong personality". But his long professional experience had bred in him an almost superhuman tolerance in dealing with voluble female witnesses. He refused to be overwhelmed by this momentous avalanche of words. After all, amid all this verbal chaff, might there not be concealed a few grains of wheat?

Mentally he catalogued the salient points of Mrs. Hagge-Smith's robust discourse.

The tragedy had been a surprise and shock to all of them.

To none more than Mr. Penpeti and herself.

Mr. Penpeti would now be called upon to shoulder the responsibilities of high office.

There was to be a meeting of the Inmost Temple that evening to elect the new High Prophet.

There was no doubt that Mr. Penpeti would be elected.

She had long suspected that Penelope Parker and Eustace Mildmann had been "platonically interested in each other".

But the subterfuge adopted by Mr. Mildmann to gain entrance into her house was not only a very uncharacteristic piece of behaviour, but certainly suggested that there had been some sort of quarrel between them.

"So she obviously hasn't yet learnt of the existence of those letters," thought Meredith. "Or of the manner in which they were to be used."

She was convinced that the Movement was passing through a phase of "adverse astrological influences". There had been the theft of a valuable piece of altar decoration from the Welworth temple.

There was the attempt on the life of Mr. Mildmann's chauffeur when returning from a dance. It was a strange coincidence that at the time Arkwright had also "very insultingly adopted the habiliments of our dear Prophet-in-Waiting".

But beyond that point Meredith refused to let Mrs. Hagge-Smith continue with her monologue. Here, suddenly, unexpectedly, was the grain of wheat for which he had been hoping. Curtly he dammed up the boisterous flow of Mrs. Hagge-Smith's speech with:

"When and where was this attempt made on Arkwright's life?"

"I beg your pardon?" Mrs. Hagge-Smith was dumbfounded. She was unaccustomed to interruption once started on a verbal gallop. She eyed the inspector with undisguised hostility. Meredith repeated his question. "But does it really matter?" asked Alicia. "It was several months ago now and it was only poor Eustace's chauffeur. Nobody of any importance. I'm sure you don't want to be troubled with such irrelevances."

Meredith flatly disagreed.

"It's essential that I should know the details." Mrs. Hagge-Smith supplied them in a surly voice and tried once more to get into her stride. Again Meredith drew her up snorting. "There was, I presume, a police enquiry into the matter."

"Yes."

"But no arrest?"

"No."

"Do you recall who handled the case?"

"No, really I…oh yes, of course…an Inspector Dubby or some such curious name. Or was it Duffy? Yes—Inspector Duffy of the Welworth Borough Police."

Meredith made a note.

"Now tell me, madam, have you any ideas about this unfortunate affair?"

"Emphatically," boomed Alicia. "There can be only one explanation. A suicide pact. I think Mr. Mildmann had some form of hypnotic influence over poor dear Penelope and that he willed her to do this dreadful thing. I imagine that she had given him his congé and, realising that she was lost to him, he mesmerised her into taking the poison. In the fond belief and hope," added Mrs. Hagge-Smith, "that they would meet and communicate in perfect amity on a Higher Plane."

"Had Mr. Mildmann any enemies?" asked Meredith practically.

"What a ridiculous question!" exclaimed Mrs. Hagge-Smith. "It's quite exhausting enough to find out who are one's *own* enemies. How can I conceivably give you a list of poor Eustace's? Hostility is also a matter of degree. Dislike and hatred are poles apart."

Meredith smiled and nobly curbed his impatience.

"Let me put it another way. Was there anybody in his immediate circle who might have had cause to dislike him?"

"At times *I* had cause to dislike him!" retorted Mrs. Hagge-Smith. "Over matters of policy and even theology he often irritated me to distraction. I know Mr. Penpeti felt exactly the same. We represent, shall I say, the progressive element in Cooism. Poor Eustace was a reactionary. And then, of course, that great overgrown boy of his, Terence... he and his father were always at loggerheads. Though in this case my sympathies were all with Eustace. A rebellious, ill-mannered, gross young man. He had the temerity to make love to my secretary. Eustace soon put a stop to that!"

"Is this young lady still with you?" Mrs. Hagge-Smith nodded. "Then perhaps the lad is still in love with her?"

"Of course he is!" said Alicia shortly. "But since Eustace and I have forbidden him to see the girl, I've no doubt his infatuation will die a natural death."

"I see. And what about Miss Parker?"

"I can't imagine anybody disliking poor dear Penelope. I think she was adored by nearly everybody. I, myself, found her a trifle vapid, a little too disorganised…but a sweet and charming disposition." Mrs. Hagge-Smith added, with what might be described as "an aristocratic leer": "Men, apparently, found her highly desirable."

"She sounded like an estate agent," thought Meredith, "describing an item of house property!"

III

But it had been an interesting interview. So Terence had been up against his father, had he? In love with a girl, whom his father had refused to let him see. A dangerous policy in the case of a hot-headed youngster who was probably in the throes of his first wild infatuation. Was there motive here? Yes, possibly. But according to Arkwright his employer's visit to the Dower House was a secret shared only between them. Then, if Terence were desperate enough to want his father out of the way, how could he have anticipated that visit? Well, as a member of the North Lodge ménage, he might have overheard his father talking with the chauffeur. And Penelope Parker? He had no grudge against her. Quite. But she may well have been a mere victim of circumstances. Terence had crept into the house, poisoned the sherry and *both* she and Mildmann had taken the rap.

"But whoa!" thought Meredith wryly. "This won't do. Mildmann was a strict T.T. Terence would have known that. Pointless to dope the sherry decanter when he knew that, in normal circumstances, his father wouldn't have touched the stuff."

And yet—that hatless lurker by the lily-pond in the belted rain-coat. Was that by any chance Terence Mildmann? Tall, well-built, with fairish hair—well, that certainly footed the bill. On the night of the murder, however, he claimed to have been in Downchester with the housekeeper. They had left the North Lodge shortly after lunch and not returned until eleven o'clock. Exactly! But, in the circumstances, wouldn't it be as well to check up on these details?

Meredith decided to drop in at the North Lodge on his way back to The Leaning Man. He could at the same time warn young Mildmann that an autopsy would have to be performed and that the ambulance would doubtless call to remove his father's body.

On reaching the North Lodge he decided first to interview the housekeeper. It was his idea to get her story about that alleged visit to Downchester and then check up with Terence afterwards. Mrs. Summers, herself, answered his ring and, at his request, preceded him into the little parlour. Once inside Meredith closed the door and began his cross-examination.

It did not take him ten seconds to realise that Mrs. Summers was nervous. Her replies at first were so vague and evasive that Meredith's suspicions were quickly aroused. He began to pin her down to more circumstantial details. What time had they arrived in Downchester? About three-fifteen off the Tappin Mallet bus. What had they done on their arrival? She had gone off to do some shopping. And Terence? Mrs. Summers didn't know. He said he was going to take a look round the book-shops. Had they met for tea? Mrs. Summers hesitated. Meredith repeated the question. Mrs. Summers admitted that they had, by arrangement, at four-thirty. Where? Again the hesitation—then finally: "Patty's Parlour in Castle Street." And after that? Oh, they had taken a walk down to the river-bank and eventually gone on to the theatre where there was a good variety bill. Had Mrs. Summers got a programme? Yes. No. She wasn't sure if she'd kept it. Then she suddenly made up her mind and produced it from her hand-bag, which was on the book-case.

"May I keep this a moment?" asked Meredith.

"Yes, of course."

"Good. Now will you ask Mr. Mildmann to come in and have a word with me?"

"But I don't...I'm sure he..." Mrs. Summers appeared confused. "Oh, very well then—I'll fetch him."

"Good!" reiterated Meredith, concealing a small, malicious smile.

The moment the housekeeper had retired, he closely scanned the contents of the programme, noting carefully the various items that were billed. Then, as Terence came in, he slipped the programme quickly into his pocket. After Meredith had explained about the autopsy, he began his cross-examination. The boy's answers came readily and certainly corroborated all that the housekeeper had already told him. Then they came to the show in the evening.

"A good programme?" asked Meredith casually.

"Yes—jolly good."

"I see that John Merridew, the Yorkshire comedian was on."

"Yes, he was jolly good, too."

"And Lou Shelton's band?"

"Oh jolly good. Really top-notch."

"And what about the juggler chap on the bicycle? I can't recall his name at the moment. But I've seen his act once or twice at the Coliseum."

Terence appeared to hesitate a second or so, then he was off again on his eulogistic gallop.

"Yes—he was frightfully clever, Inspector. Wonderful balance and all that. Jolly good show!"

Meredith smiled. He pulled out the programme and handed it to Terence.

"Just cast your eye through that, will you?"

Terence did so, and when he had fully absorbed the contents of the programme he reddened violently.

"Well?" rapped out the inspector.

"I say…that's queer…I seem to have got a bit muddled. The chap on the bicycle—"

"Quite!" cut in Meredith. "There *was* no juggler on a bicycle. Curious, eh? I mean, curious that you should have thought a non-existent artist so thundering good." His voice hardened. "Now look here, young fellow, you may as well come clean about this. You didn't go over to Downchester yesterday afternoon with Mrs. Summers. You didn't see a single item in this variety show. You merely glanced at this programme when Mrs. Summers got back and learnt up a number of details from her to suggest that you made this visit. Unfortunately I succeeded in catching you out first ball of the over. It's true, isn't it?" Terence looked down blankly at his bare and brawny knees, shifting uncomfortably in his seat. He said nothing. Meredith went on sternly: "For your own sake I advise you to tell me just why you didn't go to Downchester and what you did during yesterday afternoon and evening."

"I didn't want to go," muttered Terence sulkily. "So I just stayed back and mooned about the park."

"For about nine hours, eh? In the drizzle!"

"Well, I don't see why not. I like walking in the rain."

"Were you wearing a rain-coat?"

"Of course."

"Could I see the coat?"

"Yes, I suppose so. It seems a dappy request but you know best. It's in the hall. I'll fetch it."

A few seconds later Meredith knew that he had solved at least one outstanding problem in the case. Big, broad-shouldered, fair-haired, wearing a belted rain-coat! But what the devil *was* Terence Mildmann doing by the pond? Bluntly he posed the question. For the second time Terence reddened and remained stubbornly silent.

Meredith warned him:

"You realise that if you refuse to give your reasons for all this queer behaviour, young fellow, the police are bound to suspect the worst. I happen to know you were up against your father. That pond is only a few hundred yards from the Dower House. You see the implication?"

Terence sprang up, goggling.

"Good Lord, Inspector!—you're not suggesting that I had anything to do with my father's death? You can't be such an outsized cad as that!"

"Oh, can't I!" said Meredith grimly. "Unless you'll be frank with me, I'm bound to suspect anything. Why the devil can't you come clean about all this?"

"Because…because I can't," said Terence weakly. "I was just mooning about—that's all. Killing time. I didn't want my father to know that I hadn't been to Downchester. I had to hang about until Mrs. Summers returned. You see that?"

"In a way—yes," admitted Meredith. "But what did you tell Mrs. Summers in the first place? You must have offered her some excuse."

"Naturally. I told her how much I loathed buses and tea-shops and stuffy theatres and all the rest of it. I told her I wanted to go for a thumping long walk. And, as she's a jolly good sport, of course, she understood."

"Just that?" commented Meredith.

"Just *that*," echoed Terence with a challenging look.

IV

As Meredith left the lodge, Sid Arkwright came down the track that led to the barn. With Mrs. Hagge-Smith's evidence fresh in his mind, the inspector took the opportunity to question him about the shooting incident at Welworth. It was in this manner that Meredith first came to hear about the Man in the Teddy-Bear Coat.

"Was Inspector Duffy convinced that this man had been responsible for the shooting?" asked Meredith.

"I can't say, sir. He naturally didn't tell me much. Anyway, there was never an arrest, so I reckon the inspector got bogged down and had to call it a day. He seemed pretty certain that I got winged in the leg because I happened to be dressed like Mr. Penpeti."

"Interesting. And this man, I take it, has never been seen again?"

Sid looked round quickly, drew Meredith a little further into the barn, and said in a low voice:

"That's just where you're wrong, sir. He has been seen again."

"Oh? By whom?"

"Me," said Sid.

"You? When?"

"About ten days ago, sir, before the convention actually started."

"Where?"

"Well, believe it or not, sir, I'm damned if it wasn't in that little upstairs sitting-room where Miss Parker was found last night."

"The devil it was!" exclaimed Meredith, profoundly interested. "Why the deuce didn't you tell me this before?"

"Because I couldn't see that it mattered," answered Sid simply.

"And how was it you came to be in that particular room?" demanded Meredith.

Sid gave a lengthy and detailed explanation of the whole matter, the reason for his visit, his attempt to recover the letters for his employer, his startling encounter with the man in question. Meredith demanded a description. Tall, broad-shouldered, middle-aged, obviously educated. And his hair? Oh, darkish, turning grey at the sides.

There and then, while Sid respectfully waited, Meredith drew up the following memorandum:

> *Man seen by Menthu-Mut—Tall, broad-shouldered, fair-haired, belted rain-coat, hatless.*
> *Man seen passing gardener's cottage—Tall, well-built, of middle-age, gentlemanly, soft hat, tweed suit.*
> *Man seen by Arkwright in girl's room—Tall, broad-shouldered, of middle-age, educated, darkish hair.*

"One other point, Arkwright," went on Meredith. "Was this fellow wearing his teddy-bear overcoat when you entered the room?"

"No, sir. It was lying on the sofa."

"Did you notice what sort of suit he was wearing?"

"Yes—rough tweed affair, it was. Expensive-looking."

"What about his hat?"

"Brown tweed cap, sir. That was on the sofa near his coat."

Meredith closed his notebook and slipped it into his pocket. He took up his well-worn attaché-case which he had set down on the running-board of the Daimler.

"Well, thank heaven you had the good sense to tell me about this, Arkwright. It may have an important bearing on my line of investigation." Meredith moved towards the door. "Well, I won't keep you any longer."

In a flash Sid was after him.

"Half a mo', Inspector. There's something else I want to tell you."

"Well?"

"It was about a statement I made this morning. It come to me afterwards that I hadn't been quite as exact as I should have been, sir."

"Oh?"

"No, sir. I said as the only other person besides Miss Parker 'oo knew about them love-letters was Mr. Penpeti. That's not true. I didn't recall this fac' until after you'd left, Inspector. It was last Saturday week, just after closing-time at The Leaning Man…I was coming back down the Tappin Mallet road when…"

And there and then Sid told the inspector of Penpeti's clandestine meeting with the unknown man in the moonlit lane. For the second time Meredith whipped out his note-book and made a series of detailed notes. In particular he found the scraps of conversation overheard by Arkwright by no means the least interesting part of this fresh evidence. Who was this man? Why had Penpeti elected to meet him? And what hold had this mysterious person over the man who was about to be elected High Prophet of this queer religious sect?

By the time he left the barn, Meredith's head was full of new and startling theories about the crime. He decided to have a meal at the inn and spend the rest of the evening up in the privacy of his bedroom, trying to make sense out of these apparently unrelated odds and ends of evidence.

Chapter XVII

Pow-Wow with Penpeti

I

Seated in the commodious but rickety basket-chair in his oak-beamed bedroom after a really excellent meal, Meredith opened his notebook and began his first unhurried analysis of the facts.

Of two things he now felt sure. (1) Terence Mildmann had been lurking near that pond. He was there for some nefarious purpose, since it was evident that he was hedging on the real reason for not accompanying Mrs. Summers to Downchester. (2) The man whom Arkwright had met up in the Parker girl's room some ten days before was the same man seen by the gardener and his wife passing their cottage window shortly before ten the previous night. True, on that second occasion, he hadn't been wearing his teddy-bear overcoat and he had evidently changed his tweed cap for a shooting-hat; but for the rest the two descriptions matched up perfectly. And further, wasn't it safe to assume that it was this man Hilda had heard upstairs and later in the hall? And further still, wasn't this the man who had taken a crack at Arkwright in Welworth, when the lad was returning from a fancy-dress dance dressed as Penpeti?

At once Meredith's deft mind pounced on another possibility. This man had made an attempt on Arkwright's life, thinking him to be Penpeti. *Did it mean that poor Mildmann had lost his life for the same reason?*

By heaven, it was a plausible assumption! Very plausible! Mildmann had been poisoned, not because he was Mildmann, but because the murderer had believed him to be Penpeti. For some reason this mysterious intruder had a grudge against Penpeti. In the light of all the evidence to date, a very suggestive line of thought. This man was obviously well-acquainted with Penelope Parker. He knew all about her habits and his way about the Dower House. He had known her, without doubt, at Welworth. Was he *more* than a mere friend or acquaintance? Was he, by any chance, her lover? Or more precisely, had he at one time been her lover? An exalted position he had held in the girl's life until Penpeti came along and threw a spanner into the works.

Meredith grinned. The same old motive—jealousy. The same old triangular set-up—two men, one woman. But in this case the most logical of all the theories he could put up. Accept this relationship between the three of them and so much was explained away. The shooting affair in Welworth; the secret visits to the Dower House; perhaps the murder itself. Doubtless Inspector Duffy could help him to make a more precise assessment of this relationship, for during his investigations at Welworth, Duffy had probably unearthed far more information than Arkwright realised.

Well, The Leaning Man was on the telephone. So was the Borough H.Q. of the Welworth Garden City Police. So what was he waiting for? If he wanted the best information—Duffy had it!

Ten minutes later Meredith was speaking with Inspector Duffy. He had left H.Q., but the sergeant-on-duty had given him the number of Duffy's private residence. Luckily the inspector was in.

He talked well and he talked a lot. A nice stream-lined summary of what he called the "Mayblossom Cut Case". And when some twenty minutes later Meredith rang off, he knew he had been barking up the right tree. This middle-aged, well-set-up gentleman *had* visited Penelope Parker, late one night, at her Welworth house. In fact, almost directly after the shooting incident in the Cut! Penpeti, too, had been seen by Duffy himself, paying the girl a visit. Good heavens, yes! It was all lining-up a treat. Duffy was posting off the dossier of the case that night.

"Right!" thought Meredith, now brimful of mental energy. "Accept two facts. This man in the teddy-bear coat—we'll call him 'Ted' for short—is the murderer. Mildmann was poisoned because Ted thought he was actually Penpeti. Now how does this fit in with the circumstances surrounding the case? First, the murderer must have seen Mildmann in the guise of Penpeti approaching the Dower House. Otherwise how could he have anticipated his arrival? No point about Ted having overheard any conversation between Arkwright and his employer about the proposed visit. If he'd done that, he'd have known that Mildmann *wasn't* Penpeti. No—somehow he must have spotted the disguised Mildmann coming towards the house. But is this possible? Accept Hilda's evidence and the answer is definitely 'Yes'. It was for this reason that Ted nipped out via the french-windows. Precisely! And if he'd nipped out through the french-windows, he couldn't have nipped back up the stairs and poisoned the sherry. There just wouldn't have been time to do this and get clear before Mildmann was in the room. Besides, the Parker girl wouldn't have stood there quite calmly, while Ted dashed in, doped the sherry and dashed out again. So what? The theory's a dud. Unless, of course, the Parker girl told him that Penpeti was coming to visit her that evening. But, confound it, he wasn't! Only Mildmann dressed as Penpeti. And the girl didn't even know that Mildmann was going to visit her. So that theory also went up in smoke. Just one other possibility, eh? Ted doctored the sherry on the off-chance that, sooner or later, Penpeti would turn up and take a swig of the stuff. Umph—not worth a second thought. Too chancy. Too indefinite. After all, the girl might have taken a drink immediately after Ted's departure. Result—instantaneous death. Body discovered. Sherry found to be poisoned and removed before Penpeti ever came near the damned decanter. So the theory that Ted had murdered Mildmann, thinking him to be Penpeti, was a wash-out. Cul-de-sac! Boomp! Just like that!"

Meredith pattered off on a new scent.

"Suppose Ted's intention was simply to murder the girl and that Mildmann's death was merely an unfortunate P.S. to the main plot? Quite. I've thought of this before. Objection to acceptance? Simply this—if Mildmann's death were accidental, why the devil had he troubled to put on his gloves once inside the Dower House? So I'm back where I started, eh? Mildmann poisoned the sherry in order to kill the girl and then committed suicide. This means that Ted merely sneaked into the house to see Penelope, had a talk with her, crept down the stairs, saw Mildmann approaching the house and cleared out through the french-windows. Ted didn't tamper with the sherry at all. Well, what about it? The most common-sense of all explanations to date. No need to evolve elaborate reasons for the lack of Ted's finger-prints on the decanter. They weren't there for the simple reason that Ted didn't touch the decanter."

Meredith sighed, burrowed deeper into his basket-chair and idly watched his pipe-smoke mounting to the ceiling. So he was back where he had started and progress in the case was, precisely, nil! No—that was wrong. Surely he had now identified and vindicated two persons whom he might have considered as possible suspects—Terence Mildmann and this mysterious friend of Penelope's. Although both had been seen near the locale of the crime on the evening of the double tragedy, neither could, according to the available evidence, be implicated. What Terence *was* doing by that pond at nine o'clock on a wet night, the Lord only knew! Why that other fellow had broken into the Dower House and waylaid the Parker girl...well, the Lord only knew that, too! But the answers to these teasing questions didn't matter a damn. They were quite irrelevant. What mattered was this—it now left Eustace Mildmann as the only possible suspect. And he'd already half-convinced himself that Mildmann *couldn't* have done it. After all, if Mildmann were to be accepted as the murderer, then the motive for the crime was obviously the recovery of the letters. Penelope had refused to hand them over, so Mildmann had slyly poisoned the sherry, persuaded her to take a drink, waited until she collapsed, broken into her desk and removed the letter-case. A drastic bit of skullduggery, to say the least of it, when he could have bound and gagged the girl whilst rifling the desk. So even the motive seemed a thin one. But what followed seemed even more illogical. Having recovered the letters, Mildmann suddenly decided to commit suicide. But, in heaven's name, why? The whole business just didn't add up. Why take such care to leave no finger-prints when, ten minutes after the crime, he knew he'd be a dead man? What had he done with his gloves? Why had he succumbed far more slowly to the effects of the prussic acid than the girl? Yet, unless he had entered the Dower House without intention to murder the girl, why had he carried the poison phial on his person?

"Oh hell!" thought Meredith, suddenly feeling tired and depressed. "Where the deuce do I go from here?"

II

The next morning June came into her own again with a shimmering blue sky and the dew lying late on the grass, with the birds in full song and distant cuckoos calling to each other over a countryside rich with the scent of a new-washed earth and foliage. As Meredith gazed from his wide-open window into the village street below, his overnight depression vanished. After all, hadn't he been expecting a little too much of providence? A complicated case is not to be broken wide open in a mere twenty-four hours. Experience had taught him that a major crime was usually cleared up only after weeks, even months of patient, hum-drum work.

Over a substantial breakfast in the low-ceilinged dining-room Meredith began once more to turn over the circum-stantial evidence and the peculiarly tricky problems which the lay-out of the crime had postulated. Perhaps the most difficult aspect of the case was his inability to state with any conviction just what type of crime he was investigating. Was it a double murder? A murder plus suicide? A double suicide? Or a couple of deaths from misadventure? During the course of the previous day he had reviewed all these possibilities, analysed the pros and cons in each instance and gone to bed with an open mind. There was, however, one set-up he had so far failed to consider. Remiss of him but, in the rush of events, perhaps excusable. It was this. Had Penelope Parker, by any chance, murdered Eustace Mildmann and then taken her own life?

It was a new slant that definitely demanded exploration. Motive? Well, suppose Penelope were violently in love with this queer fish, Penpeti, and suppose it had occurred to her that once Mildmann were out of the way, Penpeti would become the top-side prophet of the Movement? Perhaps the position carried a worth-while stipend, which would put an even keener edge on her motive! And the modus operandi? Well, the poisoning of the sherry must have been more of a spontaneous act than a deliberate piece of malice-aforethought. After all, Penelope didn't know that Mildmann was to visit her that evening. On the other hand there *was* a feasible reconstruction of events.

Mildmann gets into her room by means of the Penpeti trick, and once there demands the return of his somewhat impulsive love-letters. Penelope refuses to hand them over. Whereupon Mildmann draws out his wooden revolver (Arkwright's evidence) and frightens her into revealing where the letters are kept. While he's busy at the desk, Penelope seizes the chance to poison the sherry, suggests in a sporting sort of way that he's the winner and what about having a drink to celebrate his cleverness. Whereupon Mildmann—

Meredith shook his head. Good God! The theory was riddled with holes. He mentally tabulated them. (1) If Penelope were frightened into handing over the letters, she would have saved him the trouble of breaking open her desk by handing him the key. (2) How did she come to have a phial of prussic acid all ready and waiting on her person? (3) Could she have persuaded Mildmann, who was a strict teetotaller, to have joined her in a drink? (4) Finally accepting the above motive, what was the point of taking her own life? Could she have acted with such altruistic fervour even if she were desperately in love with Penpeti? After all, the idea of Penpeti becoming High Prophet would surely include her participation in the event?

Meredith hastily finished his last cup of coffee and lit a cigarette. As he did so, a neat black "sports" swished into the commodious inn-yard and a figure in uniform jumped out. Meredith called out through the open window.

"Sergeant from Chichester, eh?"

"Yes, sorr."

"Good. Come on in. Door there on your left. I'm Inspector Meredith."

One glance at Sergeant O'Hallidan and Meredith knew that Rokeby had picked him a winner. Irish, tough, blue-eyed, broad humorous mouth, and a lilt in his voice that would have made poetry of the telephone directory. The inspector nodded to him to be seated and, since the dining-room was at that moment deserted, he quickly outlined the salient factors in the case. When he had concluded, O'Hallidan chuckled.

"An' it's meself the Sooper has seen fit to send to you in your throuble, sorr. If iver there was a more bemusing case then Oi've to meet it! Accident, suicide, murther—'tis even money on any of 'em. Sure an' it's a case demanding the patience o' Job an' the determination o' Hercules. But, by the Holy, sorr, an' 'tis ourselves that won't rest until we're through with it."

"An echo of my own sentiments, O'Hallidan!" laughed Meredith. "Now I tell you what I—" He suddenly broke off with a warning nod over the sergeant's shoulder. "Tsst! Take a careful look round, Sergeant. This, if I'm not mistaken, is a gentleman in whom we have a very natural interest. Must be staying here. I'd no idea."

Cautiously O'Hallidan edged round in his seat and eyed the eccentric figure that had just occupied a table in a far corner of the room. The bearded, slightly sinister features, the fez and the caftan—he had no difficulty in recognising the man from Meredith's description.

"Will ye take a look at that now!" he said in a hoarse whisper. "If 'tisn't the craytur ye suspect to be in love with the dead girl, sorr. And, by the Holy, 'tis himself looks more like a murtherer than a ladies' man!"

"Well, whatever he looks like," commented Meredith, sotto voce, "I've no doubt by now he's the High Prophet elect of this mumbo-jumbo crowd in the park. I've wanted to have a word with him, and as there's no time like the present…"

Meredith rose and took up his attaché-case. "Stay here a minute. I'll try and get a line on the fellow."

With a casual air the inspector sauntered across the dining-room. Penpeti glanced up sourly as Meredith, with an affable nod, greeted him with:

"Good morning, Mr. Penpeti. I've been hoping to run into you. My name's Meredith. Detective-Inspector Meredith. I've no need to tell you why I'm down here in Tappin Mallet."

"It's easy to imagine," retorted Penpeti, waving Meredith ungraciously into a vacant chair. "A tragic, unsavoury affair. I suppose it's out of order for me to ask if you've made any progress in solving the mystery?"

Meredith grinned.

"Well, I'm not allowed to talk out of turn, you know. Miss Parker was a very close friend of yours, eh, Mr. Penpeti?"

"She was a staunch colleague of mine inside the Movement," corrected Penpeti acidly. "I have, as you can imagine, many close friends inside the Movement."

"Is it premature of me to congratulate you on your promotion? Mrs. Hagge-Smith—hinted to me yesterday—"

Penpeti inclined his head.

"I was informed of the honour late last night after an Extraordinary Meeting of the Inmost Temple. But it grieves me to think that I should have been elected to this high office in such tragic circumstances."

"You've heard, of course, that Mr. Mildmann adopted a disguise in order to get into the Dower House? Miss Parker had, I understand, refused him admittance."

"Yes—I'd heard that."

"And you realise the nature of his disguise?"

"Yes."

"The point I'm trying to make is this, Mr. Penpeti." Meredith had already exchanged his easy friendliness for a more official attitude. He sensed that Penpeti was watchful, on the defensive. "Mr. Mildmann disguised himself to look like you because his chauffeur had found out from the domestic staff at the Dower House that they had orders to admit you without question at any time of the day or night. This rather suggests that Miss Parker *was* a close friend of yours, doesn't it? A *very* close friend. That you had a privileged place in her private life, eh?"

"Well, as a fellow member of the executive committee of—"

Meredith broke in sharply:

"Good heavens, Mr. Penpeti! Why the devil can't you be frank with me? I happen to know that you and Miss Parker were on terms of the greatest intimacy. Why trouble to hedge?"

A fleeting expression of uneasiness crossed Penpeti's swarthy features. He snapped out:

"I really can't see what this has to do with your investigations. May I be allowed to finish my breakfast in peace? I've an extremely busy day in front of me, as you can imagine."

"I'm sorry, Mr. Penpeti. But I can't let anything stand in the way of my duty. I'm investigating a very serious case. Now, on the night of the tragedy, where were you exactly?"

"You're not suggesting—?" began Penpeti with a truculent look.

"I'm not suggesting anything!" commented Meredith. "I

want to know just what you did, say, between the hours of eight and ten last Thursday evening."

"I don't know what you're trying to insinuate, Inspector," sneered Penpeti, "but whatever your suspicions, I'm afraid I must disillusion you. I had dinner as usual at the Manor and left there about ten minutes to nine. I then walked through the park to the Chinese summer-house."

"A minute." Meredith drew out his sketch-map, studied it closely for a second or so and placed his finger on a small blacked-in circle near the point where the main drive forked into the subsidiary drives that led to the Manor and the Dower House respectively. "You mean this building just here, eh?"

Penpeti glanced at the map and nodded.

"Mrs. Hagge-Smith has had the place converted into a temple. During the convention we have organised what we call an Unbroken Chain of Meditation. Members have pledged themselves to attend the temple and give themselves up to an hour's meditation on certain aspects of our faith."

"You mean a roster has been drawn up for the whole fortnight of the convention?"

"Precisely. And it so happened that one of my promised hours of attendance occurred between nine and ten on Thursday evening."

"So you left the Manor, walked down the drive to the temple and stayed there until ten o'clock?" Penpeti nodded. "You were alone in the temple?"

"No. We have our official times of attendance but anybody is free to make use of the temple at any time of the day or night. As far as I can recall there were at least half-a-dozen other members present when I arrived that evening. Some only stayed for a short period—others were still at their meditations when I was officially relieved at ten by my successor on the roster."

"From whom did you take over at nine o'clock?"

Penpeti hesitated.

"Really, Inspector, I can't be expected to…No—wait a minute. It was a member from one of our north London temples—a Mr. Abingdon. But, if you consider all these details relevant to your investigations, why not consult the official list? I'm certain our camp-commandant, Mr. Boot, would only be too happy to assist you."

"Thanks, Mr. Penpeti." Meredith rose. "A most useful pow-wow. You're staying at The Leaning Man for the duration of the conference, eh?"

"Yes."

"Well, I'm glad you've been so frank and concise in your information."

"Is there any point," asked Penpeti with a sardonic smile, "in being otherwise, Inspector? I have, over a long period of time, been able to develop considerable psychical powers. But I can assure you that I've had no cause to exercise those powers during the last ten minutes. My common-or-garden savoir faire has been more than sufficient to reveal to me just what was in your mind. When you sat down at this table, you rather suspected that I might have had some connection with the tragic events at the Dower House. But I warned you that you would be disillusioned. Good morning, Inspector."

III

Once outside, seated in the police-car, Meredith said:

"Drive towards the park, O'Hallidan. When we find a nice secluded spot, draw in off the road. I want to consider our immediate plan of action."

Some five minutes later, O'Hallidan swung the car on to the broad verge under the shade of some overhanging elms and shut off the engine. Meredith pulled out his pouch and slowly filled his pipe.

"A queer devil," he observed. "A pretty cool and callous customer, too, when you come to think of it."

"Mr. Penpeti, sorr?"

Meredith nodded.

"According to Arkwright's evidence Penpeti was in on this ramp to blacken Mildmann's character by making public these letters of his. I'll bet you a penny to the Bank of England that he put the Parker girl up to that nasty little game. Yet to hear him talk just now you'd think butter wouldn't melt in his mouth! Has it occurred to you, Sergeant, that it's Penpeti who has benefited most from Mildmann's death? Particularly if this new office of his carries a good salary."

"Oi suppose it's not the murtherer you're making him out to be, sorr?" asked O'Hallidan with a knowing glance.

"I admit that idea was chasing through my mind when I questioned him just now. But he seems to have got his alibi all right. A seamless alibi, eh?"

"But ye've only got his word to go on, sorr."

"No—you're wrong there. Arkwright told me when I first interviewed him that Mildmann had chosen the time and date of his visit to coincide with Penpeti's official period of attendance in that temple. As Arkwright said, they couldn't risk Penpeti showing up at the Dower House that night or accompanying Miss Parker back from the Manor. For all that, we'll check up at once. Penpeti mentioned the camp-commandant. Suppose we make his H.Q. our first port of call?"

"Sure an' you're still not convinced, sorr."

"Frankly, Sergeant, I'm *not*! I don't see how Penpeti could have murdered either Mildmann or the girl. In the latter case I don't see why he should *want* to, considering that he was obviously very friendly with her. But I've got a sort of hunch about that fellow. And my hunch tells me that he's a rotten egg. I mentioned that queer meeting of his with an unknown man when I first primed you with the main facts of the case?" O'Hallidan nodded. "Well, the few phrases Arkwright was able to overhear are suggestive of shady business. No doubt about it." Meredith drew out his notebook and consulted it. "Yes—here we are. *'Parker girl's all right, though...' 'Mildmann will take the rap'* and so on. That's all in reference to the letters, of course. Needs absolutely no explanation. But now listen to this. *'Asking you to wait a few weeks...must have patience...pay you out then O.K.' 'Safe bet, I assure you...in clover if things go...'* Not much to go on, but surely enough from which to draw a few plausible conclusions?"

"'Tis blackmail you're hinting at?"

"Looks remarkably like it."

"With Penpeti in the divil of a tight corner?"

"Exactly."

"And himself onable to pay the blood-money at all an' his blackmailer a-turning the screw."

"A situation," pointed out Meredith, "that he hoped to rectify the moment he was promoted to Mildmann's position in this confounded Movement. Which suggests, O'Hallidan, that this High Prophetship, or whatever they call it, carries a money prize, eh?"

"Sure an' that seems the way of it, sorr."

"And then there's another thing," went on Meredith. "You notice the wording of Penpeti's phrases? The use of the colloquialisms *'O.K.', 'Safe bet',* and *'In clover'* and so on. Well, that wasn't the kind of phraseology he used a few minutes back. If anything, I thought he was rather pedantic. As for that touch of the foreign accent, Arkwright said he seemed to have dropped it entirely. The point is this, when in private he appears to use this slangy sort of speech. In other words, the man's a poseur, a fake, two-faced. With Penpeti the Prophet as the least natural of his two selves." Meredith pushed away his notebook. "At any rate, we're now going to check up on the fellow's movements and find out a little more about this office of High Prophet. Suppose you drive me now to the camp-commandant."

Chapter XVIII

The Poison Puzzle

I

During the last few weeks there had been a profound change in Hansford Boot—not only a physical but a psychological change. The threat of exposure which Penpeti held over his head was a Damoclean sword that had undermined his sense of security and screwed up his nerves to breaking-point. He paid his blood-money without a murmur. Quite. But the threat remained. At any minute Penpeti might turn ugly. He might go to the police. And from that instant he would be doomed. There was no eluding the fact that it would mean a stretch in "stir", probably a long stretch. The useful, interesting, respectable life he was now leading would be over and done with. He'd never recapture it.

It was easy to imagine Hansford's feelings, therefore, when Meredith, followed by the uniformed sergeant, walked into his office as camp-commandant. He scrambled to his feet with a little grunt of alarm and stood facing the two officials with an expression of the wildest anxiety.

"Morning," he jerked out in his peculiar shorthand English. "Anything I can do? Something you want? An enquiry to make? Eh?"

Meredith introduced himself and quietly explained the reason for his visit. Hansford appeared to relax a little, though Meredith had been quick to note his reaction to their sudden appearance. But his readiness to help was undeniable. In no time he had produced the "Chain of Meditation" roster for Meredith's inspection and sent a runner round the camp to find Mr. Abingdon, whose hour of meditation had preceded Penpeti's, and Miss Mummery, who had taken over from him at ten o'clock. While the messenger was away, Meredith wasted no time in digging out a little more information.

"You're on the executive committee of this movement, Mr. Boot?"

"I am."

"Then you can probably tell me all I want to know about this office of High Prophet. Does it carry a stipend?"

"It does."

"How much?"

"Considerable amount. D'you want it exact? *Sub rosa*, really. But if you insist…"

"I'm afraid I must."

"Five thousand a year."

Meredith whistled.

"Five thousand—phew! And what about the position originally held by Penpeti—was it an honorary one?"

"Five hundred," said Hansford shortly.

"I see. So Penpeti has gained considerably through Mildmann's death?"

"To the tune of four thousand five hundred a year. Exactly four thousand five hundred more than he's worth."

"You don't like the fellow, eh?"

"Don't trust him. Never have. Ambitious. Hypocritical. Cunning."

Meredith nodded but made no comment. Inwardly he was thinking that Boot's assessment of Penpeti's character ran counter to his own. And if Penpeti were two-faced and all that he appeared to be, then, with such a financial gain in the offing, he might well have poisoned Mildmann. The motive was there. But what about the time-factor?

With the arrival of Mr. Abingdon and Miss Mummery, however, Meredith's suspicion fell flat on its face. Abingdon swore that Penpeti had arrived at the Chinese temple at nine o'clock. Miss Mummery swore that she had taken over from Penpeti at ten. Both claimed that several other members were in the temple at the time.

"So that it would have been impossible for Mr. Penpeti to have left the temple between the hours of nine and ten without his absence being noticed?"

Both witnesses agreed that it would have been utterly impossible. Abingdon went on:

"But why not question Miss Minnybell? I understand she came into the temple shortly after Mr. Penpeti arrived and stayed there until Miss Mummery took over. I warn you, Inspector, she's a most extraordinary little woman. But observant. Extremely so."

Meredith turned to Boot.

"Could you send somebody to find Miss Minnybell. I want to make quite sure about this point."

And when, some ten minutes later, Miss Minnybell arrived, Meredith received final proof that Penpeti was not the wanted man. Miss Minnybell was at her most excited and voluble. It was a long straggling tale, pitted with irrelevances, but too full of circumstantial detail to be anything but true. She had, so she said, chanced to be outside the Manor when Penpeti had left the place after dinner. She had, in fact, followed him down the drive to the Chinese summer-house. Once there she had decided to enter, and she had chanced to stay there until it was time for him to be relieved at the end of his official period of meditation. Then she had chanced to follow him half-way down the drive towards the North Lodge, at which point she had turned aside to the Ladies' Compound.

"There seems to be a very generous element of chance in your movements on Thursday evening," commented Meredith with a twinkle. "You're quite sure it *was* chance, Miss Minnybell? You weren't following Mr. Penpeti for any specific reason, eh?"

Miss Minnybell suddenly emitted a sharp little whinny of astonishment.

"Oh, how clever of you, Constable! How very clever of you! I thought it was my own little secret. But I see it's no use trying to keep any little secrets from you. In fact—no really, I think it would be foolish of me to do so. I ought to have thought of this before."

"Of what?" demanded Meredith, amused yet puzzled.

"Why the law will protect me, of course." She lowered her voice and drew Meredith away from the others into a far corner of the little marquee. "The fact is, Constable, my life is in danger! At any moment now he may make up his mind to strike! He's only awaiting the opportunity until I'm off my guard and then—"

Meredith broke in:

"A moment, Miss Minnybell. Let's get this straight. Who will strike?"

"Why Ali Hamed, of course. I thought, perhaps, you'd realised."

"Ali How-much?" shot out Meredith, astonished.

"But surely you've guessed that Mr. Penpeti's not his real name? Oh dear me, Constable, I felt sure you'd guessed the whole story. He's really Ali Hamed, you know. And I have to watch him. I have to watch him very, very closely. Yes indeed, for months now I've..."

And bit by bit the whole fantastic tale was unrolled. Chancing to catch the inspector's bewildered glance during this gabbled recital, Hansford tapped his forehead meaningly and nodded towards Miss Minnybell. However, when she had at length concluded, Meredith assured her that she had no further cause to worry. The police would now take the whole matter in hand. He commended her on her sensible decision to place the whole affair in the hands of the law. Then, gently, Meredith dismissed her.

"Phew!" he exclaimed, mopping his brow.

"'Tis fey she is an' no mistake, sorr," observed O'Hallidan.

"Borderline case," explained Hansford. "Quite harmless. Lives at Welworth. Well-known character there."

"Do you think her evidence about following Penpeti is reliable?" asked Meredith.

Hansford nodded. Already he had regained his self-possession, aware that on this occasion, at any rate, the police had not come to "pick him up."

"Certainly I do. I've noticed it myself. Acting like Penpeti's shadow. Thought it odd. But knowing how it was..." Hansford lifted his shoulders.

"Well, thanks for your assistance," said Meredith, edging towards the entrance. "Come on, Sergeant."

II

Barely had the two officials left the tent when O'Hallidan exclaimed:

"Sure an' there's somebody wanting to see us by the look of it, sorr. In the divil of a hurry, too."

Meredith followed the line of his outstretched arm and saw a figure advancing rapidly down the drive, waving wildly to attract attention. A second or so later, Meredith recognised the gardener from the Dower House cottage.

"Hullo—what the deuce do you want?" he asked.

"You, Oi reckon, surr," he said breathlessly. "'Tis something that's come to my notice. To do with that little talk we had yesterday afternoon over to the Dower House. And in case you don't catch on, Oi'm 'Erbert 'Uskings, the gardener at—"

"Oh I recognised you all right. What's the trouble? Suppose we stroll towards the Dower House while you tell me. Too many people about here."

As they set off over the springy turf beneath the shade of the great oaks and elms, Huskings began to talk.

"'Tis this way, surr. Last night down to the White Harte at Brocklebye chaps got a-talking natural like about this y'ere to-do at the Dower House. Seems they all got h-ideas as to 'oo dun it and why they dun it. Oi reckon we can take that with a darn good pinch o' salt, o' course. But one thing Oi did 'ear which struck me as h'odd. Chap named Charlie Bates—cowman up at Major Dobells 'e is—was going 'ome by the road south o' the park, see? Tidy dark night 'twas as you know. Well, Charlie suddenly walks slap into a car what had been parked off on the road-edge. No lights on, 'e said, an' nobody in it. Anyways, thinkin' it a bit queer, Charlie strikes a match or two an' has a good look-see. Stanmobile Eight, 'e says it was—saloon. Maybe you don't know, but there's a bit of a wood edging that stretch o' the road. Well, Charlie suddenly 'ears somebody blunderin' through that there wood, an' 'e crouches back under some 'azel bushes to see what's cookin'. Well, to cut a long story short, chap crashes through the 'edge and makes for the car with a small pocket-torch in his 'and. Charlie 'ad a good view of 'im afore 'e druv off. There weren't no mistake about it, Oi reckon, surr. 'Twas same chap as me an' Ruth seed pass our cottage a-Thursday night. Shooting 'at an' no coat an' everything."

"And a very useful piece of information, too," exclaimed Meredith, with a nod of approval. "Now what time was this? Did your friend happen to say?"

"Oi asked 'im the very same question myself. Just after ten, 'e reckoned. An' that, surr, fits in pretty tidy with what we already knows!" Huskings' Sussex burr took on a note of triumph. "Ar! An' that's not all, surr!"

"Well?"

"Charlie's a likely lad. Bin a Boy Scout 'e 'as. 'E chanced to notice the number o' that there car, 'e did!" Huskings drew out a grubby dog's-eared envelope. "Took it down there an' then in the White Harte, surr. AHL-2414. Aye, that's it right 'nuf. Smart lad 'is Charlie Bates!"

III

Twenty minutes later, ringing from the Dower House, Meredith was in touch with the Car Registration Department of the County Offices at Hertford. His request was simple. He wanted the name and address of the owner of car number AHL-2414. Hertford promised to do their best.

"As you know, sir," the clerk pointed out, "we can't guarantee any result. The car may have changed hands since its original registration here. Or the owner may now be living in another county, in which case he'll no longer be applying to us for a renewal of licence. Sorry, Inspector, but if your luck's in I'll ring you back in half-an-hour."

Barely had Meredith turned from the 'phone, when O'Hallidan, who had been waiting by the front-entrance of the house, came in to report that a despatch-rider had just arrived from the Yard.

"Good!" exclaimed Meredith. "That'll be the report from the police analyst. Sign for the receipt of the package, Sergeant, and tell the constable he can report back to Chichester."

A few minutes later Meredith was devouring the analyst's report with unconcealed eagerness. O'Hallidan watched him with a speculative eye. Suddenly Meredith snapped his fingers and slapped the report down on the hall table.

"Well, I'll be—!"

"It's something ye didn't anticipate, sorr?"

"You've said it, Sergeant! Something totally unexpected and, to my mind, completely inexplicable. I asked Luke Spears, the chief analyst at the Yard, to make an analysis of the contents of the decanter and the liquid residue in the two glasses. This is his answer." Meredith snatched up the typewritten sheet and read: "*'Conclusive tests show that the amount of prussic acid in solution in the two glasses was equal—in each case a high concentration of HCN being present. In the case of the decanter, however, a far weaker concentration of the acid was noticeable. It appears, therefore, that the two glasses were not filled from the decanter; or, if so, an extra dose of acid had been added after the solution had been poured out. There is little doubt that the poisoned sherry in the glasses would have been sufficient to bring about an instantaneously fatal effect. That in the decanter, however, was diluted enough to have given the victim a fair chance of recovery if medical treatment were available within a reasonable period of time.'* Well, O'Hallidan, what the devil are we to make of that? A further complication, eh? I just can't fathom it."

"An' it's myself that can't make head or tail of it either, sorr. But 'tis most likely as the analyst suggests—an extra dose o' the prussic acid was added after the weaker solution o' the poisoned sherry had been poured out."

"But, in heaven's name, why?" demanded Meredith with a flash of irritation. "Why trouble to poison the sherry in the decanter at all, when the acid was to be poured *direct* into the glasses? It just doesn't add up."

They fell silent for a moment, wrestling with this queer unexpected twist in the evidence. Suddenly O'Hallidan observed:

"Sure an' there's one ither way it might have happened."

"And that?"

"P'what if one of the poisoned glasses was poured into the decanter, sorr? Each o' the glasses would then contain a residue o' equal strength but the decanter, being half-full o' sherry, would then contain a far weaker solution."

"Good God, Sergeant! I believe you've got something there. It's certainly a possible explanation. But I can't for the life of me see why it was done. If Mildmann had poisoned the girl, and wanted to suggest that he had poisoned himself and then disappeared, it might make sense. But Mildmann happens to be dead and we *know* that he died of prussic acid poisoning. It just doesn't work out. On the other hand—"

The telephone on the nearby table began to ring stridently. Meredith snatched up the receiver.

"Hullo—yes? So my luck's in, eh? Splendid! Half-a-minute—I'll make a note. John Keith Dudley, The Grove, Bridge Street, Hitchin. O.K.—yes. I've got that. Most useful. Thanks. Good-bye." As Meredith hung up, he swung round, elated, on O'Hallidan. "Well, that's something on the credit side. Hertford have traced the owner of that car. I'll get on to the Hitchin police at once and get them to take a statement." He was already dialling exchange. "Perhaps if we get a line on this mysterious gentleman, we shall be half-way to solving the rest of our problems. Hullo! Hullo! Exchange? Give me the Hitchin police will you? No—I don't know the number. All right, ring me back the moment you're through. It's an urgent police call."

Chapter XIX

A Young Lady Gives Evidence

I

The moment Meredith had concluded his long and detailed call to Inspector Baker of the Hitchin police, he set out to walk from the Dower House to The Leaning Man. As in the case of Rokeby the day before, he had sent O'Hallidan ahead in the car. Once more he was anxious to do a little hard and solitary thinking.

The biggest jolt he had received since the case opened had been handed to him that morning by Luke Spears. Weak solution of the prussic acid in the decanter. Concentrated solution in the glasses. Why? Well, more and more, it could be assumed that the set-up of the double tragedy was far more complicated than he had originally supposed. The mystery surrounding the tray of drinks seemed insoluble. It wasn't merely a question of *who* had poisoned the sherry, but *how* they had doctored it. O'Hallidan's theory that one glass of strongly poisoned sherry had been emptied back into the unpoisoned sherry in the decanter was full of good sense. But why had the murderer done this? What was he to gain by it? There must be a reason for such a crazy action. If so, what was it? Exactly. What? Meredith gave it up. The mystery, so far, *did* seem insoluble.

His next consideration was Terence Mildmann. That he had withheld his true reason for not accompanying Mrs. Summers to Downchester was undeniable. It was equally undeniable that just prior to the tragedy Terence Mildmann had been lurking about not four hundred yards from the Dower House. And if that wasn't significant…!

"All right," reflected Meredith, "accept the fact that Terence is well up on my list of suspects. Could he have worked the crime? Assume he managed to creep into the house— what then? Did he sneak upstairs and break in on his father's tête-à-tête with the Parker girl? Did he then manage to slip the acid into the sherry when they weren't looking and persuade them to take a drink? But why poison the girl? He had nothing against her. His father—yes. In that case he had motive, since they were at loggerheads over most things, including his friendship with this Miss Blake. Not a strong motive, I admit. But in a moment of blind anger…But even then, how does this explain away the queer allocation of the prussic acid? Oh hell! That lad's concealing something from me and I'm damned if I know exactly what it is. He may be the murderer, on the other hand there's a kind of likeable naivete about the young fellow that half-convinces me he isn't!"

And Penpeti? Well, Penpeti would make a very nice murderer. His appearance, his character, his strange two-faced behaviour—all dovetailed beautifully into such a rôle. And Penpeti, above all others, had motive. Strong motive. He had a great deal to gain by Mildmann's sudden death. The kudos of the High Prophetship; the very handsome annual salary that went with the position. And the girl? Well, he had been in league with Penelope Parker over the threatened publicising of those foolish letters. Suppose the girl had ratted at the last minute and sworn, not only to burn the letters, but to tell Mrs. Hagge-Smith and the other big-wigs in the Movement of Penpeti's plot to discredit Mildmann to his own advantage?

Meredith's pulse quickened. By heaven! This new theory had a sound ring about it. Beside it his previous assumptions seemed half-baked. Wasn't it possible that the idea of using those letters had *originated* with Penpeti? The girl had been persuaded against her will to play this underhand trick on the High Prophet, then at the last minute her conscience had rebelled. What then? Penpeti could see the High Prophetship and that five thousand a year dissolving before his eyes. So he acts. He acts quickly. He must get rid of, not only Mildmann, *but the girl!* And somehow he had learnt that Mildmann was to visit the girl that night, and somehow he had managed it so that they had both drunk a glass of poisoned sherry.

Wonderful! Superb! A faultless piece of reasoning. Except for two factors. How *did* Penpeti get the poison into the glasses and persuade them to drink it? And how *could* he have been near the Dower House when he, above all other suspects, *had a perfect alibi?*

The theory was good. But the objections to the theory were far, far better. To suspect Penpeti of being the murderer was to walk into a blind-alley with one's eyes shut on a foggy night! No—Penpeti was definitely "off the menu".

II

Then came more startling news. More bewildering evidence. This time it was Maxton ringing The Leaning Man from Chichester shortly after lunch.

"Well, Meredith, I've performed the autopsies."

"That's fine."

Maxton's sardonic chuckle floated down the line.

"Is it? You wait until you've heard the details of my findings. They're going to knock you for a six. I won't trouble you with analytical minutiae and percentages of concentration and that sort of thing. I'll just give you the plain facts."

"I'm a plain man," Meredith reminded him.

"Well, here's something to be getting on with. I've analysed the stomach content in each case, as I said I would. Point A is this—the girl died of a fairly concentrated dose of prussic acid diluted with sherry. Point B is this—*Mildmann died of a far more concentrated dose of prussic acid that had not been diluted with sherry!*"

"Good God!"

"It's my considered opinion that Mildmann took that poison neat. A four per cent Scheele solution. He must have gone out like a snuffed candle."

"But damn it all…!" blustered Meredith.

"Oh and that's not all," said Maxton smoothly. "Miss Parker was going to have a baby. Not immediately. But in about six months' time. Not particularly noticeable at a cursory examination, but in the case of an autopsy…" Maxton paused, uttered another short sardonic guffaw and concluded: "I wouldn't be at all surprised if she were murdered on account of her condition. And since Mildmann had been writing her those intimate letters…Well, au revoir, my dear fellow. We'll meet at the inquest on Monday, I imagine."

III

"Well, Sergeant," said Meredith, when he had handed on Maxton's information to O'Hallidan, "where do we go from here?"

"'Tis back to Chichester Oi'd be an' no question asked, sorr, if Oi had me way. There's no future in this case—no future at all there isn't. Oi'd have said that Mildmann mur-thered the poor colleen because it was herself that was going to have a baby. An' having murthered the girl, Oi'd have said it was himself who committed suicide to diddle the hang-man's noose. But Oi've a notion you won't be agreeing with me about that, sorr."

Meredith shook his head.

"How the devil can I? If Mildmann had wanted to commit suicide he'd have taken a glass of that poisoned sherry. Point is, he didn't. He died of a concentrated dose of unadulterated prussic acid."

"Which he couldn't have drunk before leaving the house, sorr."

"Exactly. To have reached his car after such a dose would have been impossible. So what?"

"Would he have poisoned himself now, after he was back in the car?"

"He could have done. But what about his condition as he came down the drive? Arkwright said he was staggering and obviously in pain. In fact, the poor devil gasped out that he was ill and told Arkwright to get him back to the North Lodge as soon as possible."

"Would it have been play-acting at all?"

"If so I can't see the point of it," objected Meredith. "Frankly I can't see the point of anything. You'd never have thought that one decanter, two glasses and a shot of hydro-cyanic acid could have set such a bamfoozling problem." Meredith looked up sharply as the landlord of The Leaning Man came into the now deserted dining-room. "Looking for me?" he asked.

"Aye, surr. There's a call just come through for you from Hitchin."

"Splendid!" said Meredith, jumping up. "I'll take it at once." A few minutes later he rejoined O'Hallidan. He looked as pleased as a kitten with two tails. "Progress at last, thank God! Hitchin have picked up Dudley at his house and he's prepared to make a full statement. He's already admitted that he was down here on the night the girl died. Hitchin are driving him down at once so that I can cross-examine. They hope to get here in about three hours' time. In the interim, I suggest we—" Meredith broke off and jerked a finger towards the window. "Hullo, who's this? I wonder if they're looking for us, Sergeant?" He crossed quickly to the latticed casement and asked politely: "Can I help? You don't seem to know your way about. Are you looking for the landlord?"

"No, I…as a matter of fact…I was told that I should find the police inspector here. The detective who's investigating—"

Meredith smiled.

"Then you needn't look any further, young lady."

"Oh thank heaven! If you're Inspector Meredith, may I come in?"

"Please do."

After Meredith had introduced O'Hallidan, they settled themselves about the table.

"And your name," asked Meredith, "is…?"

"Oh, I'm Denise Blake. Mrs. Hagge-Smith's secretary."

"You have all my sympathy," chuckled Meredith. "And what exactly brings you to me?"

"Well, it's something that I've heard—a rumour that's going around the camp. You've no idea how swiftly things get around here. It's startling."

"It's the divil!" exclaimed O'Hallidan. "Oi'll be wagering ivery soul in the place knows me middle name is Corny, though me own mother would have long since forgetten the fact."

"And what is this rumour, Miss Blake?"

The girl hesitated, blushed becomingly and then murmured:

"It's something I've heard about Terence Mildmann. You've met him?"

"Oh yes, I've met him," said Meredith with a meaning glance at O'Hallidan.

"Well, it's all so disturbing and beastly that I felt I just had to come and see you. Mrs. Hagge-Smith doesn't know I've slipped away like this, so I've got to be quick." For the second time Denise hesitated and then blurted out: "Inspector! It isn't true that Terence had anything to do with this terrible affair at the Dower House, is it? They say the police suspect that he may have...have been responsible for his father's death. But it's untrue! I know it is. Terence didn't like his father, I admit, but to do anything like this...he just *couldn't*! It's horrible of people even to suggest it. I just can't understand them. They're supposed to be living a Higher Life and all that sort of thing and yet they can talk about Terence in this vile way. They're such awful hypocrites."

"You're fond of young Mildmann, eh?"

"I...no...yes..." Then rather defiantly: "Yes, I suppose I am. He's such a helpless sort of mutt. One can't help liking him."

Meredith said quietly:

"I'm afraid the rumour is not entirely unfounded, Miss Blake. The police never suspect anybody of anything without good reason. And in this case we have a good reason. You see, shortly before the tragedy at the Dower House occurred, the lad was seen only a few hundred yards away and he refuses to—"

"That's what I've come to see you about," broke in Denise eagerly. She snatched up her handbag, opened it and handed Meredith a folded slip of paper. "Please read that, Inspector. I think then you'll realise how this foul rumour began."

Meredith flattened out the sheet and, for O'Hallidan's benefit, read the brief missive aloud.

> *Darling Denise,*
>
> *If I don't see you soon I'll go haywire. We've simply got to meet. Now, please listen. I'm supposed to be going over to Downchester with Mrs. Summers next Thursday, but I've persuaded her to keep mum if I give this date a miss. I shall wait for you near the lily-pond at eight o'clock, so do your damndest to slip away directly after dinner. I shall hang on there until I have to go and meet Mrs. Summers off the Downchester 'bus. My darling Denise, you know I'm crazy about you.*
>
> *Lashings of love,*
>
> Terence.

"Well, well, well," said Meredith as he handed back the note. "So that's the reason for the young man's reticence. He refused to tell me why he was waiting near the pond. He didn't want to compromise you, young lady. That was rather nice of him, eh? In view of the circumstances, I mean."

"Oh, it was marvellous of him!" cried Denise with shining eyes. "Marvellous! But it's no more than I should have expected of him. Terence is like that. So thoughtful and… and so *decent* about everything."

"And you were unable to keep the tryst—is that it?" asked Meredith.

Denise nodded miserably.

"The Blot suddenly took it into her head to dictate a whole batch of letters. She kept me at it until well after ten."

Meredith's grey eyes twinkled.

"The Blot, I imagine, is your somewhat graphic pseudonym for Mrs. Hagge-Smith?" Denise nodded again. "And so the poor lad hung about there until it was time to meet Mrs. Summers?"

"Yes, I suppose so. I haven't had the chance to see him since. He probably thinks I didn't *want* to meet him."

"Well, I'll soon disillusion him on that score, young lady. Don't you worry. And thank heaven you had the good sense to show me that note. It explains everything. And if anybody dares to link that boy's name with what happened on Thursday night, you can tell them from me that he's entirely cleared of suspicion."

"That's nice of you," concluded Denise warmly.

"Well," said Meredith to Sergeant O'Hallidan, when Denise had left, "that knocks one more off the list. A charming and level-headed young lady. And if Dudley goes the same way as Terence Mildmann we're back where we started. Mildmann poisoned the girl and then poisoned himself."

"Oi've been thinking, sorr."

"The devil you have!"

"About the gloves, Oi have."

"What about the gloves?"

"It was yourself who was wondering how Mildmann could have got rid of his gloves once he was in the car."

"That's true."

"Well now, sorr, will ye consider my theory that Mildmann was only play-acting when he came out of the house. That he didn't take the poison at all until he was on his way back to the North Lodge. Faith now, an' it's a good an' simple explanation, as you'll admit."

"At the moment," agreed Meredith, "it's the only explanation. It means that somewhere on that drive home, Mildmann opened the car window, threw away his gloves, closed the window again and then settled back to shuffle off his mortal coil, eh O'Hallidan? Why he did all this we can't say. Why there were *two* used glasses beside the decanter we can't say. Why Mildmann waited until he was in the car before poisoning himself, we can't say. Why he broke into the desk and removed those letters when he knew he was going to commit suicide, we can't say. The only thing of which we can be certain was his motive for the crime. It wasn't only the threat of those letters which worried him. Good God, no! He had something far more unpleasant to conceal. He killed Penelope Parker because she was with child, and he, the High Prophet of this fanatical bunch of High Lifers, was the father of that child!"

"Sure an' Oi won't be disagreeing with you about that, sorr."

Meredith rose and picked up his hat.

"Very well, Sergeant, we'll put your theory to the test. If Mildmann got rid of those gloves by throwing them out of the car window, there's a chance that they're still lying somewhere on the verges of the drive. Suppose we take a slow and careful walk from the North Lodge to the Dower House. After all, if we do find those gloves, we've got to approach the whole modus operandi of the crime from a new angle."

IV

A couple of hours later, after a gruelling, back-aching search, Meredith and O'Hallidan returned to The Leaning Man. They had not found the gloves. Near the Dower House drive-gate, however, lying close to the rhododendron bushes in the long grass, O'Hallidan picked up a child's water-pistol. The utter irrelevance of this discovery infuriated Meredith. He observed sarcastically:

"We comb the ground for a top-line clue and what do we come back with? Damn it all, Sergeant, a kid's toy! And don't you start putting up any airy assumptions about it being connected with the crime. It probably is, but for God's sake don't suggest it! The whole set-up's quite complicated enough as it is. Come on, let's see if mine host can conjure up a nice strong pot of tea!"

Chapter XX

Mr. Dudley Talks

It was about half-an-hour later when a police car, driven by a uniformed constable, swished into the courtyard of the inn. Meredith had once more arranged to have the landlord's private parlour placed at his disposal, and in a few minutes he, O'Hallidan, Inspector Baker of Hitchin and Mr. Dudley were snugly behind its closed doors. The latter, a well-built, middle-aged man, looked tired and worried. But Meredith liked at once his open expression and unaggressive manner. Right from the start it was evident that Dudley was prepared to be as helpful and outspoken as the occasion demanded. Ordering O'Hallidan to take down a verbatim report of the interview, Meredith began his cross-examination.

"You realise why Inspector Baker asked you to come down here and make a statement, Mr. Dudley?"

"Only too well, I'm afraid."

"And you're prepared to answer my questions?"

"To the best of my ability—yes."

"Very well. Information has come to hand which suggests that you paid a visit to the Dower House last Thursday evening. That you saw Miss Parker for a few minutes shortly before she was found dead in her sitting-room. And that, subsequently, you left the house by the french-windows and returned to your car which you had left on the road to the south of the park. Is this correct?"

"Perfectly correct. May I say 'startlingly' correct?"

"This wasn't your first visit to the Dower House?"

"No. I had come down on two previous occasions after… er…Miss Parker had moved from Welworth."

"And on one of those occasions a young man came into the room where you were waiting for Miss Parker?"

"He did."

"And may I suggest that on each of these occasions, Mr. Dudley, you managed to slip into the house without the knowledge of the domestic staff?"

"That's perfectly true."

"But why?"

Dudley smiled, uttered a weary little sigh and leaned back with an air of resignation in his armchair.

"Look here, Inspector—you already appear to know a good deal about my recent movements and my attempts to make contact with Miss Parker. Wouldn't it save time if I told you the whole story from A to Z?—the circumstances which have prompted me to act as I have, the reasons for my somewhat underhand behaviour, a full, straight-from-the-shoulder statement, in fact?"

"Nothing would suit me better," said Meredith approvingly. "That is if you're prepared to—"

"I'm prepared to tell you everything!" exclaimed Dudley, suddenly raising his voice and emerging from his previous lethargy. "What can I gain now by concealing any of the details? I've acted like a damned fool! I admit it. And now, like any other damned fool, I've got to take the rap. But believe me, Inspector, I refuse to look on myself as a criminal fool. A misguided one, perhaps. You see, I'm one of those unhappy devils to whom providence delights in dealing out one shabby hand after another. Five years ago the barometer of my existence seemed to be at 'set fair'. But now…well, it's no good whining. I'll cut the cackle and come to the goose, eh?" He was now sitting bolt-upright in his chair, obviously in a state of acute nervous tension, yet in perfect control of his speech and emotions. He went on jerkily: "Five years ago I was a contented married man. I was interested in my job as a chartered accountant. I was deeply in love with my wife and I fondly imagined that she was as deeply in love with me. That was my first illusion. She wasn't. I found it out by degrees. A tiff here, an argument there, an ever-increasingly critical attitude to all I said and did. I'm an ordinary average sort of chap, as you may have gathered. I'm interested in the ordinary average things of life. Well, my wife wasn't. I say 'wasn't' advisedly, because she's now dead and—beyond the reach of my abortive attempts to bridge the gulf between us."

"Good God!" rapped out Meredith. "You mean to say—?"

Dudley nodded wearily.

"Yes. *Penelope Parker was my wife.* When she left me, she retook her maiden name and did her damnedest to forget that she'd ever been Mrs. John Keith Dudley. The trouble was, Inspector, she 'got religion'. She got it badly. *De mortuis nil nisi bonum* and all the rest of it, but I can't be less than honest with you. I went through hell on account of Penelope's high-flying notions. I wasn't tuned up to lead the Higher Life. To her I wasn't far short of a gross and unteachable savage. Well, I won't drivel on about our wretched married life. I only thank heaven there weren't any children to complicate matters. Two years ago she left me and went to live at Welworth Garden City. She chose Welworth, needless to say, because it was the Mecca of Cooism—the one place where she felt she could spread her wings and soar onto the High Plane or whatever they call it." Dudley paused, mopped his brow, sank back again into his chair and went on brokenly: "The hell of it was that I still loved her to distraction! Once or twice I was driven in desperation to see her and plead with her to return. Oh, I admit she wasn't exactly unsympathetic, but I couldn't shake her. She was devoting her life to a cause and I no longer entered into the picture. That was her argument in a nut-shell. Me versus the Higher Life. And the Higher Life won all along the line! Then one day, after some hesitation, she confessed that she had fallen in love with a member of her confounded religion. You can guess, of course, to whom I refer?"

"Naturally," said Meredith. "To Eustace Mildmann—the late C in C of the Movement."

Dudley sat up with a jerk and stared at the inspector with an expression of incredulity.

"Mildmann? Good heavens! What are you talking about? She didn't give a damn about him except as leader of the cult! It was that dago she'd fallen for, that slimy two-faced wog, Penpeti!"

"You're sure?" demanded Meredith sharply.

"Am I sure?" cried Dudley with a scowl of exasperation. "Haven't I watched her making a fool of herself with him for months? Haven't I had his virtues flung in my face every time I visited her? Of course it was Penpeti. I believe Mildmann made a few innocent advances, but he meant nothing to her as a man. You can imagine how I felt. If she'd fallen for a decent upstanding sort of chap, perhaps I shouldn't have taken it so hardly. But that dolled-up apology for a man gets me under the collar!"

"You met him at the house?"

"No—never face to face. But I used to hang about the place to watch his comings and goings. Penpeti never realised I was watching him. Hitchin is only a few miles from

Welworth and it was easy for me to drive over and act the amateur detective. And in the end…well, I just lost control. I decided to—shall I say?—erase him."

Meredith consulted the dossier which Inspector Duffy had forwarded the day before.

"With the result," he observed, "that on the night of Saturday, December the third of last year you made an attempt on his life in an unfrequented lane known as Mayblossom Cut."

"Good heavens! Is there anything you *don't* know, Inspector?"

"Little enough in broad outline," said Meredith with a smile. "But quite a lot in detail."

"All right. I'll tell you just how that happened. I never meant to make the attempt that night. It was just chance. I'd driven over to Welworth with the intention of making yet one more appeal to my wife to give this fellow up. Just outside the big corset factory there, I had a tyre burst. And while I was changing the wheel, I'm damned if I didn't see Penpeti himself entering the building with a girl. I learnt that there was a dance on in the factory and, in a sudden fit of fury at his hypocrisy, I decided to wait for him to come out. For some time past I'd been carrying an automatic, so I realised I was all set to act if the opportunity occurred. Well, when Penpeti came out I heard him arranging to take the girl home via Mayblossom Cut. I knew it was a deserted and badly-lighted spot, so I jumped into the car and…" Dudley paused, slowly shook his head and said in a dull voice: "But why go on? You seem to know the rest of the story."

"Quite," agreed Meredith. "But do you, Mr. Dudley?"

"What the devil do you mean?"

"Do you realise that the man you attempted to kill that night was *not* Penpeti."

"Not Penpeti? What on earth are you talking about?"

In a few brisk sentences Meredith explained. Dudley was flabbergasted. More than once he muttered: "I'd no idea. No idea at all!" At length he said:

"Then the fact that my shot was not fatal is luckier even than I suspected." He was thinking, too, of that night when the knife he had thrown had missed Penpeti's head by inches. But of that incident he was not going to speak. He went on: "To have killed Penpeti would have probably put a noose about my neck, but at least I should have had the grim satisfaction of knowing that the fellow was beyond the reach of my wife. On the other hand, to have killed an innocent young man by mistake…no, thank God! My aim was too low."

"And that same night you visited your wife?"

"Yes—before I drove back to Hitchin."

"And then?"

"I kept clear of Welworth for a time. My description as a wanted man was in the local papers, though the name of my victim was not publicly divulged. I soon realised that whatever had happened to Penpeti, he was still very much alive. Only two days later I saw that he had given a lecture in the town. And then I learnt about this impending conference and Penelope's intention to take up temporary residence at the Dower House. Once more—you see what a persistent fool I am?—I made contact with her. I pleaded with her to give up all this religious nonsense and make a home with me again. She flatly refused. But I was still unprepared to take no for an answer. Finally, on Thursday night, we had a violent quarrel and, for the first time, I realised the hopelessness of my position. She spoke again of Penpeti and suggested a divorce." Dudley slowly shook his head, his face devoid of expression. The weight of his misfortunes seemed to overwhelm him. Then he added quietly: "You see, Inspector, that night she told that she was going to have a baby and that Penpeti was the father."

"Penpeti!" cried Meredith. "So *he* was responsible for your wife's condition. Not Mildmann."

"So you know all about—?"

Meredith nodded.

"Yes. I naturally received a full medical report from the police surgeon. But I never suspected Penpeti. What you've just told me, Mr. Dudley, alters the whole aspect of the case. Thank heaven you decided to make a full statement. And now, with regard to your exact movements on Thursday night?"

Dudley gave a wry smile.

"This is the part that really matters, eh?"

"How did you approach the Dower House?"

"As you know, I parked my car on the road to the south of Old Cowdene. I managed to get into the Dower House garden, without being seen."

"What time was this?"

"Just after eight-thirty."

"And you entered the house—how?"

"Through one of the hall windows. You see, Inspector, by then I knew pretty well where everybody would be at that hour. The domestic staff having supper in the kitchen. My wife at dinner over at the Manor. It was all dead simple."

"And then you went up to your wife's room?"

"Yes—and hung about there waiting for her return."

"Did you smoke?"

"Yes. A cigar. It helped to steady my nerves"

"And then?"

"Well, about half-past nine Penelope walked in. I've already explained what happened. She told me about the child that was on the way and asked me to divorce her. I confess I lost my temper then. I told the poor girl just what I thought of her *and* Penpeti! After that I walked out, intending to leave the same way as I'd entered."

"And you didn't?"

"No. I was just getting through the hall window when I saw somebody coming up the drive. Although it was nearly dark, I had no difficulty in identifying the visitor. It was, of course, Penpeti."

"And then?"

"I had to act quickly because I didn't want to meet the fellow. If I met him face to face, I was frightened of losing my self-control. So I dodged into a room to the side of the house and let myself out through some french-windows."

"And the time then would be?"

"About a quarter to ten. I can't say with any accuracy."

"And you managed to get away from the house without being seen?"

Dudley hesitated and then said cautiously:

"I can't give a hard and fast answer to that question. On my way out I took the path that led by the gardener's cottage. As I went by I thought I saw faces at the window. I may have been wrong, of course. But that was my impression."

"Quite right," said Meredith briskly. "You *were* seen. By both the gardener and his wife. Shortly before ten o'clock, Mr. Dudley."

"I see," said Dudley.

"Shortly before ten o'clock," repeated Meredith with emphasis.

"I don't…er…follow."

"The point I'm trying to make is this. You let yourself out through the french-windows, on your own evidence, at about a quarter to ten. The gardener's cottage, as I happen to know, is less than a hundred yards from the house. Do you realise, Mr. Dudley, that you took *at least* ten minutes to cover that hundred yards. Not exactly a world record, is it?"

"I hid for some time in a clump of shrubs just outside the window. I wanted to make sure that Penpeti was inside the house before I attempted to get away."

Meredith said with a penetrating glance:

"You're quite sure, Mr. Dudley, that during those ten minutes, you didn't return to your wife's room?"

"Most certainly I didn't!"

"Tell me, did you happen to notice a tray of drinks when you were in the room? A decanter and a set of glasses?"

Dudley replied with a bewildered expression:

"I may have done. I really can't say. I wasn't in a particularly observant mood, but I've a vague idea that there was a tray of drinks set out on a small table somewhere in the room."

"I see." Meredith suddenly got to his feet. "Well, that's about all I wanted to ask, Mr. Dudley. I'm glad you've been so frank. Sergeant O'Hallidan will escort you out to the car. I want to have a private word with Inspector Baker."

The moment Dudley had gone out, Baker asked:

"What do you make of him?"

"My instinctive reaction is to take him at his word. My professional caution warns me that he could have slipped back into the house during that ten minutes lapse. You'll be holding him in the interim, I imagine?"

Baker nodded.

"A warrant has been drawn up for his arrest on a charge of attempted murder. He's bound to get a stretch for that Mayblossom Cut affair. My personal feeling is that the poor devil has been the victim of circumstances. I've an idea that he's been telling us the truth."

Chapter XXI

Death Down the Lane

I

"And what now, sorr?" asked O'Hallidan some minutes after the Hitchin police-car had swung out of the inn-yard.

Meredith chuckled.

"Well, Sergeant, I really don't see why you shouldn't call it a day. There's a beautifully polished brass-rail in the saloon-bar and I'm sure your foot's just itching to rest on it. For myself, I'm going to put young Terence Mildmann out of his misery. I made a promise to that young lady, remember."

Although the sun was already lowering, the June air was still warm and fragrant as Meredith set off down the lane to the North Lodge. But the inspector was far too preoccupied to notice the tranquil beauty of the evening. When he wanted to think, he was able to shut himself away from his surroundings, and at that moment his mind was brimming over with speculation. He was still uncertain of Dudley. His explanation of that ten minute wait in the shrubbery might well be the simple truth. On the other hand…Precisely!

Terence was now cleared of suspicion. Penpeti had his alibi. The latest evidence suggested that Mildmann could *not* have been the murderer. And if he dropped Dudley from the list, where the devil was he? Some other person presumably, so far unsuspected, was responsible for the crime. All fine and dandy—but who? Hilda? Sid Arkwright? The redoubtable Mrs. Hagge-Smith? Possibles, of course, but by no means probables. No apparent motive. But if all his previous suspects went up the spout, then dammit he'd *have* to start looking around for new ones.

There was no question, after the fresh evidence put out by Dudley, that Penpeti had the strongest motive for the crime. He'd realise well enough that if it became known that he was the father of Mrs. Dudley's child his chances of that five thousand a year and the High Prophetship would be slim. The double-murder, from his point of view, would be a logical step towards the realisation of his ambition. With the girl silenced, there was a good chance that the secret of their intimacy would die with her. With Mildmann snuffed out; the way was clear for his promotion. But Penpeti's alibi was perfect because it could be vouchsafed for by several disinterested witnesses. In a nutshell: motive—strong; alibi—stronger.

And with these arguments and counter-arguments processing through his brain, Meredith arrived at the North Lodge. Both Terence and the housekeeper were in, but to say that they welcomed his appearance would be grossly to exaggerate. They opened the door to him with about as much fervour as a couple of canaries might have opened their cage to a cat. But in less than five minutes the transformation was magical. Terence, at his best an inarticulate young man, just sat in the parlour and beamed. To be cleared of this foul suspicion and to hear that the girl he adored had pleaded with the police on his behalf…it was overwhelming, marvellous! He tried to thank the inspector, then he rubbed his bare knees with his ham-like hands and returned to his inane beaming. It was Mrs. Summers who stepped in and saved the situation. She insisted that Meredith should join them at supper. Meredith accepted. He was not particularly enthusiastic about nut rissoles but, hang it all, he'd got to eat somewhere.

To his astonishment Mrs. Summers served some excellent lamb cutlets with green peas and new potatoes.

"Good heavens!" he observed to Terence. "You're straying from the straight and narrow, aren't you?"

Terence reddened.

"Matter of fact, you know," he mumbled. "I've been gastronomically repressed. Mrs. Summers, too. It may not be cricket, but we're having a bit of a fling now. You can't blame us, sir."

"He used to have dreams," put in Mrs. Summers with a maternal smile, "about carnivorous food. Poor boy! Astral manifestations and all that sort of thing."

It seemed to Meredith that, apart from the shadow of the recent tragedy, Terence Mildmann was a young man whose real life was just about to begin!

It was dark when the inspector left the North Lodge to return to Tappin Mallet. Not pitch dark, for the stars were brilliant in a clear sky. There was, in fact, sufficient light for him to recognise the figure preceding him through the drive-gate on to the road. It was, without question, Penpeti; doubtless returning from some lecture or service to The Leaning Man. Meredith's rubber-soled shoes made no sound on the macadam surface of the lane and, more from instinct than for any specific reason, he began to tail the newly-elected High Prophet. Little did he realise at the time that this inconsequent action marked for him the "beginning of the end" of an extremely complex and tricky case.

He had not progressed more than a hundred yards down the lane, however, when he was aware of a second person coming quietly down the lane behind him. Still some distance away, but to judge by the footsteps gradually drawing nearer. Again it was no more than professional instinct that forced Meredith to leave the road and crouch back in the deep shadows of the hedge. He had an idea that the approaching figure hadn't actually spotted him. In this he appeared to be right, for a few seconds later the figure rapidly passed him and went on, quite unconscious of his presence, down the lane. In a flash Meredith was tagging along at the tail of this little procession.

Soon it was evident that the distance between Penpeti and this second figure had considerably decreased, for suddenly the man slackened his pace and began to proceed more cautiously. Meredith also slowed up. Then, unexpectedly, the man ahead stopped dead. From further down the road came the sound of a low whistle. The man ahead moved onto the grass verge and, bending low, began to creep forward. Meredith did likewise. Five, ten, twenty yards—and, suddenly, Meredith realised that Penpeti had been joined by yet another figure and that the two of them were engaged in a murmured conversation. For a brief instant all was immobility. Then, without the slightest warning, everything seemed to happen at once.

There was a flash, a deafening report, a stifled cry. Then, after a moment's pause, a second ear-splitting report and the sound of running feet receding down the road.

Almost before the echo of the last shot had died away, Meredith had reached the crumpled figure on the verge. He took out his pocket-torch and flashed it onto the man's upturned face. He gave a start of surprise. It was the camp-commandant, Hansford Boot! That he was dead Meredith had no doubt. There was a blackened and bloody patch on his right temple where he had pressed the muzzle of the weapon, which he still clutched in his right hand. It was all very obvious. Hansford Boot had just committed suicide by blowing out his brains!

Twenty feet away a second figure sprawled like a patch of deep shadow against the starlit grass. This time the man lay face-down and Meredith was forced to roll the body over before he was able to focus the rays of his torch on the man's features. And what he saw told him nothing. The man was a stranger. And yet, at that moment, he had a strange feeling that the face was not entirely unfamiliar. Peculiar and perplexing. Annoying, too! He straightened up and looked around. Of Penpeti there was no sign. Evidently the moment the shooting had started, he had taken to his heels and dashed helter-skelter towards the village.

The man at his feet was also dead. The bullet had entered his neck. The whole set-up of this totally unheralded and dramatic incident was as clear as crystal. Boot had been trailing Penpeti with the intention of murdering him and then committing suicide. Then the other man had joined Penpeti. Boot had fired and, in the semi-darkness, his aim had been indifferent and he had killed the wrong man.

Well, what now? Somehow he must get the bodies to The Leaning Man where he could ring Chichester and let them know what had transpired. Maxton would have to come over and make his medical examination. He, himself, would do well to go through the pockets of the dead men. After all, he still had to identify Penpeti's companion and there was a good chance that Penpeti would refuse to talk.

His line of thought was interrupted by the sudden glare of a car's headlamps fast approaching down the lane. Meredith stepped out into the middle of the road and flashed his pocket-torch. The car came to a standstill.

"Hullo! Hullo! What's all this?" demanded a gruff voice. "Anything wrong?"

Rapidly Meredith explained the situation and demanded of the burly old gentleman in the car if he were going to Tappin Mallet.

"I am. Farmers Union meeting at The Leaning Man. I'm over-late already. And now it looks as if I'm going to be a darn sight later! However…"

He shrugged his massive shoulders and with perfect aplomb, as if he had been lifting no more than a couple of sacks of grain, he helped Meredith to place the bodies in the car. Five minutes later they were drawn up in the inn-yard.

II

An empty garage had been earmarked as a temporary mortuary and it was there, by the light of a hurricane lamp, that Meredith and O'Hallidan went through the dead men's effects. First Hansford Boot, from whose inside breast-pocket Meredith withdrew a sealed envelope bearing the terse inscription—*For the police.*

"Well, now," observed O'Hallidan with a broad grin, "if he hasn't sent us a little billit-do, sorr. 'Twill be a confession or the loike maybe?"

"Explanation would be a better word, Sergeant. However, let's take a dekko."

He split the envelope, drew out a single sheet of folded paper and spread it out on the garage-bench. O'Hallidan craned over his shoulder.

"For heaven's sake! Don't breathe in my ear!" cried Meredith. "Sit down on that oil-drum while I read it to you. It certainly looks interesting."

In order that there should be no confusion at the Coroner's inquest, read Meredith. *I have prepared here a careful statement giving the reasons for my actions. I am quite sane. My mind, in fact, has never seen more clearly into the realities of the situation in which I am now imprisoned and have been imprisoned for some months. Penpeti (though I am convinced this is not his real name) has been blackmailing me. I have been forced to pay over a considerable amount of money in order to buy his silence. It so happens that I don't trust Penpeti. There was, of course, no guarantee that he would hold his tongue. The fear and uncertainty of this has driven me to take desperate measures. Some days ago I realised that I should never have any real peace-of-mind as long as this threat of exposure hung over my head. I decided, therefore, to kill Penpeti and then take my own life. By the time you read this my decision will have been translated into action and both of us will be beyond the reach of the law.*

I wish to add some personal data to the above statement. Hansford Boot is an alias. My real name is Sam Grew. For many years now I have been wanted by the police for my part in illicit drug traffic. I have tried to reform and build up for myself a new and decent existence. But Penpeti recognised me as Sam Grew and threatened to go to the police. Why he should recognise me I can't say. He claimed to have seen me in Soho many years back at a place known as Moldoni's Dive. I can, in the circumstances, only suppose that Penpeti himself had some connection with the crowd that forgathered at Moldoni's. Be this as it may, I have no compunction in killing him. I do this with a sober and clear-headed deliberation, knowing well enough that I shall have rid the world of a hypocrite, a scoundrel and a rat.

Signed, Sam Grew.

"Well, well, well!" said Meredith softly as he refolded the slip of paper and replaced it in the envelope. "Wheels within wheels, eh? Poor devil. I wonder how he'd feel now if he knew that the 'scoundrel and rat' was sitting only a few yards from here doubtless congratulating himself on a darned lucky escape. Penpeti must have known that the bullet was intended for him. A vile customer, O'Hallidan. Not only has he alienated the affections of another man's wife, but now he takes his bow as a fully-fledged blackmailer. Some time or another, we shall have some pretty staggering information to impart to the bigwigs of these Children of Osiris. Penpeti will be out on his ear. Damned and defrocked, eh?"

"It's the two-faced brazen bedivilment of him that fills me with the wrath o' God, sorr. I suppose this statement's not the outcome o' mental disorder or the loike? Sure an' suicides will concoct the quarest explanations for their actions. Would we do better, sorr, to take all this evidence with a pinch o' salt?"

"Good God, Sergeant!" rapped out Meredith, "where's your memory? Don't tell me you've forgotten the Sam Grew case?" He tapped his forehead. "I've still got the main details on file. Fellow came under suspicion. His hide-out discovered. Habits and *modus operandi* ascertained. The net was cast but the big fish wriggled through the mesh. The hue and cry went out even to us County blokes, but Grew was never pulled in. The perfect vanishing act. All this was before I went to the Yard, but I'll wager the f-p experts have got his dabs on file. We can identify all right. But the point is that the circumstantial details are correct. Moldoni's Dive *was* Sam Grew's hide-out and trafficking in drugs his racket. And there's another thing."

"Well, sorr?"

"Moldoni's was cleaned up about five years ago and Moldoni himself got a six-year stretch as a fence and an accessory both before and after a good many unsavoury facts. Do you realise what this means?"

"Oi'm bewildered, sorr!"

"Moldoni's available to give evidence."

"Evidence?"

"Concerning Penpeti. Suppose Grew is right. If Penpeti first saw him at Moldoni's it means that Penpeti was probably as bad as the worst of 'em in that rotten joint. Moldoni may be able to identify Penpeti. He may be able to tell us a few plain facts about him that Penpeti would prefer to remain secret. He may be able to tell us if Penpeti's his real name. In short, O'Hallidan, he may enable us to pull in this pseudo-prophet before he can do any more harm inside this innocent circle of self-deluded mugs!"

But O'Hallidan refused to echo the inspector's sudden elation. He dragged Meredith down to earth with a bump.

"Well now, an' Moldoni can tell us a lot maybe. But there's one thing he won't tell us."

"And that?"

"Who murthered Penelope Parker."

"Dammit! You're right there," admitted Meredith. "I mustn't allow this incident to side-track me from the main issue. Penpeti may be a scoundrel and a rat, but all the evidence to date suggests that we can't brand him as a murderer. Now let's take a look at this other chap. Not a particularly prepossessing specimen, eh? Semetic flavour about him. Cheap and rather flashy suit. Not exactly down-and-out but a type that lives by his wits rather than honest toil and sweat. Touch of the kerbside tout. Olive complexion, dark eyes, full lips, high-bridged nose…umph, suppose we go through his pockets. Hold the tray, Sergeant, while I set out the exhibits."

And replacing his rubber-gloves, Meredith gingerly thrust his hand into one of the voluminous side-pockets of the bright blue, pin-stripe suit. His groping fingers encountered something soft and springy which he gradually eased from the pocket. O'Hallidan craned forward.

Then: "By the Holy, sorr!" he exclaimed. "Phwat the divil is it?"

For a few seconds Meredith gazed at the unexpected object with utter bewilderment. Then suddenly, with an inward leap of excitement, he sprang to his feet. A swift procession of thoughts streamed through his brain—thoughts that he analysed and collated as quickly as they were formed until, as if by a miracle, he was faced with an inescapable deduction. As he turned to O'Hallidan, his smile broadened into a grin—a grin of triumph. He said quietly:

"It's the answer to a problem, Sergeant. Or more precisely, to two problems. I've a very shrewd idea now who killed Penelope Parker and how Eustace Mildmann met his death. Give me time. Give me a little time and I'll get the facts on parade and drill 'em into some semblance of order. After that…well, if we can't write 'Finis' to this case, I'll become a Child of Osiris. Damned if I won't!"

Chapter XXII

Final Facts

I

Although the next day was Sunday, it was certainly no day of rest for Meredith. Overnight he had been inspired by a red-hot theory. Now he was tumbling over himself to check up on its plausibility.

His first visit, directly after breakfast, was to the Manor, where he had a long and serious interview with Mrs. Hagge-Smith. From there O'Hallidan drove him back to The Leaning Man in time to catch Penpeti before he left to conduct his morning service in the lecture tent. The High Prophet seemed worried and impatient.

"I'm sorry," said Meredith shortly. "I know it's an awkward moment, but I didn't have a chance to interview you last night about this shooting affair. I was busy with the police surgeon until midnight."

"The whole thing," answered Penpeti icily, "was the work of a madman. I can't understand it! Hansford Boot always seemed a reliable and enthusiastic member of the Movement. I never suspected that he was in any way abnormal."

"In my opinion he wasn't. It may interest you to know that he left a written statement. Perhaps you'd care to read it? It concerns you."

"A...a statement?" stammered Penpeti, obviously disconcerted. "But—"

Meredith thrust the note into his hand.

"Read it!" he rapped out.

Penpeti did so.

"Good heavens! But this is monstrous, Inspector. Libellous, too! A tissue of lies. Surely you don't imagine that I *was blackmailing* this man. Me, the High Prophet of—?"

"Sorry—but I can't ignore the implications of such circumstantial evidence. There's no smoke without fire. I've naturally got to follow up this accusation. But it would save me a great deal of time, Mr. Penpeti, if you told me here and now the true facts of the case. Had you some hold over Hansford Boot or had you not?"

"Most emphatically...no!" snapped Penpeti. "The man must have been utterly unbalanced. He must have been suffering from what I believe the psychologists call a persecution mania."

"All right, Mr. Penpeti. We'll leave that subject for a moment. Now what about this friend of yours, this man you met in the lane?"

"Friend of mine!" exclaimed Penpeti. "I don't follow, Inspector. Until last night I'd never set eyes on the fellow. He stopped me in the lane and asked me for a light."

"For a cigarette, eh?"

"Yes."

"Then how was it his cigarette-case was empty and that no cigarette was found anywhere near his person?"

"I really can't say. But that was the reason he gave for stopping me."

"You realise, of course, that Hansford Boot intended that shot for you?"

"Now that I've read his fantastic statement, it's evident."

"So you had a lucky escape, Mr. Penpeti?"

"A miraculous escape, I imagine."

"Why did you run away immediately after the shots were fired?"

"I wanted to fetch help from the village. But before I could get back to where the shooting had taken place, I saw the bodies being taken from a car in the yard of the inn."

"I see. And you've nothing further to say on the subject?"

"Nothing."

And at that Meredith allowed the High Prophet to pass on his way.

II

From The Leaning Man he was driven to the North Lodge, where he picked up Sid Arkwright and returned with him to the inn. Once there he ushered the young man into the empty garage. The two bodies lay side by side on the concrete floor, covered with two rough blankets.

"I'm sorry about this, young fellow. Not a particularly agreeable task, I'm afraid, but I want to see if you can identify this man for me." And stooping over, Meredith gently drew down the blanket from the face and shoulders of the man Penpeti had met in the lane. "Well?"

Sid took one look and straightened up. He stared at Meredith, open-mouthed with amazement.

"Good Gawd! Inspector. It's that chap I was telling you about."

"What chap?"

"The one Penpeti met that night in the lane. The chap he spoke to about them letters of the guv'nor's and what he intended to do with 'em."

Meredith smiled.

"It's no more than I anticipated. It may interest you to know that his name's Yacob Fleischer of Fourteen Salmon Street, Camberwell. We found several letters addressed to him in his pocket. That name doesn't convey anything to you—in connection with Penpeti, I mean?"

"No, sir. Nothing."

"Well, Arkwright, I don't think you can—No, wait—there's just this. You did say that when you drove Mr. Mildmann over to the Dower House last Thursday evening the drive-gate was shut?"

"Yessir, because of the sheep in the park, as I told you afore, sir."

"You got out, opened it and closed it behind you?"

"Yessir."

"And on your return journey you did the same?"

"Yessir, as quick as I could, on account of the guv'nor's condition."

"One other point, Arkwright. While you were waiting outside the Dower House for Mr. Mildmann to reappear, what exactly did you do?"

"Well, sir, I was naturally feeling a bit hoppity. So I lit a cigarette and strolled about on the drive. As I explained, we'd parked just out of sight of the house, so there wasn't any chance of me being seen. There's a big clump of bushes and trees in front of the house, as you may have noticed, sir."

"Thanks. That tells me just what I wanted to know. All right, Arkwright. No need to wait."

"O.K."

Sid moved towards the door of the garage, hesitated, turned back and said uncomfortably:

"There's just one thing, sir. Can I have a word with you outside? This place sorta gives me the willies."

Meredith stepped out into the deserted inn-yard, followed by O'Hallidan, who locked the door behind him.

"Well?"

"It's about that there Crux Ansata, sir."

"Oh yes. I recall Inspector Duffy's report on the case. It was stolen from the temple at Welworth and then, for some mysterious reason, returned."

"It was me, sir," said Sid simply.

"You?"

"I stole it, sir. Been on my conscience ever since it has and I felt I just had to come clean about it. I come across the key of the temple in the guv'nor's overcoat. He'd left it by mistake in the Daimler. That's what first put the rotten idea into my head, see? Courting a girl I was then—an expensive sorta judy she was, too. Big ideas! Like a fool I wanted to cut a dash and go over big with the girl. Presents and the like."

"I see. Well?"

"Well, all this happened just afore the dance at the corset factory and that nasty business in Mayblossom Cut. I'd got my fancy-dress rig-out for the dance up in my room, see? So just in case I was spotted, I shoved on the togs afore I set out for the temple. Idea was that if anybody *did* spot me, they'd just think it was old Penpeti and leave it at that."

"Sound logic," observed Meredith dryly. "Go on."

"Well, I'd got an uncle of mine who owns a pop-shop in Hammersmith. He was ready to advance me a nice little bit on the thing and no questions asked. With the money I bought my girl a dimind bracelet. Kinda crazy thing one does when a chap's in luv, I suppose! Well, then came that business in the Cut, which put me on my back for a time. Seeing as I'd guyed his pet religion and all that, I was ready for the guv'nor to cut up rough. Point is—'e didn't,

Inspector. Looked after me as if I was a kid. 'Eaped coals of fire on my head, as the saying is. Made me feel as cheap as dirt, that did. So the moment I'm on my pins again, I forces my girl to give back the bracelet and I nips up to Town and argues my uncle into giving me back that there Ansata affair. And within twenty-four hours, I'd 'borrowed' the key of the temple again and put the Ansata back in its proper place, see?" Sid took a deep breath and exhaled gustily, as if with profound relief at a difficult corner now rounded. "Well, thank Gawd, that's out and done with! It's up to you now, Inspector. I'm ready to take what's coming to me. The guv'nor was a grand guy and it's been sticking in my gullet for months, this has. But I feel a damn sight better now and that's straight! Tell me, sir, am I for it?"

Meredith shook his head.

"It's sometimes better to let sleeping dogs lie. This is one of those dogs, Arkwright. But I'm glad you've told me. I'll make matters straight with Inspector Duffy and get him to write 'Case Closed' at the bottom of his dossier."

"Coo! Thanks, Inspector. It's decent of you."

"It's hard-headed common-sense," Meredith corrected him gently. "Go on, young fellow. Scram!"

III

Twenty minutes later, Meredith was waiting impatiently on Tappin Mallet station for the London train. He had, as he knew, a busy day in front of him. First a visit to the Yard, where he intended to leave one of the exhibits in the case for expert examination and analysis. Then he intended to go down to 14 Salmon Street, Camberwell, where he hoped to unearth more information about this seedy, shifty, mysterious individual known as Yacob Fleischer. And after that? Well, he had an idea that Moldoni had "gone over the wall" to serve his six-year sentence at Maidstone jail. And he wanted to talk to Moldoni—a quiet, exhaustive talk. He was hoping against hope that Moldoni's stretch in stir had not impaired his memory. At that moment Moldoni's memory was a vital element in his final reconstruction of the tragedy at the Dower House.

It was a full programme and Meredith plunged into it with his usual zest and efficiency. He had already phoned the Yard from The Leaning Man, with the result that Luke Spears was waiting in his office when he arrived. Meredith apologised for having dragged him out on the Sabbath.

"Don't apologise," chuckled Luke. "There's something in the wind. That sticks out a mile! Damn it all! Meredith, you needn't look so smug. You've broken the back of the case—is that it?"

"Possibly," assented Meredith with his customary caution. "I shall know more about that when I've had time to digest your report."

"What exactly do you want me to do?"

Meredith, having gingerly unwrapped his exhibit from the tissue-paper, explained in detail.

"The point is, I want to return to Tappin Mallet to-night. Can you get me out a report by, say, six o'clock this evening?"

"It won't be for want of trying," said Luke dryly.

And Meredith knew that with Luke Spears this was tantamount to an affirmative.

Thereafter he kept on the move. A police-car was available and, after a highly satisfactory interview with the tenants of Number 14 Salmon Street, he headed all-out for Maidstone. There again his luck held and, by the time he was ready to return to Town, Meredith was in a mood of undiluted elation.

On his desk at the Yard he found Spear's neatly-typed and beautifully stream-lined report awaiting him. It only needed this to round off a perfect day's investigation. Luke's findings set the seal on his previous suspicions. His theory, in short, was no longer a theory. Just one or two links to be welded into place and his chain of evidence would be complete. To-morrow he would press for an open verdict at the inquest. Say another forty-eight hours to collect and collate the extra material he needed. And after that?

Well, barring unforeseen complications, he would be all set to make an arrest!

Chapter XXIII

Meredith on Form

I

The inquest on Mrs. Dudley (née Parker) and Eustace Mildmann was held in the long sitting-room of the Dower House at eleven o'clock on Monday morning. It passed off without any unexpected incident. Mr. Paley, the Coroner, had elected to sit without a jury; and, as soon as all the formal evidence had been given, he brought in an open verdict as Meredith had anticipated.

After the inquest, Rokeby drew Meredith aside into the Dower House dining-room.

"Well, and when can we expect an arrest?" he asked in sarcastic tones. "This side of Christmas?"

Meredith smiled.

"My dear fellow, it's never safe to prophesy in a major investigation. But if the information I'm after comes in from the Paris Sûrete by to-morrow, I think you can stand by to snap the bracelets on the wanted man by, say, the day after."

"The Paris Sûrete!" exclaimed Rokeby. "But what the—?"

"Sorry, Rokeby. I'm saying nowt until we go into conference with your Chief. I hate airing my opinions on a case
until I've been able to prove my contentions up to the hilt.
I've still one or two further depositions to take here at Old
Cowdene, before I can sit down and draw up a really comprehensive report. In the meantime I'd like you and the Chief
to glance through this preliminary affair. It incorporates all
the evidence and clues I've so far been able to rake in. But
for my final statement—well, can you curb your impatience,
say, until Wednesday morning?"

Rokeby made a wry grimace.

"I seem to have no option. O.K., my dear fellow. Until
Wednesday, then."

"Until Wednesday," thought Meredith when Rokeby
had left. "Precisely. Just forty-eight hours in which to tie
up all the loose ends and ring in a convincing summary of
my deductions."

From Rokeby he went to Miss Minnybell. From Miss
Minnybell to that unfailing source of information, Sid Arkwright. After an excellent and solitary lunch (for O'Hallidan
had already been detailed to report back to Chichester) Meredith went up to his room, opened the dossier of his case,
read and re-read every deposition, sorted out his notes and
began to rough out the main paragraphs of his final report.
But until he received the anticipated data from the files of the
Sûrete, there was bound to be an hiatus in the continuity of
his story. He felt keyed-up and restless, waiting with impatience for the despatch-rider who was to come down from
the Yard, the moment the Paris statement was handed in.

That night he slept badly. More than once he got out of
bed, lit a cigarette, prowled about the room or returned to a
fitful perusal of the documents of the case. The next day his
impatience reached fever-heat. He hung about the precincts
of The Leaning Man, not daring to wander far afield in

case the expected despatch-rider put in an appearance. And then, shortly after two o'clock, he droned into the yard and handed over the precious papers from his neat black wallet. Meredith signed for the receipt of the package and made an undignified dash for his room. There, he broke open the official seal, spread out the enclosed papers on his bedside table and scanned them with undivided attention.

Within five minutes his expression of grim anxiety resolved itself into a smile; within ten he was chuckling to himself with unrestrained delight; within twenty he knew, without any shadow of doubt, that the last piece of his puzzle had clicked faultlessly into place. The case was in the bag!

He went down to the telephone and rang up the H.Q. of the West Sussex County Police at Chichester. A few minutes later Rokeby came on to the line.

"Well, Meredith, do we call that conference in the Chief's office or do we not?"

"We do," said Meredith decisively. "If convenient, at ten o'clock."

"Ten o'clock? Good! I'll let the Chief know at once. And I'll see to it that he damn well *makes* it convenient! Cheero."

"Till to-morrow, then," concluded Meredith.

II

A long, wax-polished table; five people seated around it; two uniformed stenographers stuck away discreetly in a corner; long rays of bright June sunshine slanting through the tall windows; somewhere in the room the drowsy buzzing of a trapped bluebottle.

At the head of the table sat Major Sparks, the Chief Constable—massive, shrewd, grey-haired, good-natured. On his right, Detective-Inspector Meredith; on his left, Superintendent Rokeby; and beyond them, Sergeant O'Hallidan and Chief-Inspector Braintree of the Yard. As strong a team of crime-breakers as had ever been assembled in that austere but airy room at County H.Q. The atmosphere, despite the fact that they were all hard-headed experts in this exhaustive and often thankless game of criminal investigation, was tense and expectant. The Chief Constable mopped his brow, cleared his throat and said in his husky bass:

"Well, gentleman, I'm not here to-day to do the talking. We're leaving that to Inspector Meredith. You've all seen his preliminary report on the case, so I suggest we now ask him to go ahead with his final report. If there's any point that you feel needs elucidation, for heaven's sake, speak up at once. I know the inspector's as anxious as we are to take this matter to court with a foolproof case for the Crown. O.K., Meredith. Fire ahead!"

And, taking a deep breath, Meredith began talking. Somewhat hesitantly at first; then, gaining confidence, with more fluency and pace. He set out the report in his own words, only referring to his written summary in order to make sure that he had left out none of the salient facts.

"Well, if you'll excuse the paradox, gentlemen, I'll begin at the end and end, so to speak, at the beginning. In other words, with the murder of Yacob Fleischer by Hansford Boot on the night of Saturday, June the eighth. More correctly I should say the 'inadvertent murder', because the bullet that killed Fleischer was really intended for Penpeti. But first let me give the full motive for Hansford Boot's actions." And with masterly precision Meredith detailed the facts concerning the relationship between Boot and the newly-elected High Prophet. He went on: "Now this fellow Fleischer interested me a lot, particularly when he was identified as a man who had already been making secret contact with Penpeti. My witness, Arkwright, who overheard a conversation between them some weeks ago, left no doubt in my mind that this fellow Fleischer had some sort of hold over Penpeti, in the same way that Penpeti had a hold over Hansford Boot. In other words, the blackmailer was, in turn, being blackmailed. But why? Well, gentlemen, you know as well as I do that no man can be successfully blackmailed unless he has done something that he is anxious to conceal. Naturally I asked myself—What *was* this 'something' in the case of Penpeti? Luckily, I didn't have to seek far for an answer. In fact, no farther than Camberwell—Number Fourteen Salmon Street, Camberwell. There I found a very useful witness in the shape of Hannah Fleischer, Yacob's wife. After a little verbal pressure, and under the stress of learning that her husband had been killed only the previous night, Mrs. Fleischer's reserve collapsed. She began to talk and, thank God, talk a lot! Well, I won't withhold this very interesting and significant piece of information. *Peta Penpeti and Yacob Fleischer are—or should I say were—brothers!* Her information didn't startle me quite as much as you might imagine. For this reason. When I first saw Yacob's features, just after he was shot, I was convinced that I'd never set eyes on the fellow before. And yet, in some odd way, his features were familiar! Later I realised why. There was between him and Penpeti a strong family likeness, only modified by the fact that Penpeti wore a beard." Meredith paused, looked around the table and asked: "Any questions, gentlemen?" There was dead silence. "Very well, I'll pass on to the next phase of my investigations. Mrs. Fleischer, once she'd got off the mark, was more than lavish with her evidence. She told me that Yacob and Marcus—that was Peta's real Christian name—had always been up against each other. She, herself, hated Marcus because, as she expressed it, 'he put on airs and threw his weight about' inside the family circle. Well, to cut a long story short, this is the pith of what Mrs. Fleischer told me. Marcus, at one time, had been working the charity racket in the States. He'd just cleaned up a packet when the F.B.I. got on to his tail and Marcus had to make the long-hop across the Atlantic. Eventually he and Yacob landed up in Paris in the early 'thirties. Their new racket appears to have been dope. What exactly happened in Paris, Mrs. Fleischer didn't know. But suddenly the brothers turned up in Camberwell, where Marcus went to earth. For three months he never shoved his nose outside the door of Number Fourteen. But from then onward, Mrs. Fleischer noticed that Yacob was no longer under his brother's thumb. The rôles had changed. It was now Yacob who seemed to call the tune. In fact, it wasn't long before Mrs. Fleischer realised that her husband was blackmailing her brother-in-law. After a time, Marcus began his old game again—the bogus charity ramp. Yacob went in for small-time dope peddling. The favourite rendezvous of their particular gang was Moldoni's Dive in Soho." Meredith turned to Chief-Inspector Braintree. "You may recall the place, sir."

Braintree smiled grimly.

"A hot-spot of dope peddling, an exchange mart for stolen goods, an underworld gossip-shop! Oh, I recall the place all right! We cleaned it up about four years ago and Moldoni, if I'm not too wide of the mark, is still serving his stretch."

Meredith nodded.

"I'm coming to Moldoni directly, sir. But the point is that it was at Moldoni's where Marcus Fleischer alias Peta Penpeti first got a line on Sam Grew alias Hansford Boot. Marcus had a good memory for faces. Sam was not so gifted. The result was that Marcus was in a position to blackmail the poor devil without fear of retaliation. I imagine in his Soho days our Mr. Penpeti didn't wear either a beard, a fez *or* a caftan! Those charity racket boys usually favour a clerical rig-out. It inspires confidence in their victims."

"And Moldoni?" put in the Chief Constable eagerly.

"I'll come to him now, sir. I interviewed him last Sunday in Maidstone jail. A most satisfactory little pow-wow. I asked him if he remembered the Fleischer brothers. Oh yes—he remembered them all right. Yacob and Marcus. Well, gentlemen, I fired a shot in the dark then and, Sunday being my lucky day, I plugged the bull! I pumped Moldoni about their relationship, suggesting to him that Yacob was blackmailing his brother. Well, where Mrs. Fleischer couldn't talk because she didn't know, Moldoni talked a lot because he *did*. He *knew* what had happened in Paris. An ordinary, sordid affair with a woman in the case. A woman called Minette Desfaux. I'll just give the bald facts. Minette was Marcus Fleischer's mistress until she fell in love with a fellow called Pierre Gaussin. Then she left Marcus high and dry, and later, in a fit of jealous rage, Marcus shot her. Yacob knew this. And he knew that Gaussin was hopping mad and one of the slickest knife-throwers in Montmârtre. So the brothers cleared out and returned to Camberwell. Of course the Sûrete started to investigate the murder. Got hold of a lot of facts, too, including a photo of the wanted man. But the man they never got. He'd acted first. Well, when I interviewed Mrs. Fleischer in Camberwell last Sunday, I wheedled a photo out of her—a photo of Marcus Fleischer before he cultivated a beard and called himself Peta Penpeti. I sent this by special courier to the Sûrete. Yesterday I received their report. There's no mistake about it. Peta Penpeti's the murderer of Minette Desfaux right enough!" Meredith paused, glanced round the table with an apologetic air and added: "No need to tell me what you're thinking, gentlemen. What the hell has all this got to do with the death of Penelope Parker and Eustace Mildmann at the Dower House on Old Cowdene estate?" Meredith suddenly unclasped his battered attaché-case and drew out an object which he placed in the middle of the table. "There's the answer."

"A beard!" exclaimed the Chief Constable. "A false beard! But what the deuce—?"

"I'll explain, sir. When I first saw the photo of the beard-less Penpeti I was startled by his astonishing resemblance to his brother Yacob. Naturally, I argued like this. If Penpeti minus a beard looks very like Yacob, surely Yacob plus a beard would look very like Penpeti. I found that false beard in Yacob's pocket after he'd been accidentally shot by Sam Grew. You see daylight, gentlemen?"

"You mean there's been some sort of impersonation?" asked Rokeby.

"Just that. But no rough-and-ready disguise such as Mild-mann adopted. That wouldn't have fooled a really observant person for a brace of shakes. The only reason why it might have been effective was that he only had to fool the maid at the Dower House. And even then only for a second, when she opened the door to him. It was dark, too. Above all, the maid was used to letting Penpeti into the house at all odd hours of the day. She probably wouldn't have given him a second glance."

"But in Yacob's case it was different, eh?" demanded Braintree.

"Yes, sir. Yacob could have stood up to a pretty close scrutiny and fooled the best of us. Complexion, colour of eyes, build, even the timbre of the voice—all would help to build up the deception. Add the characteristic fez and caftan, and Bob's your uncle!"

"But why did Yacob *want* to impersonate his brother?" asked Rokeby sharply. "What did he get out of it?"

"A rake-off, I imagine. A handsome rake-off, no doubt, of the five thousand a year stipend payed by that addle-pated old martinet, Mrs. Hagge-Smith, to the High Prophet of her pet cult. You see the implication?"

"You mean," cried Rokeby with a sudden flash of under-standing, "that Penpeti—?"

Meredith nodded.

"Just that, my dear Rokeby. Penpeti no longer has one murder on his conscience. *He has three! Minette Desfaux, Penelope Parker and Eustace Mildmann!*"

"Did ye hear that now!" boomed O'Hallidan. "Well Oi niver—did ye iver! Eustace Mildmann murthered!"

Meredith chuckled.

"Knocked you edgeways, eh Sergeant? And yet it was you who first put me on the right track."

"Me, sorr?"

"Yes. When you picked up that water-pistol near the Dower House drive-gate."

"But Oi don't—"

"All in good time, O'Hallidan. First things first, eh gentlemen? Well, this is only an assumption, but when I've concluded my report I think you'll agree that it's a safe one. Penpeti overheard Mildmann and Arkwright discussing their plan for the recovery of those letters. You'll recall all about the letters from the preliminary report I put in after the inquest. So I won't go further into the matter now. Now again it's a mere matter of assumption. To my mind Penpeti had persuaded Penelope Parker to show those letters to the bigwigs of the Movement in order to vilify Mildmann's character. At the same time, the child she was carrying was to be fobbed off as his. Well, I think, at the last minute, the girl ratted. Her conscience just wouldn't let her do it. You can imagine how Penpeti felt after that?"

"Scared stiff, eh?" said Rokeby. "Frightened that the girl might blurt out the truth about her baby and ruin his own career in the Movement."

"Exactly. Not only would he fail to get Mildmann degraded from the position of High Prophet, but he, himself, would be kicked out of his position as Prophet-in-Waiting. On the other hand, with the girl out of the way, he was safe. The letters would come into the right hands. Everybody would suspect that Mildmann was the father of the unborn child." Meredith paused and added with slow emphasis: "And even more would they suspect this, gentlemen, *if Penpeti so arranged things to suggest that Mildmann had killed the girl and then taken his own life!*"

"Which is precisely what he did, eh?" put in the Chief Constable quickly.

Meredith nodded.

"And the modus operandi?"

"Neat but not gaudy, sir. It was, of course, all based on a devilish clever alibi."

"Provided by Yacob Fleischer, is that it?" asked Rokeby.

"Just that, my dear fellow. Again, all very simple and damn near foolproof. I'll deal with the alibi first. Yacob hid in the rhododendron bushes outside the Manor and waited until Penpeti left the place after dinner on Thursday night. Well, Penpeti turned aside into the bushes and Yacob walked out. In my preliminary report I mentioned that crazy old biddie, Miss Minnybell. You know how she was always trailing Penpeti. Well, when Yacob moved off down the drive towards the Chinese summer-house, Miss Minnybell tailed him. You see, the very fact that Mildmann had planned to enter the Dower House at a time when Penpeti was due to make an official appearance in the temple, simply played into the brothers' hands. Penpeti was expected to be in the temple from nine until ten. It was dark outside, remember, and the temple itself, as I was quick to note, is lighted by a single blue lamp let into the ceiling. Above all, it's an unwritten law that nobody should utter a word once they've crossed the threshold of the temple. It's a place of meditation only, and members are expected to treat it as such. But you see the significance of this? During his hour in that temple Yacob knew he wouldn't be called on to speak a word. I tell you, gentlemen, the provision of this alibi was a stroke of genius."

"And Penpeti?" demanded Braintree. "What did he do on parting from Yacob?"

"Made straight tracks to the North Lodge, presumably, by some unfrequented route across the park."

"And once there?"

"He waited his chance and hid himself, probably under a rug, in the back of Mildmann's Daimler. Either before Arkwright drove it out of the barn, or when it was drawn up in front of the North Lodge waiting for Mildmann to get in. Don't forget, gentlemen, that when Mildmann set out for the Dower House it was practically dark. It was a dirty night, with low rain clouds. I tell you, everything conspired to make things easy for our Mr. Penpeti."

"And once in the car?" asked Rokeby.

For the second time Meredith opened his attaché-case. This time his exhibit was the water-pistol.

"We now come to O'Hallidan's exhibit," smiled Meredith. "An ordinary kid's water-pistol, fitted with a rubber bulb at the point of grip."

"And with this, I presume, Penpeti suddenly emerged from under the rug and threatened Mildmann," said Rokeby sarcastically. "With the result that Mildmann died of heart failure. The perfect murder, eh?"

Meredith said with a tolerant smile:

"Oh, it's not quite as simple as all that. I think Penpeti *did* threaten Mildmann with the pistol once the car had started. Doubtless, Mildmann would have seen it silhouetted against the faint wash of light still left in the sky. But that's only half the story. Perhaps you'll find it easier to follow if I tell you, gentlemen, *that the rubber bulb of that water-pistol was charged with a highly concentrated solution of prussic acid!*"

"Good God!" cried Rokeby. "You mean to tell us—?"

"As much as I possibly can," broke in Meredith. "The precise details, I hope, will in due course be filled in by Penpeti. But I've good reasons for my assumption. You see, Maxton noticed that there was a slight chip out of one of the teeth in Mildmann's upper denture. We can only presume that the chip occurred when Penpeti forcibly thrust the muzzle of that lethal weapon into Mildmann's mouth. I suggest he pinched Mildmann's nose, thus forcing him to open his mouth, then jabbed the muzzle between his teeth and pressed the bulb. With such a concentrated dose of the poison, it would need only a few drops to produce a fatal effect. I imagine Mildmann collapsed at once and that in a few minutes he was dead."

"And then, sorr?" asked O'Hallidan breathlessly.

"Well, Penpeti opened the car window, tossed the pistol into the bushes, while Arkwright was opening the gate of the Dower House drive."

"And the man, confound it, who entered and left the Dower House," broke in the Chief, "was not Mildmann disguised as Penpeti. It actually *was* Penpeti!"

"You've said it, sir! It *was*. And when he came out to the car again there was nothing wrong with him. You recall Arkwright's evidence which I incorporated in my preliminary report? Ill, staggering, gasping for breath. All fake, of course. But this play-acting served two useful purposes. Firstly, it enabled Penpeti to disguise his voice by gasping out only a few words in a husky, choking sort of way. This completely foxed young Arkwright. Secondly, it was a nice lead-in to the subsequent discovery of Mildmann's dead body in the car. His apparent condition on leaving the house meant that Arkwright wasn't all that surprised when he arrived at North Lodge and found his employer *kaput!*"

"But look here, Meredith," broke in Braintree, "if Penpeti entered that car, how was it that Arkwright didn't discover him when they reached the North Lodge?"

"It was the Dower House drive gate, sir. Arkwright had to get out, drive the car through and shut it again behind him. This gave Penpeti the perfect opportunity to sneak out and vanish into the darkness."

"But surely Penpeti took a chance," said the Chief, "in leaving Mildmann's body in the car, while he was inside the house? Suppose the chauffeur had looked in and discovered the body? Pretty tight corner for Penpeti, eh?"

"Well," admitted Meredith, "it *was* a risk, sir. But not a big risk. Arkwright would have no real cause to look into the back of the car, because he naturally thought it was empty. I daresay the body was actually lying on the floor and that Penpeti had thrown the rug over it. Before he got out he probably hauled the body into a sitting posture on the seat. During the drive, of course, Arkwright would have overheard nothing, because of the sound-proof glass panels between the front and back of the car. No—take it all round, gentlemen, I think we've got to hand it to Mr. Peta Marcus Penpeti Fleischer!"

"And the girl?" asked Rokeby. "How do you think she actually died? We know she was poisoned, of course, but what were Penpeti's actions once he was in the room with her?"

Meredith smiled.

"In the circumstances, I imagine Penpeti was naturalness itself. And why not? He often visited her there. Seeing the sherry decanter, he merely proposed that they had a drink together and the girl merely accepted. Nothing odd in that. Penpeti had probably often had a drink with her. He knew from previous visits that the sherry decanter and glasses would be set out on the table. All he had to do was to pour out the sherry, stand between the girl and the table and empty the phial of prussic acid into the glass."

"And into his own glass, too?" asked Rokeby, puzzled.

"Good God, no!"

"But hang it all—!" began Rokeby, cantankerously.

"I know what you're thinking, my dear chap. The second glass contained a residue of concentrated prussic acid and the decanter a diluted dose. But it's all very simple. Penpeti didn't doctor the sherry that he drank with the girl. He waited until she'd collapsed, poured out a second portion into his own glass, added a second phial of prussic acid and poured the whole lot back into the decanter."

"'Tis as Oi suggested, sorr," said O'Hallidan with a smirk of satisfaction.

"But what the devil did he do it for?" asked the Chief Constable.

"A red-herring, sir. It was all part of his build-up to suggest that Mildmann poisoned the girl and then took his own life. The rifling of the desk and the removal of the letter-case was all part of the same trick. After all, Arkwright knew that his employer had gone there to recover the letters. Penpeti knew it, too, since he must have overheard them making their plans. And when Arkwright actually found the letter-case beside the dead body of his master, it was no more than he expected. It all helped to preserve the illusion that the man who stepped out of the Daimler and, later, staggered back to it, was Mildmann in disguise and not the genuine article. If," added Meredith with a twinkle, "there *is* anything genuine about this particular article!" He ticked off the items on his fingers. "Charity racketeer, dope pedlar, blackmailer, false prophet, treble murderer! And add to this imposing list the fact that he's intelligent and devoid of all moral restraint and you have the almost perfect criminal. As far as I can see he made only one mistake."

"The gloves?" shot out Rokeby.

Meredith nodded.

"He remembered to put them on when he entered the house, but he forgot to remove them before he returned to the car. It's been a puzzling factor in the case from the start." Meredith leaned back in his chair, stretched his legs and concluded: "Well, gentlemen, I think that more or less foots the bill." He turned to the Chief Constable. "Do I get that warrant of arrest, sir?"

Major Sparks chuckled.

"You do, my dear fellow. *And* something more!"

"And that, sir?"

"A pat on the back, a feather in your cap, a headline in the Press and a well-deserved drink. And when I say 'well-deserved', I damn well mean it. A good show, Meredith. A *very* good show."

Only Major Sparks did not actually use the word "very". He employed a less polite but far more emphatic adjective that more correctly expressed his professional approval and admiration!

To see more Poisoned Pen Press titles:

Visit our website: poisonedpenpress.com/
Request a digital catalog: info@poisonedpenpress.com